Pride F

MW00773392

Single Books
Love Burns

LOVE BURNS

ADRIAN J. SMITH

Love Burns
ISBN # 978-1-83943-724-3
©Copyright Adrian J. Smith 2021
Cover Art by Erin Dameron-Hill ©Copyright August 2021
Interior text design by Claire Siemaszkiewicz
Pride Publishing

Published in 2021 by Pride Publishing, United Kingdom.

Pride Publishing is an imprint of Totally Entwined Group Limited.

LOVE BURNS

Dedication

To my husband, who has always encouraged me
to be me, to write, to love, to be better each day.
Thank you for loving me through my strengths
and my faults.

Chapter One

Becca carefully set the last of her picture frames into the cardboard box then shoved two shirts around them, making sure they were tight against the sides. Folding over the flaps, she pressed down lightly as she pulled the packing tape across to seal the box. This day had come far sooner than she had hoped, but the twins she had watched over for the past year were officially on track with life, and she was no longer needed. It was time for them *and* her to move on.

The agency, Kiddie Academy, was sending her to a new home. They had warned her it would most likely be a temporary position. No one lasted long at this appointment. Becca had heard the rumors before Kiddie Academy had even decided to send her there. The other nannies all talked, all shared, and she had seen a vast number of women go through that house in just two short years.

Nerves ramped up in her belly as she picked up the box and walked it out in a light March rain to her run-down car. After opening the back door, she slid it in, her entire life fitting into the small sedan. Sighing and brushing away a few tears, Becca went to the house, triple-checked that she had everything, then set the alarm and left. All her goodbyes had been said, and this was how she'd wanted it — quiet and without fanfare.

Slipping behind the wheel, Becca turned the engine and backed out of the drive. A year had been a good run, her longest nanny position yet, but it was time for a new life — perhaps her last before she finally finished her degree. She was the fixer, the one who went into struggling homes and helped the kids turn around. That was what her employer Kiddie Academy called her, anyway. With a steadying breath, Becca headed to the address on the files she'd acquired, ready to begin her new job.

When she pulled up outside the house, she was gobsmacked. The house itself was beautiful, but it was also huge. This was the upper class. They routinely had nannies and maids who were live-ins and had their own sections of the house. That was why she'd opted to work for those families, to cut down her costs, pay more for school — that'd been her theory, anyway.

But this house? There was something different about it. The tans and browns blended together to look like a vast desert in the middle of a rainforest because of the number of trees and shrubs and green things that surrounded the building. Stepping out of her car, the glimmer of the sun off the waters in the pool caught her eye. She took a step to the side of the house to get a better look and let out a deep breath. Clenching her jaw, Becca flipped through the papers in her hand again and looked for the name of her new employer.

Kimberly Thompson.

Adrian J. Smith

Something about it rang a bell, but she couldn't place the name. Still, the niggling feeling in the back of her mind didn't leave. Turning on her toes, Becca headed for the front door. Nerves swelled in her belly, but she tamped them down before pressing the bell. The ring echoed through the house. There was a loud thump then pattering feet as their owner no doubt raced toward the door.

Becca heard a small voice on the other side, squeaky but clear.

"Can I open it, Mama? Can I? Can I?"

"Wait until I get there, please. You know better than to just open doors for strangers."

"But can I open it?"

Becca smiled to herself, knowing she'd likely have the same conversation with any child in her care. It was only a few more seconds before the handle turned and the left side of the French door snicked open a crack, revealing the bright brown eyes and red cheeks of a small, cheery boy. Becca planted the softest smile she could on her face and bent down to his level.

"Afternoon," she offered. "I'm Becca. You must be Michael."

"Open it all the way, kid." The woman's voice, still behind the door, was solid and strong, but her admonition to Michael was said with a tone of love.

Michael shoved the door the rest of the way open, the door itself flinging rapidly toward the wall. A small hand with thick, short fingers caught it before it slammed to a stop.

"Michael…we don't open doors like that."

"Who are you?" His small voice was full of curiosity. He completely ignored the beautiful woman now standing fully revealed before Becca.

9

Becca had to work hard to pry her eyes away from her, but she managed to glance again at Michael and hold her hand out for him. "I'm Becca. It's good to meet you."

The woman stepped behind Michael and pressed her fingers to his shoulder in a protective manner. "Are you from Kiddie Academy?"

"I am." Becca straightened her back and turned her smile toward whom she presumed was Kimberly, her new employer, hoping it would disarm some of the hostility coming off her in waves. "I know I'm a little early."

Kimberly waved her away before stepping forward and extending her own hand. "It's all right. I'm Kim. This is Michael. We just finished dinner. Come on in. Michael can give you the grand tour while I clean up."

"Sounds like a plan." Becca put her focus on Michael as she swallowed the lump in her throat. First impressions were everything, and while she was there for Michael, her impressions of Kimberly mattered far more, since she was the source of Kiddie Academy's problems. "What are you going to show me first?"

Michael bounced on his bare feet briefly before running inside. "My room!"

Chuckling, Becca waited for Kimberly to move to the side so she could come in, but Kimberly hesitated. Their eyes locked, and Becca found herself lost in the pale hazel with a hint of yellow. Becca raised an eyebrow and cocked her head to the side, surprised when Kimberly jerked and held her hand open for Becca to walk through the doorway.

As soon as Becca was inside with Kimberly behind her, out of her immediate sight, she was able to relax briefly. But she was just as lost as ever. Michael was nowhere to be found, and the inside of the house matched the outside. It was huge. The living area took over most of what she could see, and from there, all she saw was a kitchen.

Kimberly stepped beside her. "His room is down the hall off the kitchen. Third door on the left."

"Right. Thanks."

Becca headed away from Kimberly, hoping she'd masked the shudder racing up her spine. The niggling feeling that she knew Kimberly came back sharply, but Becca ignored it and focused on Michael—the main reason she was there. She knocked on the door and grinned.

"You left so fast that I missed where you went. You must be as fast as Flash!"

Michael stopped where he stood and cocked his head to the side, the toy tractor slipping from his fingers onto the floor. "Who's Flash?"

"What? You don't know who Flash is?"

Michael shook his head. Becca stepped onto the carpet and curled her legs under her to sit down on the floor in front of him. She grabbed the tractor and set it the right way. "Flash is the fastest man alive. He was struck by lightning, and he became as fast as lightning. He can run for days and never stop. He can run so fast that you can't see him."

"Is he a superhero?"

"He sure is."

"Cool!" Michael plopped down on the floor and grabbed the controller for his tractor. He drove it in circles around Becca, and she laughed as he ran into things and narrowly avoided her. Occasionally, she would pretend she was scared he was going to scoop her up and dump her somewhere else. Michael roared with laughter as he attempted to run her over.

Becca had no idea how much time had passed, but when she glanced out of the window after hearing footsteps down the hall, she realized it was dusk. She glanced around the room for a clock, found none then looked at her watch. "Michael, do you suppose it's getting close to bedtime?"

He sheepishly crossed his legs and looked down at his hands in his lap. "I guess."

"Do you think we should clean up your toys before bed, so your room is nice and clean in the morning?"

"I guess..." he muttered.

Becca smirked and picked up the tractor. "Where does this go?"

He jumped up, took it from her and put it in a cubby against the wall. It didn't take them long before the room was cleaned, and when he turned to look toward the door and not Becca, Becca was taken off-guard.

"We cleaned my room!" He beamed.

"That you did." Kimberly's voice was like silk, floating over Becca's skin and warming her. "Did you show Becca anywhere else other than your room?"

"Ummm. I did."

Becca glanced up in time to see Kimberly give Michael a look that meant business. "*Did* you?"

"No. We just played."

The smile that brushed Kimberly's lips was one of pure love. "Why don't you get changed into your jammies, and I will show Becca the rest of the house."

"Okay!"

He jumped up without another question. Becca, however, rolled to her side then got up to her feet. When she stood, facing the door, she found herself within an arm's reach of Kimberly. Her heart rate ratcheted up and her breath left her lungs.

"This way."

The curt tone was back, and Becca couldn't figure out if it was just her Kimberly wasn't liking or if she was like this with everyone. Doubling down on her efforts, Becca knew she'd have to make progress, otherwise her name would end up back on the available list like everyone else who had been through this house.

Becca followed Kimberly the way she had come before, her eyes focused on Kimberly's swaying hips. Kimberly had generous curves and a rounded butt covered by skin-tight leggings. Her shirt billowed a little more as she moved, her dark hair straight down her back.

"There's a bathroom at the end of the hall that Michael uses. The kitchen's here, living area... There is a den down that hall, along with two guest rooms. There's also the sunroom that leads to the pool that way. Michael is not allowed near the pool or in the backyard without you or me. You are CPR trained, correct?"

"Yes, ma'am," Becca answered.

Kimberly wrinkled her nose. "No need for that. You can call me Kim."

"Kim. Kim Burns." The click in Becca's head was nearly audible. "You're Kim Burns. How did I not put that together?"

Kimberly hummed to herself. "I am. Didn't think you recognized me. I tell Kiddie Academy not to share, so I'm not surprised they didn't tell you. That, and Burns is my maiden name, not my married name."

Becca's eyes widened again, her muscles locking up with a touch of fear and worry. "I'm so sorry. I should have recognized you. I've seen your cooking show."

"I don't expect people to know who I am, but thank you."

Becca grinned and winked. "I didn't say I liked your show. I just said I'd seen it."

Kimberly smirked, and it was the first time Becca felt she'd made a chink in Kimberly's thick and solid armor. It was a small one, but a chink at that. Kimberly pushed open the door to a room down a hallway the complete opposite direction from Michael's.

"This is your wing...bedroom and bathroom. You'll have to share the kitchen with us. I do apologize for that, but I rarely cook when I'm home."

"Don't blame you for that. I can't imagine cooking all day then coming home after work and wanting to cook again."

Kimberly let out a snort. "Exactly. We can discuss everything else once you get a bit more settled and once Michael is asleep. I'd rather not mess up his routine any more than necessary."

"Absolutely. I'll just bring in my stuff then."

"Here's a key." Kimberly held out the single key between her thumb and forefinger, dangling it in front of Becca. "I've got a file for you with the alarm code and everything else that you'll need to know."

"Got it." Becca reached forward and held her hand open so Kimberly could drop the key into her palm. She would much prefer to avoid touching Kimberly if at all possible. Something about her set Becca's nerves on fire.

* * * *

Michael was already tucked in bed, asking for anything and everything to delay bedtime once again. It was a song and dance Kimberly and her son had played many times. Smiling down sweetly at him one more time, she kissed his forehead.

"It's bedtime. Seriously."

"Okay," he whispered. "Water?"

"No," she answered, sternly. "I'll see you in the morning. Night-night."

"Night. Love you!" He gave her a cheeky grin with far too much energy for a four-year-old about to fall asleep.

"Love you, too."

Kimberly stood up, ran her fingers over Michael's cheek then exited the room, shutting the door as quietly as she could. The lights were still on in the kitchen and living area, and she could hear Becca going in and out of the front door. Rubbing her lips together, Kimberly paused in her tracks and debated where to go. Normally, she wouldn't help. It wasn't that she was cold or didn't have a generous bone in her body. It was because she'd done the in-and-out-of-boxes so many times in the last two years that she loathed the idea of doing it even one more time.

When she heard the door close, she shook her head at herself and headed down the hall toward the main part of the house. Becca had disappeared into her room. Kimberly followed her silently, stopping in the doorway. This was Becca's room, and she felt like an intruder to go beyond without an invitation. She knocked gingerly on the doorframe and leaned against it, crossing her arms over her chest.

"Do you need any help bringing your stuff in?" She tried to make her tone sound warm, but she feared it came off as cold. She often did that—and usually when she didn't want to.

Becca spun around as if surprised by her presence. Her dark red hair spiked perfectly behind her head, not moving with the no-doubt crazy amounts of gel in it, and her pale blue eyes widened.

Kimberly put her hands up. "I didn't mean to scare you."

"You didn't. Well, I guess you did. I didn't hear you at all."

"I have been accused before of being too quiet."

Becca wrapped her hands together in front of her. Kimberly straightened, tensing with nerves. She had to make this one work. Michael would start kindergarten soon enough, but Kiddie Academy had told her they would be canceling her contract if she fired another one of their nannies. She needed someone to help her.

"Do you have more things?" Kimberly asked again, not quite sure where to put her anxiety.

Becca shook her head. "No, this was the last of it. Did you want to talk about routine and everything else?"

"Sure. I was just going to grab a glass of wine. Do you want one? Wait! Are you even old enough for one?"

Shaking her head, Becca headed for the door. "Yes. I am old enough for wine, but I think I'll skip it tonight and just have some water."

Kimberly debated for one second whether or not to ask but gave in to curiosity. "How old are you, then?"

Becca scrunched her nose in Kimberly's direction before snorting. "I'm twenty-eight. Yes, I'm still in college, working on my bachelor's degree. Just taking it slowly—or as my mother would say, I'm on the twenty-year-plan."

"Sounds like my mom," Kimberly muttered as she reached the kitchen. "Glasses are in the cabinet to the right of the sink."

Becca pulled down a drinking glass for herself and a wineglass for Kimberly. She handed it over, and their fingers brushed. Kimberly jerked and opened the white wine a bit more forcefully than she had to. She poured herself a glass—a full one, almost to the rim—before she headed for the giant island in her kitchen and sat. Becca soon followed with her glass of water and took up the next stool over.

Kimberly pushed a manilla folder over and took a long sip of her wine. "This is the basics of what I have. My schedule, mostly. I'm in the middle of building the television part of my career, so my schedule is crazy."

"I Wiki'd you."

"You *what*?" When she looked at Becca, there was a slight blush to Becca's cheeks, and Becca refused to look Kimberly in the eye. "What did you find?"

"Random crap that may or may not be true."

Kimberly hummed and took another long drink from her wine. "At least you don't believe it all."

"I don't believe most of it."

Kimberly narrowed her eyes at Becca. "I appreciate that. Short story? My ex and I split over two years ago, although we lived pretty separately before that, if we're being honest. It was mutual, no hard feelings. We co-parent very well, mostly because Bradley has a hands-off tactic to parenting, but I have primary custody. Michael goes over there for one weekend a month and for two weeks in the summer—if Bradley ever actually takes him for two weeks."

"That sounds very amicable."

Turning on her stool to fully face Becca, Kimberly tried to judge where the tone was coming from. "You sound like you don't believe me."

"No divorce is amicable."

"It was when he admitted finally that he is gay. No point in staying married to a woman."

Becca's lips formed into a perfect 'O' shape and color rushed to her cheeks.

"Wasn't on Wiki, was it?" Kimberly snapped, this time allowing the anger to lace her tone. "He's a doctor for the rich and famous, so he has a busy schedule and isn't as interested in being a full-time daddy, but he does love Michael, and that's all that matters in the long run. You will have those weekends completely off. I am home as much as I can be, and when I am home, you do not have to do a thing with Michael. However, my schedule is long and has random hours. I'm often gone for days when I'm shooting a show or for twelve-to-fourteen hours when I'm in the restaurant. I'm the executive chef at Gamma's. That is when I need you to fill in the gaps."

"That's what I am here for." Becca spun the glass of water on the counter between her fingers.

Kimberly bit the inside of her cheek, sure she had already screwed up what was her last-ditch effort to provide some sort of stability for her son while she was a single working mom. Silence carried over them. Kimberly was hesitant to break it, not sure what to say, but knowing she probably should. Exhaustion fluttered through her bones, and she rubbed the heel of her palm sharply against her thigh, as it ached.

Becca was the one who spoke first. "So, if you don't cook at home, what does Michael eat?"

Kimberly snorted. "What I cook at the restaurant that's left over."

Becca hummed. "And you?"

"Doritos."

"Seriously?"

"What? That wasn't on Wikipedia?" Kimberly asked with a hint of sarcasm.

Becca clenched her hands, and her eyes drooped in sadness.

Kimberly wished she could take back her accusation, but she wasn't the kind of person to filter herself.

"I shouldn't have done that. I'm sorry."

Astonished, Kimberly shook her head. "No, it's natural for you to be curious. You'll have to learn I have a very odd sense of humor. It'll take a while for you to get used to it. Until then, feel free to just ignore me or call me crazy."

"I'll take that under advisement."

Kimberly finished her wine. "I have a short day tomorrow, so I'll be around in the morning if you have any questions."

Standing, she set the empty glass in the sink and turned to face Becca. Becca looked so young compared to how Kimberly felt. They were twelve years apart in age, but it felt closer to two lifetimes. Becca's life was just beginning and Kimberly's was smack in the middle.

"My room is down there, across from Michael's, if you need something."

"I think I'll be set."

Kimberly hesitated a moment before turning and heading toward her bedroom, leaving Becca behind. It had been a quiet day at home, but it had been stressful nonetheless. Kimberly turned the light on as she entered her room and shut the door behind her. After stripping out of her loose shirt and tight leggings, she pulled on loose pajamas and a tank.

Sleep was not her forte. She hadn't slept more than four hours since...she couldn't even remember when. Pulling out her laptop, Kimberly reclined in her bed and pressed the machine into her lap. She opened the top, scrolled her emails, then retrieved the one file she hadn't shared with anyone. It was a cookbook, a dream—something she'd always wanted to attempt but had struggled to get started. Even twenty years into her career, she still couldn't formulate how it should all go together. She skimmed her notes before growing frustrated and turning on the television to watch her favorite show and zone out. Perhaps tomorrow would be a new day.

Chapter Two

Becca'd been at the house for close to a week, and she'd barely seen hide or hair of Kimberly. Her employer was always rushing in one direction then another, and when she wasn't, she was spending time with Michael — and rightfully so. Their constant inadvertent avoidance of each other did not help to alleviate any of Becca's curiosity about her new boss.

What she'd learned about Michael was far more interesting. The routine she had been given for him was definitely out of date. According to it, he was still napping for three hours a day. After attempting on the first day to settle him and get him to sleep, Becca had given up and turned to just having a couple of hours of quiet time in which he might or might not sleep. Most four-year-olds didn't need hours of nap during the day.

His personality had taken a change in a wonderful direction when Becca had declared an end to nap time. Michael was a bright and bubbly kid, crazy-smart, who had a penchant for saying the most quizzical things. If she didn't know better, she'd think he meant everything he said as a joke. She smirked to herself as she put the final touches on their dinner.

"Michael, supper is ready."

He burst from the living area where he had been playing with a car in some high-speed chase. His feet pattered against the floor as he ran.

"Wait! It's not done yet!" he shouted.

"It's not?" Becca stood with her hands on her hips, scanning their plates and the skillet to see what she had missed.

"I need a towel." Michael grabbed the one settled on the rail of the oven and shoved it over his hand. He pointed a finger in the dish towel then got up on his stool, wiping his hand in a circle around the plate. He did it to one then the other.

Becca gave him a confused look when he set the towel down and grinned up at her. "Now it's ready."

"Where'd you learn to do that?" Laughing, Becca grabbed the food and headed toward the table so they could sit down to eat.

"Mom does it."

"She probably does." Becca set the plates down and pulled out the chair for Michael to climb into it. She pulled out her own chair before she slid to sit.

"I know she does." Michael grabbed his fork and stabbed a piece of the sliced chicken. He popped it in his mouth and giggled. "You're the bestest cook ever in the whole wide world!"

"Ahhh, thank you, kiddo." Becca's cheeks warmed, but her stomach dropped an instant later.

"Even better than me?"

"Mama!" Michael jumped off the chair and ran for the door. "You're home!"

Becca slowly turned in her chair, eyeing their unexpected dinner guest. Kimberly looked disheveled and not too much the worse for wear, but she had a tired look in her eyes. She opened her arms wide for Michael to run into them, but when she only closed her right arm around his shoulders, Becca narrowed her gaze even more. Kimberly winced.

"Have you eaten? We just sat down."

Kimberly sat in one of the empty chairs, leaning back and closing her eyes. "That sounds heavenly."

"I'll get it, Mama!"

"I'll help you." Becca stood and followed Michael into the kitchen.

He scrambled up the stool to grab a plate. Becca took the plate from him so he could stand near the stove. She carefully plated the chicken, the broccoli and the rice before dipping the spoon into the sauce and drizzling it over the top in a slow circle.

Leaning down, Becca whispered to Michael, "A good server always asks his customers what they want to drink."

Michael didn't hesitate before he raced over and grabbed Kimberly's hand. "What do you want to drink?"

"Water would be lovely." She caressed the back of his head before he ran to the kitchen.

Becca had already brought a glass down for him, and as soon as he got there, she handed it over. He put it up to the fridge and filled it before slowly walking to his mom with it in hand. Becca followed with the dinner plate in tow. She set it down before sitting in her own chair. Michael had already dived into his meal again, but Becca was stuck observing Kimberly.

Her face was drawn, her eyes downcast and her cheeks unusually pale. Her normally chipper attitude when returning home or seeing Michael was muted. *Something is wrong.* Becca had no idea what it was, but she knew Kimberly was off. Taking a bite of her own meal, Becca attempted to keep Michael distracted from whatever was going on while also still watching Kimberly to try to figure it all out.

Soon enough, they were finished eating, Michael's plate and hers had been cleaned, but Kimberly's was only half-touched, the chicken in particular left alone. Becca picked up the plates while Kimberly begged Michael to go get into his pajamas. Kimberly wandered into the kitchen where Becca was busy cleaning up and filled her water glass up again.

Becca held her tongue. As much as she wanted to ask what was wrong, she didn't. They didn't know each other well enough, and Becca wasn't sure how well asking a blunt question would come off, but there was something definitely up.

When, for the third or fourth time Kimberly did something and refused to move her left arm, Becca pulled out all the stops. She turned the water off and spun around, leaning against the massive sink with her arms crossed. She eyed Kimberly up and down, her gaze scanning from Kimberly's toes to her wide, luscious hips, to her breasts then her face.

"Like what you see?" Kimberly snarled.

Becca wrinkled her nose and ignored the attack. "What happened?"

"Nothing happened."

Pointing one finger at Kimberly, Becca smirked. "That right there tells me something happened. What did you hurt? You haven't used your left arm since you got home."

Kimberly rolled her eyes and spun on her heel. She turned and headed for the couch, flopping down. Becca, not willing to give up the fight she had picked, followed her and stood over her still form. She waited patiently and silently for Kimberly to give her an answer, and when she said nothing, Becca caved.

"Would you prefer Michael be in here to hear your story or would you prefer to share it before he's ready to be tucked in?"

"I slipped at the restaurant and fell down. Nothing more."

"They sent you home."

Glaring, Kimberly gave a curt nod.

"Because?"

Kimberly snorted. "Because I'm too old and sore to keep going tonight."

"Old and sore? Really?"

Kimberly waved her right hand. Becca caught it and squeezed briefly, drawing Kimberly's attention to her. Their gazes locked, and Becca sat down on the edge of the couch. She dropped Kimberly's right hand and reached for her left. Kimberly jerked it out of the way.

"Kim. It's more than just sore, isn't it?"

"Just sore."

"Let me see, then."

Huffing out a breath, Kimberly moved her arm so Becca could take a look. Gingerly taking Kimberly's hand in hers, Becca carefully inspected it. Scars from cuts and burns littered the top of her hand and even up along her wrist, but that certainly wasn't what was bothering her. Becca went to turn Kimberly's hand over, but Kimberly hissed and jerked away.

"Bend it."

"No." Kimberly glared.

"Can you?"

"No," Kimberly answered with a defeated tone.

Becca glanced at the hallway where she knew Michael was probably already done getting ready for bed. "You have to go to the ER."

"No."

"Non-negotiable. You probably broke it."

"I didn't break it."

"Kim…how exactly did you fall?"

"I'm not answering that."

"Fine. Did you land on your palm?"

Becca knew from the look Kimberly gave her that she had hit the nail on the head. Becca let out a short breath and leaned back, pressing her hand to Kimberly's thigh.

"I'll get you some ice for now, but you are going to the ER. I can either call one of my friends to come watch Michael if you don't have anyone, or he can come, but you have to get this checked out. This is your livelihood, remember?"

"I know." The sorrowful timbre was back.

Becca took it as a good sign.

"He can come. Hopefully it won't take too long," Kimberly answered, resigned.

"I'll drive then."

* * * *

They arrived at the ER to find a nearly empty waiting room. Kimberly relaxed, knowing they would most likely not be there all night, but she still wasn't happy about being dragged to the doctor. Michael bounced up and down. She reached over and placed a firm hand on his shoulder as she leaned over the admitting desk.

"Hi, how can we help you tonight?" The woman's sweet voice irked her, as did most things lately.

Kimberly took a breath and tightened her fingers on Michael's shoulder. Just before she was going to answer, Becca butted in.

"I'll take him over to the chairs. That way you can focus."

Kimberly gave a curt nod before answering the initial question, thankful someone was taking some control for once. "I had a fall at work and did something to my wrist."

After a few more questions and a clipboard of paperwork, Kimberly sat next to Becca and Michael, who flipped through a book that had magically appeared. Kimberly narrowed her eyes at it, trying to remember if it was one from home before giving up and focusing on the paperwork in front of her.

Becca and Michael chatted amicably while Kimberly waited, pain seeping from her fingers all the way up to her shoulder. She was glad Becca had come to entertain Michael, because she wasn't sure she had the wherewithal to deal with him and pay attention to her own medical needs.

Once Michael finished with the book he had been reading, Becca put it into a bag Kimberly hadn't noticed before. From the bag, she pulled out a second book, one of Michael's favorites. Becca read it to him, pointing at each word as she went. Michael followed along, saying the words he knew by heart. Kimberly closed her eyes and focused on taking deep breaths to relax herself. This was not where she'd wanted to end up. She certainly didn't want to be there with Michael in tow, but Becca had been right. She needed to get her wrist checked out.

"Kimberly Thompson." Her name rang through the near-empty waiting area.

Kimberly rustled around as she moved to stand up. Michael looked up at her with curiosity and a touch of fear, his brown eyes wide. Sighing, Kimberly jerked her head to the side.

"Come on then, the both of you. Let's get this over with."

The three of them trekked into a small room with a bed. Kimberly sat on the mattress while Michael and Becca took the chairs. She put her feet up, thankful for the place to rest, and closed her eyes. The nurse asked even more questions, which Kimberly answered, then she left.

Michael took the opportunity to sneak around the bed and pull himself up with the sheets so he could lie next to Kimberly. He snuggled under her good arm and pressed his face to her chest.

"The doctor will make your owie better, Mama. I promise."

Tears brimmed in Kimberly's eyes, and she bent her head to brush a kiss into his hair. When she looked over at Becca, she seemed enraptured in the moment. Kimberly afforded her a small smile before she closed her eyes and focused on Michael. He was her priority, day in and day out. He was the reason she wanted to advance her career — so she could care for him without any help.

She stroked Michael's hair gently as he snuggled into her side, staring beyond him at Becca. She clenched her jaw as she recalled how she'd treated her earlier that night. Even as closed off as she was, she knew she'd been nasty in a way that was unnecessary.

"I'm sorry about earlier," she confessed.

Becca jerked in her direction. "What?"

Kimberly bit her lip, annoyed she had to repeat herself. "I'm sorry about earlier. About what I said."

"You didn't say anything that offended me." Becca leaned forward, glancing at Michael before her gaze settled on Kimberly.

"Maybe not, but I wasn't exactly nice."

"Hmm. Well, I won't argue with you on that one." Becca folded her hands together.

Kimberly wanted to say something, something out of anger, but she held her tongue. "I was mean. I was in pain, which is not a valid excuse, but I'm sorry."

"There... That wasn't so hard, was it?" Becca's lips turned up in a smile. "Thank you for apologizing. I get the sense you don't do that often."

The humility in Becca's tone took Kimberly off-guard. Becca wasn't wrong, but it made her feel uneasy that someone she had known less than a week was able to pin so much of her down. Unsettled, Kimberly tugged lightly on Michael's hair.

"When the doctor comes in, you're going to have to move. Okay, kiddo?"

"Okay," he whispered, sleep lacing his voice.

They lay quiet for another ten minutes or so before there was a slight knock on the door, then it opened. Michael didn't rustle. Kimberly shifted to sit up a bit more, making sure the ice stayed firmly in place on her left wrist.

"Hi, I'm a PA here at the hospital. My name is Greg." He looked down at the chart in front of him. "Seems you had a fall and hurt your wrist."

"Slipped in the kitchen," Kimberly added. "Put my hand out to catch myself, which was only semi-successful until I landed hard on my ass."

Greg looked up without moving his head, eyeing Kimberly. "We'll probably get some X-rays of your wrist to make sure it's not broken and put it in a wrap. If it is broken, you'll need to get a cast at the orthopedist. We'll give you that referral if you need it."

"Okay."

"Let me look at it." Greg set the chart on the counter before rubbing some hand sanitizer between his hands. He came around the other side of the bed and carefully took the towel and icepack off. He lifted her wrist, didn't move it much, poked here and there then set it down with the ice on top of it. "We'll get some X-rays and go from there. It'll be a few minutes before they come in."

"Okay." Weariness seeped into her voice, and she was ready to go home, have a glass of wine, watch her favorite show and crash for the night.

Quiet fell over the room again as they waited, and waited, and waited some more. Michael snored away from his position next to Kimberly. The X-ray technician came into the room, wheeling the machine with him, and Becca stood up. Kimberly watched, curious, as Becca came over and rolled the sleeping toddler from the bed into her arms. She cradled him against her chest.

"We'll be outside until you're done," she whispered before heading out of the door.

Kimberly watched until she couldn't see them anymore. Sighing, she listened and followed instructions. She had the lead vest pressed over her chest and painfully positioned her wrist on the machine. Three times over, she had to reposition and wait for the picture to be taken. Once the tech was done, he wheeled the machine out, and Becca came in with Michael still sleeping in her arms.

"He's out cold," Becca said as she sat on the end of the bed.

"Must have had a busy day." Kimberly reached down and ruffled his hair. "I know I broke it."

"And you didn't come straight here because...?"

Kimberly stared at her shoes like she'd already been scolded. "I can't work with a broken wrist."

"Bullshit. You can. It'll just take some modifications, some serious patience and some tenacity—all of which I'm sure you can muster."

"Thanks for the pep talk." Sarcasm dripped off her tongue.

"You treat all the nannies this way? Because if so, I can see why you go through one a month. I'm surprised anyone even makes it that long." Becca stared straight at Kimberly.

The spotlight was on her. Kimberly knew her own issues with her personality. She was considered a great chef with a bad demeanor. She heard it every day in the restaurant when they thought she couldn't hear them, and she often heard it from the camera crew each time she filmed. She had been hardened over the years, for sure, but rightfully so.

Kimberly glared. "I pay well. But if you'd prefer to leave, the door is open. I'm not keeping you."

"Perhaps I pity you."

"Not my problem." Kimberly leaned against the pillows again, trying to ignore Becca as best she could. Michael was already far more attached to Becca than he had been to the last four or five nannies. And Kiddie

Academy had told her that if Becca quit or was fired, she would be dropped as a client. Backtracking, Kimberly let out a breath. "I didn't mean that. I seem to be apologizing to you a lot."

After a few moments of silence, Becca shook her head. "That wasn't actually an apology, but I'll take it as such since you admitted you were wrong."

"I...I am sorry."

Straightening her shoulders, Becca shifted ever so slightly so their thighs met. "I'll give you this round because I have no doubt you're in pain, but don't think you can treat me this way tomorrow or from here on out."

Thoroughly scolded, Kimberly chose not to speak. Every time she'd opened her mouth around Becca lately, she'd seemed to instantly regret it. Becca hadn't had to bring her to the ER, she hadn't had to take care of Michael during her off hours and she didn't have to consistently be nice to her. Kimberly was certainly better off keeping her mouth shut for at least the rest of the night.

Luckily, the PA came in and broke the awkward tension. "It looks like you have a clean break."

"Shit," Kimberly muttered.

"A nurse will come in and wrap it to keep the swelling down, and we'll get you set up with that referral, but since you work with your hands, I would strongly suggest you not work until you can see the ortho."

"That won't be happening. I'll take it easy, but I have to work."

Greg was halfway in and halfway out of the room. He stared Kimberly down, but must have given up, because he nodded and left. Becca looked surprised, but Kimberly shrugged almost nonchalantly.

"I have to work. I have shows booked that I can't cancel simply for a broken wrist. It's not my dominant hand. It'll slow me down, I'll wear a glove and I'll be careful, but I have to work. That is non-negotiable."

"He said a week, at most really. Just until you can get in to see the specialist."

"I'll give it tomorrow, but that's it."

"You're a bad patient."

Kimberly chuckled. "You are not wrong, Becca. Though I never claimed to be a good one."

They were there another hour before they were finally released to head home. Michael slept through most of it, but Becca woke him up when it was time for them to leave and had him walk next to them to the car. Kimberly slid into the passenger seat and let out a short grunt of pain when her hand hit the center console. Sore as she might be, she didn't want to let Michael or Becca know how much pain she was truly in.

The distinct clicks of the car seat let her know Becca would be joining her up front soon enough. Kimberly rubbed her eyes as the weariness of the day seeped into the rest of her unbroken bones. Of course she would break her arm a week before leaving town for a competition. She would have to make some serious phone calls come morning.

The drive home was mostly spent in silence. Becca drove carefully and pulled into the driveway. Kimberly went ahead of her, opening the doors and turning off the alarms as Becca carried Michael inside. Luckily, he was already dressed for bed, so Becca took him straight to his room and settled him in before coming back out to Kimberly.

Kimberly sat on the stool at the counter by the kitchen. Her stomach grumbled, and she remembered she had barely touched her dinner, which was very unlike her. No one would accuse her of missing a meal, ever. Kimberly stared longingly at the refrigerator, debating if she had enough energy to go find the left-over dinner.

"Want some dinner?"

"Yes... God, yes."

Shaking her head, Becca opened the fridge, pulled out the leftovers and heated them. It wasn't long before a warm plate of pre-cut chicken was set in front of Kimberly. Taking her first bite, Kimberly moaned as the flavors hit her mouth. She ate liberally and ignored Becca, who remained in the kitchen.

Once she was done, Becca was already cleaning up. Kimberly grabbed Becca's hand as she reached for a pan that remained on the counter from before they'd left. "Don't worry about cleaning."

"Habit," Becca muttered.

"My habit is to pay someone else to do it." Kimberly laughed lightly. "Advantage to working in a restaurant with dishwashers. It sucks when they're drunk and don't come to work, but eh, no dishes is a definite plus."

"I think that's the first time I've seen you smile all night."

Warmth blossomed in Kimberly's belly. As much as she wanted to ignore the feeling, she couldn't. It felt good to finally be able to talk with someone about something other than work or her ex-husband. She hadn't realized how lonely she had become over the last few years.

"Been a rough day," Kimberly answered.

"True. And with that, if you're demanding I stop cleaning, I'm going to head to bed. I imagine you won't be in fighting form in the morning."

"You are probably right. But, before you go, can I ask you one last favor?"

"Sure." Becca leaned against the counter with her hip, a smile on her face and her pale blue eyes sparkling. She looked relaxed for the first time since they'd met. "What do you need?"

Kimberly lifted her broken wrist and the tight but thick wrap job the nurse had done on it. "I'm going to need help getting my sleeve over this thing. I did not take that into account."

Becca snorted. She stepped around the kitchen island and reached for Kimberly's arm. Between the two of them, it took a few minutes to wiggle off Kimberly's chef's jacket. Becca checked the swelling briefly then told Kimberly goodnight and disappeared to her room. Kimberly turned off the lights as she walked to her own room, ready for a new day with new problems.

Chapter Three

The knocking was incessant. Becca tossed in her bed and threw the blanket over her head, trying to fall back into sleep, but the knocking kept up—pounding and pounding and pounding. Growling, she flipped the blanket off herself in a fit of rage. Pressing her feet to the cold floor, she wiped at her eyes and muttered a curse under her breath as the banging on the door got louder and the doorbell chimed in as well.

"Jesus Christ," Becca groaned and got to her feet, heading toward the front door. No one else was up in the house. The sun was up, shining brightly through the windows, almost blinding her. As she got closer to the door, Becca heard a voice shouting through it.

"Kimberly, open up! Come to the fucking door. Seriously, Kimmie. Open the damn door."

Becca glanced around to make sure Kimberly wasn't hiding in the kitchen or on the couch. She hesitantly stepped toward the door and peeked out of the small glass window before unlocking it and opening it.

"Who the hell are you?" a man with wide eyes shouted before trying to get around her.

Becca planted her feet firmly, refusing to open the door any farther.

"Who the hell are *you*?" she countered. "Don't you think it's a bit obnoxious to pound on a poor woman's door until someone comes to answer it? Aren't there better methods of getting someone's attention rather than being a beast in a suit?"

She eyed him up and down, deciding right then and there that she didn't like him. He was dressed impeccably, but his demeanor was all man, all power, all superior entitlement.

"I own this house."

"Bullshit." Kimberly's voice echoed down the hall as feet pattered heavily on the floor.

"Daddy!" Michael ran right by Becca and wrapped his arms around the man's legs, burying his face in his pants. "Why are you here?"

"Yes, why are you here, Bradley?" Kimberly snapped.

Becca decided to step to the side, thinking Kimberly had this handled better than she could, but she wasn't sure she wanted to leave all together.

"Who is she?" He jerked his head in Becca's direction and spat the question.

"Our new nanny."

Bradley wrinkled his nose at her as he picked up Michael and stepped into the house. Becca shut the door behind him, attempting to ignore the disgust in his voice and the fact that she suddenly felt like she'd been torn down two or three notches on the equality scale.

Kimberly repeated her initial question. "Why are you here?"

"I went to the hospital this morning and someone told me my wife had been in last night for a broken wrist." Again, he glared at Becca.

"Jesus, isn't patient privacy anything these days?"

"Not when it's your wife."

"I am *not* your wife."

Becca's back went ramrod straight, and she reached for Michael, ready to take him out of the room. Kimberly must have caught the move because she put a hand up to hold Becca off.

"I am *not* your wife," she repeated and smiled down at Michael.

"I am still on file as your emergency contact."

"Well, I'll be changing that ASAP," she muttered. "I fell at work. Broke my wrist." Holding up her tightly wrapped hand with noticeably swollen fingers, Kimberly smirked. "Becca here was so kind as to take me in to be seen. So, you can thank her then apologize for being such an ass."

Bradley's demeanor instantly changed. He ducked his head slightly and almost shuffled his foot like a scolded toddler. "I am sorry for making assumptions—"

"And for being an ass..." Kimberly added.

"And for being an ass," Bradley repeated. "And thank you for taking such good care of Kimmie."

Kimberly rolled her eyes but didn't add anything else. Instead, she turned around, plopped down on the stool at the kitchen island like she had the night before and relaxed. After a pause, she shot a glare at Bradley. "Aren't you supposed to be at work?"

He sighed, joining her in the kitchen with Michael still in tow. "I'll go back in a minute. I wanted to make sure you were okay."

"I'm fine," Kimberly said, exasperated.

Becca wasn't ready to fully leave Kimberly on her own yet, so she headed to start the coffee that both of them would no doubt need. She also wasn't sure Michael was going to be up for hearing their conversation. Filling the pot with water, Becca set up the coffee maker while also keeping one ear attuned to the rest of the suddenly full kitchen.

"Who did you get a referral to?" Bradley had picked Michael up and cradled him against his side. Michael melted into him.

Kimberly waved her good hand and shook her head. "I have no idea."

"What?"

"It was late. I just woke up. Let me catch my bearings."

"You need to see Jim."

Kimberly rolled her eyes. Becca leaned against the counter, both hands gripping the edge as she watched the dysfunction unfold in front of her. Michael hopped down from Bradley's arms and headed for the pantry. He came over with the box of cereal. Without thinking, Becca reached for the bowl and helped get him set up with his breakfast. The coffee percolating scented the kitchen with its deep fragrance.

"I will see whomever I want to see," Kimberly threw back. "It may be Jim. It may be someone else."

"Do you want me to take Michael for the rest of the week, so you can rest?"

"No. I'm going back to work tomorrow."

"You can't do that!"

Kimberly shot Bradley a glare that Becca was happy to not be on the receiving end of. Shivers ran down her spine as she watched anger build behind Kimberly's eyes before she tamed it to a slow roil. Her icy tone echoed throughout the house. "I will be going to work tomorrow."

"Kimmie, you could hurt yourself even more."

"That is *my* lot to lose. I am going to work tomorrow. I may not be cooking tomorrow, but I am going to work. There is certainly enough stuff to go around that I can and will find something useful to do."

Bradley put his hands up in the air in surrender. "Please take it easy, though."

"Fine." Kimberly put her head on her good arm on top of the kitchen island and closed her eyes.

Becca sensed her defeat and exhaustion. There was no masking it. Bradley stepped into the kitchen proper and pulled out a mug, filling it with coffee after reaching around Becca and getting into her space. Once again, Becca refused to move, forcing him to awkwardly angle his body to circle hers. She wasn't about to back down. When he stepped away, Kimberly watched them curiously.

Bradley headed for the door, but Michael caught on and raced over. He grabbed Bradley's leg and screamed, obviously not wanting him to leave. Both Kimberly and Becca stayed still while Bradley peeled Michael off him. "I'll see you in a couple of weeks, bud. You'll have all weekend with me. We can go to the movies and to the park."

Michael brushed away tears. "Really?"

"Really, really. I promise."

Nodding, Michael stepped away just enough for Bradley to sneak out of the front door and shut it. Within another second, Michael was at the door, on the floor, throwing the world's biggest fit. Kimberly sighed and slowly went to get up, but Becca stopped her with a gentle hand on her shoulder.

"I've got this one."

She headed over to him, sat next to him on the floor and pulled his small form into her lap. Becca leaned against the wall and shushed him gently, letting him cry. Michael curled into her, and she pressed a kiss to his head.

"What's going on, kiddo? What are you feeling?"

"I'm sad," he muttered through sniffled sobs. "I miss my daddy."

"I bet you do. But you know your daddy will come back, right? He's not gone forever. He'll always come back for you."

Michael nodded visibly calmed. His sobs became less, his sniffles further in between and he wiped his eyes, even though they were mostly dry. After a few more minutes of snuggling, Michael tensed and gasped.

"What?" Becca asked.

"My cereal is soggy." The whine was once again in his tone, and Becca knew she'd have to head it off before he had a second breakdown for the morning.

"You know what? You're probably right. Why don't you go get dressed for the day, and just this once, I'll make you a brand-new bowl."

"Really?" Michael asked sheepishly.

"Really, really," Becca answered.

Michael burst up from her lap and raced down to his room. Becca was far slower to get up, but once she got to the kitchen, Kimberly stared at her with a look she couldn't quite read. It was either surprise or appreciation, but there was something else mixed in that Becca couldn't put her finger on.

Kimberly broke the silence first as Becca set the soggy cereal into the sink. "He really is an ass, but he's also a great dad."

"I can see that," Becca answered, unconvinced.

"He really is."

"Why did he think he could just come in here like that?"

Kimberly glanced down the hallway toward Michael's room. "He wanted to stay married. I didn't. I'm not going to stay with someone who obviously isn't into me that way — or women in general. He loves me still — or the idea of me. He loves Michael. But I did not want an open relationship. I did not want to be made to feel like I was less than. So I kicked him out after I caught him cheating again and told him to go live his own life, which he is doing a really crappy job at."

Becca snorted. "I guess."

"Oh no, he is. He lives about three lives — one as an invasive cardiologist at the hospital, one as a father and one as a college boy who parties every night of the week and jumps on top of anyone who will let him."

"What?" Surprise laced Becca's tone. She grabbed another bowl and set it on the counter.

"It's true. Want to make me one of those?"

Without thinking, Becca grabbed a second and third bowl for each of them. "How's your arm this morning?"

"Sore. All of me is sore. I feel like I'm a hundred years old."

"Definitely don't look a hundred. Maybe fifty," Becca teased.

Kimberly smirked.

"Word of advice, though, before Michael comes back in here. Don't have those conversations or talk to Bradley like that in front of him." Becca wasn't sure she wanted to see Kimberly's reaction, but she hoped she'd listened.

"I know. I try, but I get sucked into it."

Becca kept her mouth shut, knowing that if she said anything else it wouldn't help the situation and would probably only push Kimberly in the opposite direction than she wanted. She finished making their breakfast and poured herself and Kimberly some coffee. Michael came running out and sat next to his mom. Becca put the bowl in front of him, and he dug into it.

"Seeing as how you're going to be here all day now, would you mind if I take the time for myself?"

"Got a hot date?" Kimberly shot back, malice edging her tone.

"No. I have an exam coming up, and I would like the extra time to study."

Kimberly turned her head slightly and narrowed her eyes in question.

"I'm working on my bachelor's degree, remember? I only have a couple of semesters left. Didn't you read my file?"

"Of course I did."

Becca could clearly see she had not. Shoving the odd feeling off, she explained, "I'm working on getting my degree in teaching. I want to teach elementary school."

"Oh."

"Anyway, I have a test. I could really use the time to study if you don't need me today."

"Sure."

Becca escaped to her room and sat on her bed with her cereal bowl in hand. That had been a far more eventful morning than she had anticipated. Settling into the quiet of her room—her sanctuary—Becca mentally took note of everything she wanted to accomplish that day. She was going to make the most of her newfound free time.

* * * *

Kimberly finally got the courage to knock on the door. Michael was busy playing, and she had to go into work. The texts and phone calls had gotten to be too much. There was some type of gastro bug going around the kitchen, and her hard, fast rule was 'do not come in sick.' Well, that meant people weren't coming into work and the kitchen was shorthanded, not to mention that they had a party of twenty coming in for dinner in the next hour. She couldn't put it off any longer.

Becca had left with such finesse that she wasn't sure she wanted to interrupt her. She'd appeared for lunch but had disappeared quickly back into her room. Kimberly had taken as much of the day to relax as she could and to rearrange her schedule so she could properly see the doctors who would surely yell at her for working, but she had no other choice.

Every time she had thought about walking down the hall to talk to Becca or check in with her, she'd had to remind herself she had no reason to do it. That, and embarrassment welled up in her belly and chest over everything Becca had witnessed that morning. Thus far she had been able to keep the nanny separate from the drama in her personal life, but Becca had seemed to slam face-first into it.

Forming a fist with her good hand, Kimberly rapped her knuckles three times against the door. Anxiety bubbled in her belly, and she had to draw in a short breath before she heard the sweet voice call her inside. Opening the door, Kimberly was not prepared for the scene that hit her.

Becca lay perched in her bed, dirty dishes on her nightstand, laptop on her lap and glasses sitting atop her nose. Her tank top was low on her chest, her shorts riding high on her long and lean legs. Becca barely glanced up to acknowledge Kimberly.

"Looks like you made yourself at home," Kimberly stated, crossing her arms carefully and leaning one shoulder against the doorframe.

Slowly looking up, Becca pulled the glasses from her face and popped them on top of her head. She raised her eyebrow in Kimberly's direction. "If you'd rather I not live here, I could leave."

"No!" Kimberly stood up straight and put both her hands out. "That's not what I meant. You just look comfy is all."

"Comfy in my own room."

"Yeah…" Kimberly trailed off. "Anyway, I have to go in to Gamma's."

"You said you weren't going."

"I have to. There's no way around it. I will take it easy, Scout's honor. But I do need to go help. They're short staffed. I won't be there all night, but I need you to watch Michael as we'd originally discussed. My schedule has changed because, you know" — she raised her wrapped hand in the air and waved it — "this. I put it on the calendar as best I could. Had to delay a trip to New York, but that's life."

"All right. When?"

"In ten minutes or so?"

"Got it."

Kimberly found her feet rooted to the floor as Becca stood up from the bed. Her gaze skimmed over Becca's curves as she sashayed toward her dresser, ignoring her still in the doorway. Somewhere deep in Kimberly's belly, heat flared, and try as she might, she couldn't tamp it down.

Before she became the creepy boss, she spun around and headed to her own room to get ready for work. It didn't take her long to dress and head out of the door. The drive was fast, and when she walked into

Gamma's, all her stress vanished. She was in her zone, and that she could control.

Once in the kitchen, she shouted out orders to help where she could, and when she realized there was no way to get around cooking, she pulled a glove over her left hand and did what she could without using it as much as possible. She shifted sauté pans around, cleaned the plates after they were finished and ready to go out, and she kept the kitchen running like clockwork.

As soon as the dinner rush was over, everything calmed and quieted. Kimberly glanced at the clock for the first time since entering the building and cringed. It was later than she'd expected, and she hadn't gotten any of her paperwork completed.

Her desk was scattered with papers and sticky notes, but she had to wade through it all to get some work done. Her wrist pulsed sharply in the wrap the nurses had done up, and her back and shoulder were just as sore. She really should have listened and stayed home, and she would no doubt pay for it when she got back later that night. Kimberly checked the profit and loss statement from the previous night and week, set up the final touches on the menu specials for the weekend that was fast approaching and reworked the schedule to avoid the sick and the injured personnel as much as possible.

Grimacing, she rolled her chair out from the desk and rubbed her tired eyes. Nothing good could come out of a broken wrist for her. Flexing her fingers, pain streaked up her arm to her elbow and she groaned. Her fingers were swollen. Her hand was swollen. Her feet and ankles were as well. Regretting coming in, she shut down her computer, closed her office and headed for the kitchen door. The kitchen was under control and she could leave without everything falling apart.

The car drive home was long, but she made it. Clambering out of the driver's seat and into the house, she near collapsed on the couch and rested her feet on it. The house was quiet—blessedly quiet. She toed off her tennis shoes then peeled off her socks, wincing at how swollen her feet and ankles were.

"You're home late. Michael kept asking for you."

Becca's voice caused a cascade of shivers to run down Kimberly's spine. She let out a breath and closed her eyes, enjoying the dark. "It was a complete disaster when I got there."

"I suppose you fixed everything."

"Mostly. Can't fix stupid, though."

The cushion of the couch by her feet shifted, and Kimberly opened her eyes to find Becca sitting on the edge. They stared each other down, and Kimberly eventually shifted so Becca could be more comfortable. "Here... You'll want this."

Kimberly took the proffered ice packs and kitchen towels. She settled them against her arm and sighed as the cool hit her skin. It was exactly what she needed. "This is heavenly. Thank you."

"Michael wants to learn to read."

"I guess it's about time."

"I can teach him, if you'd like. It'll be good practice for me."

"Sure. I can't. I'm a horrible teacher. I have no patience for it." After a brief moment of silence, Kimberly licked her lips and spoke again. "I'm sorry about this morning. You really did not need to see that or be drawn into our drama."

"Don't worry about it—"

"No, really, I'm sorry. I don't apologize often, as you so cleverly pointed out, so take it when I give it."

"Yes, ma'am," Becca smarted back.

Kimberly rolled her eyes and shook her head while a smile tugged at her lips. "You're just as smart with that mouth as I am sometimes."

"You like it. Don't deny it."

Chuckling, Kimberly nodded. "Yeah, I suppose I do. It's annoying—don't get me wrong—but I would also call myself annoying, after, you know, a bossy bitch."

As soon as the words left her mouth, the air was sucked out of the room. Kimberly knew she had taken a misstep somewhere, but she couldn't figure out where.

"I wouldn't call you a bitch. Blunt, yes. Stubborn. You know what you want, and you're not afraid to get it. There's nothing wrong with that."

"Sometimes there is." Kimberly grinned and shifted the ice pack slightly. "I'll let you get to bed. I'm just going to lie here until I morph into the couch."

Laughing, Becca stood up. "See you in the morning."

Once again alone, Kimberly flipped on the television to completely zone out to whatever was on. She wasn't quite sure what she would have done without Becca there the last two days. Either way, she was very glad she had her to rely on, even if it was a struggle to admit she needed help.

Chapter Four

The afternoon was quiet. Kimberly was at work, and Michael was curled up on the couch reading his book to her for the hundredth time that day. He knew every word by heart, so Becca knew he wasn't actually reading—rather, he was reciting from memory. She smiled as he read through it once more. Becca took the book from him, hoping to distract him, and smiled.

"How about we learn to really read a book?"

"Oh! Yeah. That sounds fun! Which book?"

"I have a special one in my room just for that. Let me go get it."

Becca got up and Michael followed, bouncing on the balls of his feet as they went. She opened her door to her semi-clean room and found the book she'd left on her dresser for just that reason. After walking to the couch, they sat down. Becca opened it to the first lesson.

"We're going to learn sounds, then we'll learn the words when we can put sounds together. Okay?"

"Okay. What sound is this?" Michael pointed to a letter.

"Eh."

"What about this one?" He touched another.

"Michael. Be patient. We have to focus in order to learn, okay?"

"Okay."

"Here's the first sound." Becca read it and touched just under the sound. Michael repeated after her. They spent the next thirty minutes going through the three sounds and repeating them slow then fast then slow again—then rhyming words together. Michael looked ecstatic, but he tired of the lesson as she expected he would. Once he was fidgeting and not paying close attention, Becca put the book down and turned on the television. She found the guide and put on some music.

"Let's have a dance party."

"Oh yeah!" Michael stood up and danced barefoot on the rug in the living area. Becca made sure to set the music to something upbeat, then she joined in.

She was laughing as she tried to copy Michael's dance moves and giggling when he tried to copy hers. Neither of them were very good dancers, but they were having fun and burning energy, which had been Becca's goal. After the third song, Becca grabbed her phone and took a video of Michael dancing.

He laughed. "Who will see that?"

"I thought I would send it to my mom. She always loves to see what we're doing."

Michael grabbed Becca's phone and played the video again, laughing at himself as he did a particularly interesting and wild move. "Can my mom see this, too?"

"You want me to send it to her?"

"No. A different one. You and me dancing. We'll show her that one."

"What? I don't think your mom will want to see that."

"Yeah. Both us." Michael grabbed Becca's hand and tugged. "Please!"

Giving in, Becca set up the phone on one of the side tables, and she hit record as soon as the next song came over the television. Michael grabbed her hands and together they danced and laughed as the music blasted. Once it was done, Michael ran over to the phone, waved, told his mom he loved her then brought Becca the phone.

"Now show it to my mom."

"Give me a minute." Becca flipped through her contacts, sent it to her mom with a note. Then she sent the text to Kimberly, hesitating for only a brief moment before she picked which video to send, but Michael had told her the one with both of them. She typed out a short message, attached the video and hit send, hoping Kimberly didn't think too poorly of her.

"I'm thirsty," he said.

Becca laughed. "Let's get some water then. We can dance more tomorrow."

As soon as they made it into the kitchen, Michael chugged his glass of water and asked politely for more. He drank down his second glass and asked for a third. Becca's eyes widened. She filled it again but told him to drink more slowly this time.

Michael set his cup on the counter. "I'm hungry."

"When are you not, kiddo?"

He laughed. "What's for dinner?"

"I have no idea. What do you think we should have?"

"Hmmm..." Michael folded his arms across his chest and put his finger to his mouth like he was thinking. "Cereal?" Michael cracked himself up, laughing at how funny he thought he was.

Becca opened the refrigerator. "We had cereal for breakfast. I don't think we should have it again for dinner."

"Chicken?"

"Maybe. I think there's some leftover from the other night."

"Bleh." He pulled a face.

Becca scrunched her nose. "What? You didn't like my chicken?"

"No way!" He laughed again.

"What about pasta?"

"Lasagna?" he specified.

"Let's see if we have the stuff for it."

Becca rustled around in the fridge then in the pantry. She found most everything she usually used except one of the cheeses. Though she had never cooked with such fresh cheeses before, she pulled everything out and set it on the counter.

"Okay, kiddo. We can make lasagna, but you have to help me."

"Mom doesn't let me cook."

"What? Why?" Becca searched for a casserole dish and set it on the counter before reaching to grab a pan.

Michael pouted his lip out and put his head down. "She says I get in the way."

"Oh, honey, she's just not used to having a kid in the kitchen. Tell you what... We will make lasagna, and you get tell her all about how you helped make it. Sound good?"

"I guess." He shuffled his foot against the ground.

Adrian J. Smith

"Good. Now, Chef Michael, can you get me the oil? We're going to cook up this sausage and some ground beef."

Michael perked up immediately. They spent the next hour or so in the kitchen, Becca teaching him as much as she knew and asking him for help pouring, mixing and layering the lasagna. It was her grandmother's recipe she had stolen when she'd left the house.

Once they'd put it in the oven, Becca got down on Michael's level. She smiled. "Now, Chef Michael, you know this recipe is a family secret." She put her finger over her mouth. "So, no matter how much your mom begs for it—because she's going to love it because you made it—you cannot share with her. Okay?"

He nodded. "Got it. I promise."

"Good. What do you want to do while it cooks?"

"Read!"

"Kid after my own heart." Becca pressed her fingers to her chest and smiled. "I love that you love to read."

Michael bounded off to his room to get a book, and Becca settled in. If she were willing to admit it, she was already falling in love with Michael. He was brilliant, funny, energetic and had a bright personality. She had connected with him right away, and luckily, she was pretty sure the feeling was mutual.

* * * *

Kimberly sat in her chair in her office, finally having a minute to relax. The dinner rush was about to gear up, and luckily, she had been able to avoid most of the kitchen that day and let her body rest. Bradley had sent her a couple of texts throughout the day to check in on her, and she'd sent curt messages back but largely ignored him. His outburst the previous day had been uncalled for, and she was still sour over it.

The message from Becca made her heart skip. She opened it, not knowing what to expect, but when she saw the video, she smiled. The message was simple — *Michael wanted me to take this video and send it. He misses you every day you're gone.*

Hitting play, Kimberly watched and laughed as the two of them danced to a song playing loudly from the television. She wished daily that she could be with him all day every day, just as much as she wished she could grow her career. She wanted her cake, and she wanted to eat it too — and sometimes that wasn't possible. Her heart hurt at how much she wished she could be there, dancing with them.

The knock on the door stirred her out of her reverie. "Chef, there's a problem."

"Yeah." Kimberly's voice broke. She cleared her throat and repeated herself. "Yeah. What's going on?"

Her dishwasher summoned her with a finger and a head nod. Kimberly reluctantly got up out of her chair and headed toward the kitchen. The tension there was thick, and she wasn't sure she was ready to walk into whatever hellfire was happening. On the stainless-steel counter sat an appetizer plate with hardly anything eaten off it.

"What's going on?" she asked, authority lacing her tone.

"This was sent back," Maury, one of her head chefs, answered. "Apparently it's too salty."

"What?" She grimaced and poked at the plate with a fork she grabbed. She stabbed a piece of potato and popped it in her mouth, thinking through the flavors as they hit her tongue. Rosemary. Salt. Pepper. Sweet. Vinegar. Nodding, she took one more bite then invited Maury to take his own taste.

"I don't taste salt," he said.

Kimberly tilted her head to the side and nodded. "Correct. There's salt, but it's not overwhelming. There's too much vinegar. Make sure they're just putting a splash in *before* cooking the rest of it."

"Yes, Chef," Maury answered.

Kimberly went to her office and pressed on through her paperwork. It was her least favorite part of the job, which was why it had backed up so much, and since she couldn't cook, it was the only reason she was dedicating so much time to it. Pursing her lips, she stared at her computer screen again, a headache brewing in the front of her skull. At first it was a dull throb, then it became a sharp stab.

Downing caffeine and a couple of migraine pills, Kimberly set back to work. The ruckus from the kitchen called out to her, but she ignored the tugging sensation and focused on her work. If she were lucky, she'd get ahead for the first time ever and get to spend more time cooking once her wrist was well on its way to healing.

She had a second cup of coffee to try to dull the migraine even more, but once it started pounding, she gave up. Kimberly left her office and went out to the kitchen. She checked on all her chefs, making sure they were keeping pace with the orders and maintaining the quality of the dishes. She tested a couple, added salt to some and butter to others. Making her rounds, Kimberly relaxed as her headache eased.

Not one to miss out, she did jump on the line and chop up a few onions and bell peppers. Her cuts were precise, and the rhythmic repetition set her even more at ease. This was going to be a long couple of months while she waited for her wrist to heal, and thank goodness it was her non-dominant wrist, otherwise she'd be in even more of a tizzy.

Eventually, Maury chased her off the line, and Kimberly retreated to her office. She watched the video Becca had sent one more time before she dove into her work. It was going to be a long night.

* * * *

It was past midnight when she stumbled into the house. All the lights were off, save the one over the stove. Kimberly reached bleary-eyed for the kitchen switch so she could see. The house was clean, and it felt good to hear nothing but the sweet lullaby of Michael's sound machine echoing down the hall.

Any other night and it wouldn't have been so exhausting, but with everything else that had happened, she'd been siphoned of all her energy. It was as if the last two weeks had been never-ending, and she knew the next two were going to be just as bad. Her follow-up appointment with the ortho was in the morning, and she no doubt would have one more before she'd get a real cast—thanks to the doctor ex-husband for warning her of that in one of his many random texts throughout the last few days.

Kimberly grabbed the handle to the fridge and sighed as her stomach rumbled. She pulled the door, fully expecting nothing to be made, but was pleasantly surprised when she saw the nearly full casserole dish of lasagna sitting on the second shelf.

"Score!"

She grabbed the glass dish and set it on the counter. Not hesitating, Kimberly grabbed a fork, pulled at the foil and went to town on the cold lasagna. She was at least halfway through what might be considered a third piece when the light to the living room flashed on, nearly blinding her. She froze, fork mostly to her lips and mouth wide open. Becca stared at her with a look of amusement on her face.

"What?" Kimberly asked.

"Didn't even want to heat it up?"

"It's too good."

"Aww, well thank you. I take that as a compliment, coming from you."

Kimberly wrinkled her nose and straightened her back, the last bite of lasagna still hanging precariously on to her fork. "What's that supposed to mean?"

"You're this popular, huge, well-known chef. You like my food."

"I like a lot of food, especially food I don't cook. Especially cake. I like cake a lot."

Becca snorted and walked over to the kitchen island. She took the lasagna and cut off two heaping hunks. She grabbed a couple of plates and warmed them in the microwave. Kimberly poured two glasses of white wine then sat on the stool. It didn't take long for the beep of the microwave to sound. Becca put the plates down, grabbed herself a fork and swung around to sit opposite Kimberly.

"Oh, was that second plate for you?" Kimberly teased as she slid the plate closer to herself. "I thought you were just reading my mind and being generous."

Narrowing her eyes, Becca chuckled. "It's my grandmother's recipe."

"Italian?"

"Surprisingly, no. Polish. But she grew up living next to Italians, her best friend was Italian and she stole as many recipes as she could."

"Best idea ever," Kimberly said around another mouthful of lasagna. "Does this have sausage in it?"

"Sweet sausage and beef."

Kimberly moaned around the next bite she took. It seriously was a heavenly meal, and she had plans to eat the rest of the lasagna before she left for work the next day. "God, this is good. I may need to steal your recipe."

"Chef's secret. I'll never share."

Grinning, Kimberly leaned back slightly, fairly certain that Becca was flirting with her. It had been a long time since anyone had. The wall she kept up at all times made sure of that, but if she didn't know better, she would think Becca was — and she liked it.

"I'm sure I'll get it out of you some day," Kimberly teased. "Maybe I can figure out all the ingredients if I sit here and eat everything."

Laughing, Becca took a bite for herself. "Maybe you can, but I'll never tell you if you're right or wrong."

"Touché." Kimberly was halfway done with her newest piece of lasagna and was unabashedly planning on getting herself another.

Becca took a long sip of wine before saying, "Michael might share it with you before I do."

"Oh?"

"Yeah. He helped me cook it today. He was fully entranced by making the sauce."

"You made the sauce from scratch?" Kimberly was impressed.

Becca shrugged. "You didn't have any, but you had all the ingredients for it."

"I'll give you that one."

They ate in silence for a few more minutes. Kimberly pushed her plate to the side after finishing it. "Why are you up so late?"

"Studying."

"Ah, yes, for your test."

Becca nodded. "Educational Psychology."

Kimberly's eyebrows lifted. "That's a heavy class."

"Yeah, not my strong suit. I much prefer the method and curriculum classes. This one... This one is a doozy. I'm worried I'll fail it."

"You won't. Make sure you don't. I know I couldn't pass it, but you seem much smarter than me."

Becca smiled softly. "Did you go to college or just culinary school?"

"Both."

"What'd you major in?"

"Nothing useful." Kimberly drank the last of her wine and got up for a refill of both her drink and her plate. While the microwave buzzed to life, she turned to Becca. "Anthropology. Very interesting to learn, nothing to do with that degree without getting another degree, and let's face it, school is not my thing. I struggled just to graduate."

"So why cooking?"

Kimberly shrugged and grabbed her hot plate. "Got my first job at the school cafeteria, loved it and realized I liked working there way more than I liked school. I was decently good at it. Thought I'd keep it going."

Becca nodded. "Sounds like you found your passion."

"Why teaching?"

Shrugging, Becca smiled. "I love kids. I love watching them learn and when they have that moment when something clicks and they get it. They're so smart and don't know it. It's really quite a contrast I love living into."

"Then it sounds like you found the right major for you."

"I think I have. I've been putting off my degree because of student teaching and not being able to find the time for it and work, but I'm almost to the point that I have no other choice. I have to do it sooner rather than later if I ever want to actually be a teacher. I don't want to end up being a perpetual student."

"I hear you there." Kimberly finished her last piece of lasagna and knew she couldn't manage to shove another one down her throat, as much as she wanted to. "Was he good today?"

"He was excellent. He's so creative. I love it."

"Yes, I think he takes after me in that area, but he's definitely got his dad's brain."

Becca didn't respond. Instead, she cleaned up. Kimberly sensed their camaraderie was over and cleaned up her own mess. Becca put the rest of the lasagna in the fridge while Kimberly slid the plates and glasses into the empty dishwasher.

Kimberly made sure to catch Becca before she headed to her room. She pressed her fingers into Becca's arm to get her attention then leaned against the counter. "I have to shoot an interview early next week. I'd love it if you could bring Michael. I haven't really had anyone to bring him before, anyone he actually connected with, and it's clear to me he likes you. I know he would love to be there in person rather than just watching Mommy on the TV."

"I think he would love that."

"Good." Kimberly let out a breath she hadn't known she'd been holding. "I guess I'll see you in the morning."

"In the morning, then." Becca left, and Kimberly soon followed her cue and headed off to her own room.

It was easily two in the morning before she fell asleep comfortably after having to adjust herself and the pillows a hundred dozen times. The swelling and her wrap itched like mad, and she had to mentally talk herself down from going back to the kitchen to grab a fork and scrape it under the temporary cast. After finally clearing her mind and begging the caffeine she'd drunk earlier to stop keeping her awake, Kimberly fell into a light slumber.

Chapter Five

The car service was a nice perk, and as soon as Michael stepped out of the front door, his jaw dropped. Becca laughed and grabbed his hand to lead him toward it. Kimberly had finished installing his car seat, so when Becca and Michael got there, he was near bouncing out of his shoes. He climbed into the SUV, full of energy and talk. Kimberly followed behind him, buckling him in while Becca walked around and got in on the other side.

As soon as she shut the door, Michael's constant chatter was her friend. As they pulled out of the drive, she zoned out slightly as she listened to him continue on and on about the weather, the cars they passed, the set they were going to, his best friend Kamryn, who he missed, the episode of his favorite show he had watched three weeks ago and more. Small things made Becca smile, but she let Kimberly take the lead on entertaining him for the drive. It was her job to do it once they arrived.

They were actually going to two places that day. The first was a late morning talk show, where Kimberly was expected to cook a quick summer specialty in something like three minutes or less. Becca had shaken her head at the thought. She had no idea what to expect from a television set. The second was an actual cooking demo, where Kimberly would be spending about an hour with an audience, teaching and answering questions. That one sounded far more interesting.

"Becca." Kimberly leaned forward so she could see Becca across the car seat. Michael stopped talking and just observed. "I think they said you could watch the cooking demo from the back if you and Michael would like to. You might not want to stay the whole time—it'll be long—but if that would interest you..."

"It would, for sure." Becca gave Kimberly a small smile and settled back as Michael voiced his agreement.

"Yes! I want to watch Mama cook."

"He loves cooking," Becca commented, more to herself than to anyone.

Kimberly leaned over again, a puzzled expression crossing her features. She looked to the floor. Becca caught the glance and shifted so she could see Kimberly completely. Michael looked curiously between the two of them. After a few more seconds of silence, Becca pushed herself to ask the question on her mind.

"Does that surprise you?"

"Yeah, I suppose it does."

"I love cooking, Mom," Michael chimed in.

Tears threatened Kimberly's honeyed eyes. "I didn't know that, kiddo. We should cook dinner together tonight."

"For Becca? Can we cook for Becca?"

Kimberly's mouth opened and closed. Becca's nerves bubbled up, and she searched for an excuse. Clearly, Kimberly was not comfortable with that. Becca put a hand on Michael's leg. "Kiddo, I don't think I'll be able to do that tonight. Maybe some other night."

"Tomorrow night?"

Becca chuckled and shook her head. "You and I can cook dinner tomorrow night, because your mama has to work tomorrow."

"Breakfast. I love pancakes. Mama, can we make pancakes for Becca tomorrow?"

Once again, Becca was met with a lost look on Kimberly's face. Before she could give another rebuttal, Kimberly slowly nodded. "Yes, we can make pancakes for Becca tomorrow morning."

"Yay!" Michael clapped his hands together and kicked his legs out in excitement. Then he turned on Becca. "My mom makes the bestest pancakes in the whole widest world."

"I bet she does." Becca reclined in the seat, determined not to intrude on any more family time if she could help it. While she loved spending time with Michael, she recognized the need for space. Glancing out of the window, she watched as cars, highways and buildings passed by.

It wasn't much longer before they arrived at the studio. Kimberly had filmed the late-morning talk show twice before, and apparently the fans had particularly liked her. As soon as she arrived, it was as though she owned the building. She walked in with confidence—a complete change from what Becca had seen of her before leaving the house, which had been close to utter chaos.

Becca held Michael's hand as they followed. They were shown to a room where they would spend most of their time while Kimberly was out on the stage. Becca pulled out some small toys and books for Michael while Kimberly ran through her to-do list. The two of them played on the couch as Kimberly left for makeup and came back shortly after.

Michael nearly jumped out of his shoes when his mom came back into the room. Becca's heart flew into her throat, and she had to tamp it down. Kimberly looked so different. Her hair was pulled into a tight ponytail, but all the loose strands that tended to float around her face were smoothed away and not to be found. Her eyelashes were long and sultry, her honey-colored eyes left to stand on their own against the rest of her darker complexion.

Becca swallowed hard as she remained sitting. Kimberly smiled as Michael ran over to hug her, declaring he had missed her desperately in the last hour she'd been gone. Kimberly laughed, told him she'd missed him too then invited him to go with her to the kitchen. When Becca didn't move swiftly enough, Kimberly stopped mid-turn and cocked her head to the side.

"Coming?"

"Yes." Becca's voice broke, so she cleared her throat and tried again. "Yes."

Following Kimberly was an adventure. She'd never been backstage before. There were rooms upon rooms until she came upon a small kitchen area. It had a large oven and burners, a counter — all the bells and whistles a normal kitchen had, plus some. Michael spent the next hour helping his mom prepare three sets of the same three dishes, leaving all of them in various states of unfinished except one.

A timer resounded in the room, and Michael rushed over to the oven, jumping up and down. "It's done! It's done!" He took in a deep breath through his nose and made a slurping sound with his mouth. "It smells soooo good."

"It does." Carrie Danforth came in through the door, startling Becca. She bent down close to Michael and smiled. "I can't wait to taste it, can you?"

He shook his head then hid slightly behind his mom's leg. Kimberly reached down and pressed her hand into his back, comforting him. She turned to Carrie and smiled. "This is my son, Michael."

"Hi, Michael," Carrie replied. "I'm Carrie."

Carrie extended her hand. Carefully and slowly, Michael took it and shook before hiding behind his mom again. Becca waited for a sign that Kimberly wanted her to take him to their room before the show began, but Kimberly made no such request.

"This is Becca."

"Hi." Becca waved her hand, trying to pull herself together and not be starstruck, but never in her wildest dreams had she thought she would be meeting the host of a daytime talk show. This was so far out of her world that no one would believe her even if she told them. "I'm just the nanny."

Kimberly shook her head. "Not *just* the nanny. I wouldn't be able to do this without her."

Heat tinged Becca's cheeks. Carrie held out her hand and shook Becca's. "Well, glad you're here to help out."

Carrie turned to Kimberly. She took a few steps forward and gripped Kimberly's broken wrist tenderly. "What happened here?"

"Ah, I broke it. Stupid, really. Fell in the kitchen at Gamma's. Clumsy me."

"Can you cook?"

"Oh, yeah. I can cook. Always." A twinkle entered Kimberly's eye. "It's my non-dominant hand, so I'm lucky—but I can cook."

"Good. Just be careful, okay?"

"Always."

Carrie pursed her lips, narrowed her eyes as she judged Kimberly. "I don't believe you, but that's okay. What are you making today?"

"Grilled salmon filets with lemon, grilled veggies in a lemon-herb sauce and a peach crumble. That's what Michael here has been waiting for."

"Well, it does smell delicious. Did you help your mom make all this?"

Michael nodded vigorously, but he didn't make a sound.

"I really can't wait to try it all. I bet it tastes as good as it smells."

Shyly, Michael put his head into his mother's leg, hiding from Carrie.

Carrie turned to Kimberly. "It's always a pleasure to have you here. We shouldn't make it so long next time."

"Absolutely."

Carrie left, and Kimberly finished setting up. Michael stole leftover sliced peaches from the counter as he danced around the kitchen in joy. Becca remained fairly quiet, not sure what to say or do. Everything was a new experience for her, and she was unsure what proper etiquette was, so she kept Michael in line as best she could and watched Kimberly in her zone.

She wasn't paying attention when Kimberly turned with a fork of food in her hand and a smirk on her face. "Here... Try this."

Before Becca could even answer, Kimberly shoved the fork toward her. Parting her lips, Becca took the proffered bite and moaned around the bright bursts of lemon on the salmon. Becca put her hand to her mouth and moaned again as a second wave of flavors hit her.

"I love salmon," Kimberly whispered like it was some big secret.

"It's really good. Thank you." Becca swallowed the last of it and glanced around to try to find Michael, making sure he wasn't getting into any mischief he should be avoiding.

"We won't have time to stay afterward for the crumble...also one of my favorites. Dessert-anything, really."

"Like your sweets, do you?"

"I wouldn't look like this if I didn't."

Becca gave her a puzzled look. "Look like what?"

"Fat."

The word clung to the air in the room. While Kimberly hadn't said it as a curse or accusation, the word left all that in its wake. Becca touched Kimberly's arm briefly, unsure what to say. She gave her a sorrowful look, one with pity and disbelief, but words wouldn't come to her.

"What? It's true. I'm fat. I'm old. I'm not exactly nice. Wonder why I'm still the single one with not even one date in the last year, and he's the one out there with a new boyfriend every week? I don't."

"I don't for one second believe that."

Their conversation was interrupted by a loud bang. Michael's sobs echoed a second later. Both Kimberly and Becca twisted sharply toward the noise to find Michael clutching his hand, his face turning red and tears streaming down his cheeks.

Kimberly raced over to him and wrapped him in her arms. Becca moved over, touching his hand to check it as Kimberly continued to soothe and calm him down.

"I just… I just hurt my fingers," Michael made out as soon as he was calm enough to talk.

"Did you slam them in the cabinet?" Kimberly asked.

"Yes!" His answer sent him in another flurry of sobs.

Kimberly hugged him tight, but the door opened with someone calling her name. Becca shifted to take over as Kimberly stood. It didn't take her too long to calm Michael completely. She lifted him into her arms, and he curled into her. Kimberly came back and pressed a hand to his cheek.

"Mama has to go do some work now, okay, kiddo? I'll be back soon. You can watch on the TV in the room, if you want."

"Watch you on TV?"

"Yeah! If you want to."

He nodded and wiped his eyes again. "I wanna watch."

"Becca can take you in there and watch too."

"Okay. You go to work now?"

"I do have to go to work now. I'll see you in a little bit, then we'll go to another one of mama's jobs."

"Okay."

* * * *

It took another three hours before they were able to leave, but Kimberly found herself once again sitting in silence in the back seat of an SUV with nothing other than a car seat and sleeping child separating her from Becca. Michael had passed out as soon as they'd turned onto the highway, surely the excitement from the day overwhelming him.

Forty-five minutes later, they pulled up at a local culinary school. The morning had gone better than expected, but the afternoon was what was going to take a long time. She could only hope Michael would be able to behave through it. At least this job would be more laid back than the previous one.

She relaxed as best she could, gathering herself and her energy for what was to come next. She must have dozed off, because a hand on her arm and a soft voice calling her name woke her up. When she flitted her eyes open, Becca's baby blues stared at her.

"We're here," Becca whispered. "He's still out."

"Wonderful. He's not usually very much fun when he wakes up."

Becca hummed her agreement. Kimberly reached for the buckles on the car seat and unhooked them, jarring Michael from his sleep. He jerked, eyes popping open, then he stretched and groaned.

"We there yet?"

"Yeah, baby, we're here."

He strained his neck to look outside the window. "You work here?"

"Yup. I'm working here today."

Becca climbed out of the car as Kimberly helped Michael down. They went inside, Becca following close behind as Kimberly led the way. She got to the large classroom, and her nerves shot through the roof again. There was a reason why she preferred to be in her kitchen and on television. Fewer people.

She did not boast the best personality for dealing with crowds, and it had taken her a long time to learn how to teach well and effectively. She wasn't the most personable chef out there, which made each of these demonstrations — or talk shows, or interviews — that much harder. She had to be on her best behavior and really hold her tongue.

The room was empty of an audience when they all walked in, but Kimberly knew they were in the right place. The lights were on, and there were people up front around the kitchen on the stage, working and preparing. One woman in a button-up blazer approached with her hand held out.

"Kim Burns, good to meet you finally. I'm Jessica Reims."

"Ah, yes. Good to meet you, too."

"This is where you'll be cooking today. I'm sure you'll want to walk through and get everything set as you want it. Feel free... The room and the kitchen are yours. Kyla here will be your sous chef, so if you need anything during the demonstration, ask her and she will get it or do it for you."

"Hi, Kyla," Kimberly said as she held her hand out in a greeting.

"Chef," Kyla responded. "I always have admired watching you cook."

"Well, thank you," Kimberly answered, her cheeks flushing with a slight burn. Compliments like that always surprised her. She knew she was a decent cook, but some people made it out to be as if she was one of the best, and even with all her years of experience, she wasn't sure she agreed with that. "This is my son, Michael, and his nanny, Becca. They wanted to join today and see a bit of what my work is all about."

Becca gave a small smile, but Michael was beaming. Kimberly put her mind to the work in front of her and entered the kitchen. She put pots and pans exactly where she wanted them, moving the tomatoes and pasta from one side of the kitchen to the other. She was supposed to showcase the new pots and pans. She'd been cooking with them for a month to test them, and while they were nice in some ways, they were not in others. But she was being paid to promote them, so that was what she would do.

The pans were heavy, so lifting them with her healing wrist was going to be a problem. Grimacing as she moved yet another large pot, she gave in to the inevitable. Turning to Kyla, she rolled her eyes. "I'm gimpy. I'm probably going to need your help lifting this when it's full during the demo."

"Anything you need, Chef."

"Thanks. I'm such a klutz."

"We all are sometimes."

"Ain't that the truth."

Loud laughter shook her. Kimberly turned her head and narrowed her eyes against the light to see where it had come from. It was so familiar, the trill echoing in her mind. She made out Becca's form in the first few rows if she put her hand over her eyes to block out the spotlights. Becca was sitting, laughing with Jessica.

A pang of jealousy shot into her belly. Grunting, Kimberly tamped it down. It was stupid. Becca was her nanny, that was all, and she had no right to be jealous. She did, however, have the right to be angry if she was paying attention to some woman instead of her son, which was the whole purpose of having Becca there.

Anger boiled in her belly instead of jealousy, and she let it simmer as she continued to work, listening in on what she could hear of the conversation. It was mostly a normal one. Jessica was explaining how everything worked, how they'd gotten in touch with Kimberly's agent to see if she would even be interested in something like this and how they went about setting up the event. Michael would pop in a question every once in a while, and Jessica took the time to answer him sweetly, but it was obvious her main concern was Becca.

Kimberly's anger roiled a little more. Becca would tag on to the questions, explaining what Kimberly would be doing. It warmed her heart to hear how attentive Becca was to Michael. In fact, it made her feel something she hadn't in a very long time. Swallowing, Kimberly focused on the kitchen in front of her. They only had thirty more minutes before the doors would open, and she would need to be hidden away in the back.

Jessica came to fetch her before she knew it was time. She, Becca and Michael were led to a small conference room, where they would wait until the demo began. Kimberly grabbed hold of her chef's jacket that she had brought with her and headed to the bathroom to change.

With the door locked, she leaned over the bathroom sink, wishing she could splash ice cold water all over her face but knowing her makeup would be ruined, and that would be a disaster because she didn't know how to fix it. Sighing, Kimberly attempted to breathe out, the rage still boiling in the pit of her stomach. She would talk to Becca about it later. Right now, she had to focus in order to get through this demo, had to hold her tongue and talk through her filters. *Breathe.* She must breathe.

Dressing, Kimberly checked her hair before heading down to the conference room. Becca and Michael were having a mini dance party to some music blasting from her phone. Joy bubbled up in her as Michael came over, grabbed her hands and started to dance awkwardly with her. Kimberly twisted down then back up, laughing as there was a knock on the door.

"Ready, Chef?"

"Yeah," Kimberly answered.

"They're about to do introductions."

Nodding, Kimberly straightened her chef's jacket and kissed Michael's cheek. "Wish me luck."

"Good luck, Mama! You're the bestest cook in the whole wide universe."

"Thanks, kiddo."

The next hour seemed to vanish before it began. Everything had stayed calm, the marinara and pasta had been cooked and shared, Kyla had been a necessary and helpful resource and Becca and Michael had managed to sneak in and out a few times. Kimberly had known because she could hear his chattering as he asked Becca questions.

As they were on their way out—Michael tired from the long day and Kimberly trying to remember if she had everything she'd brought—Jessica stopped them. "It went wonderful today, Kim. Thank you for coming. I truly hope you'll join us again."

"I would love to," she answered, her eyes crinkling into a smile. "I enjoyed it. The audience had some great questions."

"They did for sure." Jessica turned to Becca and blushed.

Kimberly tensed. Michael was unaware as he pulled on her hand, trying to convince her it was time to leave already.

"Here. It's my number. If you...you know...want to call me sometime, maybe get a drink."

"I—" Becca stuttered. "Thank you." Her cheeks were as red as Jessica's, if not more. She took the proffered paper and tucked it into her back pocket.

Kimberly's rage boiled. What just happened was completely inappropriate. She turned to Michael, focusing her body and gaze on him so she wouldn't make an outburst. Becca was already headed down the hall toward the exit, so Kimberly nodded at Michael, and they made to follow.

The ride home was tense. Kimberly let her anger build. As soon as they were home and Michael was in bed, she would have a chat with Becca. What had happened could not happen again—otherwise, she wouldn't have a job. When the driver pulled up to the house, another car blocked the drive. Michael was asleep. Kimberly strained her neck to see who was at the house and cursed.

"Bradley's here," she muttered.

"What on earth for?" Becca countered.

"Who knows?"

"I can get the car seat if you need Michael for the distraction."

"Thanks."

Kimberly let out a breath, shifted her son into her arms and headed into the house, forgetting to even think about her conversation with Becca. Bradley was already inside when she opened the door. He went to speak, but Kimberly shot him a glare and he quieted down. The hour was late, and Michael would no doubt need to go straight to bed. She took him into his room, changed him as he stood half-awake then put him back down.

When she got to the kitchen, Becca was nowhere to be found and Bradley sat at the counter with a snifter in his hand. She heaved a breath and asked, "Why are you here?"

"I came to check on your wrist."

"My wrist is fine. Why are you really here?"

"You like her."

Kimberly's lips thinned in displeasure. "Quit the bullshit."

"She's your type. You've always liked them leggy."

"Why are you so obnoxious?" Kimberly reached for his glass and stole it, downing the rest of the liquid. "Thanks."

He rolled his eyes. "Really, though. How is your wrist?"

"Sore."

"You're doing too much."

"I need to work."

"You can afford to take time off."

"Financially, yes, I can. But this isn't about money. It never was."

He hummed and took her wrist in his hand. "Ice it tonight and try to take it easy tomorrow. Let it heal right. You don't want to make it worse on you in the long run."

"I know. You're still on for next weekend, right?" Kimberly's heart warmed at his concern, reminding her of who he'd once been.

"Absolutely. Got everything planned out."

"No dates?"

"I've got a date, tonight and tomorrow."

Kimberly snorted. "You always have a date."

"I do. I like it that way."

She shook her head as he grinned, the dimple in his cheek melting her like it always did. He was charming in every way, and it served him well.

"What's got you all in a tizzy today?" he asked as he poured them another drink.

Kimberly shrugged. "Nothing I can't handle."

"What is it?"

"Just training the new nanny."

"You do go through them."

She glared. "I think Becca will work out well, though—at least until Michael goes to school. He really likes her."

"So do you."

She glared again.

"You do. You can't deny it. You enjoy her company."

Changing the subject, Kimberly pointedly asked, "Don't you have somewhere to be, like a date?"

He laughed. "There you go again, always avoiding talking about your feelings."

Kimberly tensed, but he was not wrong. They'd once been best friends, someone she always shared with. The last two years had taken their toll on their friendship, but she would love to have him be close to her that way again.

He smiled sweetly. "I thought I would be nice and bring you dinner."

She grinned. "Thank you. What is it?"

"Indian."

"Perfect! Really, though, stop this overprotective 'I'm the man' macho stuff. It's so unattractive. And I want Michael to know how to respect women."

"You're right. I'm sorry. I will stop."

"Thank you." Kimberly bit her lip, feeling that it was far easier than it should have been. They'd had a mutual divorce, for the most part, but his personality was not easy to deal with. Neither was hers, if she were honest. It was a surprise they'd made it the ten years they had been married, but they had turned into wonderful friends. "Now, I'm tired. So I'm going to eat this food in bed in my pajamas and pass out. Like you said, it was a long day."

"I'll come get him Friday after work."

Kimberly nodded. "Thanks again for the food."

"Anytime, sweets." He bent down and pecked her loudly on the lips.

Kimberly growled and scrunched her nose. She hated when he called her that. As soon as he was gone, she made good on what she'd said. Relaxing in bed with the carry-out boxes next to her, she flipped on the television and zoned out.

Chapter Six

The knock on the door wasn't a surprise, and Michael jumped up from his place on the couch, racing for it. He slid to a halt before he smacked it face-first and opened the door, revealing none other than his father. Becca tensed. Her interactions with him had not been good. He put her on edge, and she very much wished Kimberly were home to deal with him.

He came through the door, shutting it behind him, a sleazy smile on his face. Becca grimaced inwardly. Michael was already vying for his attention, but Bradley stared her down, not quite ignoring his son but not letting him have all his focus.

Becca glanced down at Michael to distract herself. Bradley bent down and grabbed him by his arms to still his energy and gather his focus. "Do you have everything packed and ready to go?"

Michael shook his head.

Bradley turned his chin down and gave him a stern look. "Maybe you should get to it, then, so we can have ice cream before dinner."

Michael gasped. "Mama never lets us do that!"

"Daddy days are fun."

Becca rolled her eyes and cringed. If anything, Bradley was only going to make the situation between him and Kimberly worse. Rather than saying anything, she held her tongue and got up from her perch on the couch to clean up their snack mess. She had promised Michael he wouldn't have to do it that day if he spent thirty minutes practicing writing, and he had done it without complaint. He was well on his way to writing his name.

She turned toward the sink, turned on the water and rinsed off dishes before loading them in the dishwasher. The hand on her back forced her to jump into the sink's edge as she spun around. Bradley stood far too close to her for comfort. His smart gray suit and shiny white teeth put her even more on edge. She had assumed he'd gone down to Michael's room to help him pack. A healthy shot of fear coursed through her veins.

"I didn't mean to startle you. So sorry." He held his hands up and took a step away, straightening his two-toned blue striped tie.

Becca wasn't sure what to say, so she bit her lip and stared up at him. He was tall, taller than she would think Kimberly would be interested in. Pushing that thought to the side, she focused on his brown eyes and waited for him to let her know what he wanted.

He leaned against the counter, his elbow planted on it like he had no care in the world. He was completely comfortable, and that very fact made Becca uncomfortable. She wished she could ask him to leave, but it wasn't her house, he wasn't her ex and it was her job she'd be risking.

"She likes you, you know." His lips turned up in a slick grin, a dimple popping up on his right cheek.

Becca's raised an eyebrow in curiosity. "Who likes me?"

"Kimmie."

She narrowed her eyes. "Your point? I surely wouldn't still haven't a job if she didn't. It's not like she's afraid to fire someone."

His smooth laugh echoed in the kitchen, and Becca now understood why so many people fell at his feet and groveled. Becca wasn't sure what to make of him, so she went to the dishes to distract herself and try to put herself at ease. After a few more seconds, his hand was on her elbow, and his look was serious, unlike it had been before.

"I don't mean as an employee. She likes you enough for that, yes, but she *likes* you."

Again Becca shook her head, not understanding. This time, he glanced toward the hallway Michael had gone down, then at her, before leaning in close. His breath against her ear made her shiver.

"She likes you, Becca. You are her type to a T. You *have* to realize that."

Becca's mouth dropped open. Then she closed it tightly and clenched her jaw. She narrowed her eyes at him. "I'm not her type."

"You are. Didn't you know?"

"Know what?"

"Kimmie's bi."

"Oh." Becca licked her lips, not quite sure what to say. She always hated the double standard that those within the community could out someone, but those outside it couldn't. If someone didn't want to share their sexuality, then it shouldn't be shared. Confused by why they were even having this conversation, Becca said nothing.

"She likes you," Bradley repeated.

Sighing, she gave in to her baser urge to tell him off. Her tone was harsh when she spoke. "What is your point? She and I are not in a relationship, nor do I think we will ever be. You shouldn't be outing her to people you barely know. Her career could be in jeopardy, not to mention mine. How very selfish of you."

It was his turn to stand agape. Pride burst in Becca's chest.

"This was completely inappropriate. If there's anything I have learned about you, it's that you have boundary issues. So, let me set one right here, right now, for you. This is not your house. I do actually live here. You do not. And while I live here, you need to respect me, you need to respect my space and you need to back the fuck up."

With her last word, he took a step back and glanced down the hallway one more time. "Oh yeah, you two will be good together. I like your feistiness."

Becca heard footsteps in the hallway, so she plastered a smile on her face and turned to bid Michael goodbye for the weekend. Not much else was said as Bradley and Michael left. As soon as Becca was alone in the house, she collapsed onto the couch and pressed her fingers to the corners of her closed eyes. That could have easily been a disaster. Luckily, he had backed down. Now she could only pray there was no fallout with him talking to Kimberly about what had happened.

* * * *

Kimberly calmly walked into the dim house. It was late, well after midnight, but since she knew she didn't have to come home to take care of Michael, she'd actually gone out with some of her staff and bought them all a round at their favorite bar. It felt wonderful to spend some time with them, bonding in ways they hadn't done in years.

Setting her keys into the bowl by the door and toeing off her shoes, she sighed. Her hair was a mess, her calf muscles ached from standing so much and her wrist pounded with angry pain. She had definitely overdone it, but it had all been worth it in the end.

The lamp in the corner of the living room was on, as well as the television. The show playing softly was one of hers. Raising an eyebrow, Kimberly moved closer to the couch, finding Becca nowhere in sight. Turning toward the hallway for her room, she headed down that way, noting the light was on but the door closed.

Turning around to head back down the hallway, the door opened suddenly. Caught in the act, Kimberly smiled and shrugged. "I didn't mean to bother you. I saw the light and the TV on."

"Yeah, I just needed to grab a different book for studying."

Kimberly nodded more to herself than to Becca, and then used her thumb to point over her shoulder. "You're watching my show."

Becca blushed and then shrugged. "I like it. So what?"

"Nothing. I think it's cute. It's nice to know people actually watch it rather than just being told that they do." Kimberly swallowed. "Do you have a minute? I wanted to talk to you about something."

"I wanted to talk to you about something, too."

"Oh." Kimberly's stomach dropped. She worried Becca would be telling her she was quitting, and she really couldn't take that. She'd grown fond of her, as had Michael. This was the first time she could really see the whole situation working out. Her fear ratcheted up. "Let's talk in the living room then."

As they made their way slowly to the couch in the dimly lit living room, Kimberly could barely breathe. Her stomach was doing flip flops faster than she could count, and as she sat down, she feared she might faint. Brushing a hand against the side of her face to try and stop the spinning, she thought to herself that she might have had too much to drink earlier.

"You first," Kimberly said.

"Oh. Okay. Well, Bradley came by to pick up Michael, and I may have said something he probably didn't appreciate. I didn't want you to find out from him and think I'd gone off my rocker or that I was stepping over the line, which I may have done. I'm not sure, but—"

"Whoa. Slow down. What happened?"

"Umm…" Becca looked down at her hands twisting in her lap. Even in the dim light, Kimberly noted this was the least confident she had ever seen her. "I had to set a boundary with him about respecting me because I live here, and that while he may be Michael's father and I respect him for that, he needed to respect me."

"Oh my God, what did he do?"

"Nothing! I swear." Becca put her hands up in the air. "I promise you, it wasn't anything awful. He just got personal, and I told him he'd crossed a line and not to do it again."

"This is getting worse by the minute. What did he do, seriously? Cut the crap out of it."

Becca rubbed her lips together. Kimberly drew her anger back in, realizing she was only making the situation worse. Leaning forward, Kimberly pressed her fingers into Becca's knee and gave a slight squeeze of comfort.

"I'm sorry. You don't have to tell me what happened if you don't want to. I'm glad you said something to him. I will as well. He should not be treating you poorly, especially in front of Michael."

Becca put her hand out, palm up, to make sure Kimberly understood. "Michael wasn't there. He missed the whole thing."

"Oh, good. At least he did that. But if you do ever want to share with me what he said or did, please, feel free. I will talk to him about the rest." Kimberly left her hand where it was. Warmth seeped from Becca's bare knee into her fingers and reminded her just how real she was.

Becca covered Kimberly's hand and squeezed. "Thank you. He—actually, you know, I'll tell you, because it pisses me off."

"Okay then." Kimberly gave a small smile. "He's a good one for pissing women off."

Giving a wry chuckle, Becca nodded her agreement. "He outed you."

"He *what*?" Confused, Kimberly frowned.

"He outed you. He told me you are bisexual, and I really hate when people in the community do that. I'm serious. It's this stupid double standard. Why is it such a sin for someone straight to share another's sexuality but it's not for someone in the community? I didn't need to know that. I didn't ask. He just offered up the information like he was looking to gain some points or something. I told him right out that it was inappropriate."

Kimberly was speechless. She straightened her back and took in short sharp breaths as Becca continued to ramble.

"He shouldn't have done that. I don't care if you're gay, straight, bisexual, trans or a fucking clown. You are who you are, and you're my boss. I love Michael dearly and I don't want anything to mess that up. He's so sweet. Really, he is." Becca put her hand on Kimberly's knee this time. "He's one of the sweetest kids I have ever taken care of. He's so well-behaved and so curious about the world. I don't want to mess this up. I really need this job."

Clearing her throat, Kimberly finally spoke, her voice breaking as the words came out. "You're not going to lose your job over this."

It was as if Becca hadn't heard her as she continued to ramble on. "I get so mad when people are treated poorly, and frankly, your ex has not made a good impression on me. He's come in here yelling at me once, sneaking into the house another time. He just does not have any boundaries. And while —"

"You can stop." Kimberly's voice was barely a whisper, but Becca halted her rant.

"What?"

"You can stop. I know he's an asshole. I was married to him for ten years. He cheated on me for ten years. I'm very much aware of who he is and how he acts, but he's also a very close friend — or at least he used to be before he turned into frat boy number five."

"I'm so sorry. I didn't — I overstepped. I'm sorry. I'll shut up now."

Kimberly gave a wry smile, unsure as to why tears were forming in her eyes. "Don't worry about it. I'm used to dealing with him, and I will talk to him about respecting some boundaries."

"Thank you. And for the record, I don't care if you're bisexual."

"I assume he told you because he thinks you're my type," Kimberly added.

A nod was Becca's answer, and it was all Kimberly needed.

Unsure what to say, Kimberly drew in a deep breath through her nose and attempted to relax. Confusion swam through her, though. Bradley wasn't wrong. It had been over a decade since Kimberly had been on a date with a woman, not because she hadn't wanted to but because she'd been marked unavailable because she had fallen in love with someone—and subsequently out of love with him.

Becca's soft voice drew her attention to the conversation. "You don't have to say anything. It's none of my business."

"He made it your business. I'm sorry for that. Unlike Bradley, however, I do hold to boundaries. So you don't have to worry about anything happening between us."

"I wasn't worried."

"Good." Ready to escape to her bedroom, Kimberly made to push off the couch and retreat, but Becca's hand on hers stopped her from going any farther.

"You said you wanted to talk to me about something."

"Right. Also not a fun conversation. The other day at the demo, you"—she paused for a brief second—"you were very friendly with Jessica. While I understand attraction, when you are being paid to watch Michael, I need your focus to be on him. He is your priority."

Becca nodded. "You're right. I'm sorry. I wasn't anticipating that happening. I don't plan on calling her either, in case you cared to know. I'm pretty sure she was flirting with me to get to you."

"Oh." Kimberly's eyebrows rose in surprise. "I didn't need to know, but yes, I suppose that could happen. You're worth much more than her anyway."

"Well, thank you for that compliment. I'll try to deal with it better next time."

"I'm sure there will be a next time. You're young and attractive. You certainly don't need to tell every woman no just because you think it'll interfere with your work."

Becca shook her head. "I won't. Something about that whole thing just felt off."

Kimberly nodded, ready to drop the conversation and fully escape from the humiliation she was feeling. The house was far too empty without Michael there. Sadness seeped into her at his absence, and she wanted to retreat to her bed and work on her cookbook as best she could.

Rising from the couch, she folded her hands together. "I'll be off to bed then. Exhausting day." She rolled her eyes, smiled and didn't wait for a response as she retreated.

* * * *

Becca had spent most of Saturday hiding away in her room, studying. It wasn't until late afternoon that she sought the sun and caffeine. She had three exams coming up for midterms and desperately needed to get in quality study time. Stretching her muscles, she went out to the kitchen to grab a drink. Seeing Kimberly seated at the counter, she spun around and changed her mind.

Whatever had happened the night before had been awkward and confusing. She'd spent the rest of the night trying to figure out what had gone wrong and if she'd made the right decision to spill her guts about Bradley. In her room, Becca put on a fresh outfit, rubbed her hands through her hair, shoved her study materials into her bag and made for the front door.

She ignored Kimberly as she turned toward her and shut the door quickly. Unsure of just about everything, she stumbled into her car and blindly drove toward her best friend's apartment. She knew they'd be home. They were supposed to get together, but Becca had seen the greater need for studying. Well, Drew could study with her for a distraction.

It took her about an hour to drive through LA to get to Drew's, but when she knocked on the door, she was met with a warm smile and comfort. Drew looked confused for a brief second then they invited her in. Plopping down at the kitchen table, Becca unpacked her crap and set it all up to get to studying. Drew ignored her for the better part of an hour before sitting down next to her.

"Why you here, sugar?"

Becca wrinkled her nose. "Cut straight to it, don't you?"

Drew shrugged, and Becca felt comforted again.

"I started a new job, and I don't know. Maybe I should quit."

"Quit?"

Becca sighed and leaned back in her chair, bringing her knees up to rest against the edge of the table. "It got complicated."

"Complicated how?"

"I have a crush on my boss. And last night—well, last night it got awkward."

"Oh, do tell." Drew's eyes glistened with curiosity.

"I don't even know where to start. I don't think she likes me, not like that. I think she appreciates me, and she loves that I love her son. I love that kid, seriously. But last night and the other day, I think she was jealous."

"What?"

"Yeah, the other day, some chick gave me her number, and last night Kimberly brought it up. But—I don't know—something about how she was acting. It made me think there was more to it."

Drew raised one delicately waxed brow. "More what?"

"I don't know!" Becca's chest rose and fell in exasperation. "I really don't. I promise."

"But you like her?"

Becca gave a meek nod. "I'm not doing anything about it, though. I don't want to lose this job. I'm so close to finishing school. I have to just push through until I can start student teaching."

Drew hummed, but Becca wasn't sure if it was in agreement or disagreement. Not pushing it, she ignored Drew and focused on her conundrum. A crush was easy to ignore—at least it should be. Yet there was something in the way Kimberly held herself, confident and uncertain at the same time, brusque and soft. She was a walking contradiction. The only thing Becca knew for certain was that Kimberly loved Michael and would do anything for him. She was devoted to being the best parent for him that she could be.

When Becca looked up to see Drew staring at her, she smiled wryly. Drew was one of her oldest friends — they'd grown up with each other and she knew Drew would be brutally honest. When Drew said nothing, Becca was left in a second wake of confusion.

"What do you think I should do?"

Drew shrugged. "I think no matter your choice, someone is going to be hurt."

Nodding in agreement, Becca put her forehead against her knees and blinked back tears. Drew was right. There was no getting out of this without Michael being hurt. Dread settled into the pit of her belly, and while it was uncomfortable, Becca let it reside there and chose instead to ignore it.

"Can I stay here a couple of nights? Just until I have to go back to work?"

"You bet, sugar. You're always welcome here. And you know the charge."

"Yes, I'll cook dinner and breakfast every day." Becca grinned and rocked on her side to plant a kiss on Drew's perfectly kept-up cheek. "Love you."

"Always and forever," Drew answered. "Now get to studying. That test isn't going anywhere."

Becca groaned. "Three tests."

"Holy hell, sugar." Drew pointed a finger at her while standing up. "You better get that nose out of dreaming and into books."

Narrowing her eyes, she chose to ignore her best friend and go back to studying. It was hours later when she emerged from the books to cook them both a meal of whatever she could find in the near-empty pantry.

Drew's kitchen was the opposite of Kimberly's. Kimberly would die if she had to cook here.

Drew flittered around her as she puttered at the stove. "Where's your lady?"

"What lady?" Becca asked as she stirred the pasta in the water.

"Your cooking lady."

Becca froze. "My cooking lady?"

"Yeah, you usually watch her when you cook. Or have you seen her do this recipe so many times you have it memorized?"

Clearing her throat, Becca turned to Drew her cheeks drained of heat. "My cooking lady, as you so nicely put it, is my new boss."

"What?" Drew laughed, obviously thinking Becca was joking.

"My new boss, Kimberly...her stage name and maiden name is Kim Burns."

"You're shitting me."

"I'm not," Becca answered.

"Oh my God. Let me see."

Drew whipped out a phone and pulled up a video. With the phone set in front of the both of them, Becca watched as Kimberly, in all her pride and poise, taught whoever was watching how to make the perfect summer salad with squash and watermelon. Becca could barely look at the small screen, and instead, occupied herself with the boiling water.

"She's your boss?"

"Yes."

"This chick, right here?"

"Yes." Each time Drew asked ramped up the dreadful feeling in the pit of Becca's belly. "She is my boss. You can drop it now."

"No freakin' way. How did that even happen?"

"I have no idea—but it did."

"What's her house like? What's her kitchen like? Oh my God, does she cook for you?"

"No, she doesn't cook for me. Why would anyone want to cook another meal after cooking all day?"

"Good point." Drew tapped one long thin finger against two very thin and painted lips. "So...the house."

"It's huge. Yes."

"Come on, sugar. Give me some details."

Rolling her eyes, Becca regaled them with all she knew about Kim Burns the chef and even more she knew about Kimberly Thompson, the ex-wife and mother. By the end of the night, they were yawning with full bellies and happy hearts, and she realized she should have visited sooner. Drew always knew how to lift her spirits and set her on the right path.

Chapter Seven

Becca had never been to New York City in her entire life, and she'd spent days planning out what she and Michael could do together while Kimberly would be holed up at the studio. Excitement was an understatement about how she felt when Kimberly had shared that she and Michael would be going on the trip with her. The bubbling sensation in the pit of her stomach hadn't stopped in days.

The hotel suite was huge. Becca followed Kimberly and Michael inside, dragging her own small suitcase behind her. Michael beelined it for every room in the suite, checking it out. He ran back.

"I want to sleep in this bed, Mama." He pointed toward one of the rooms.

"Does it have one bed in the room or two?" Kimberly asked.

"Two."

"Okay, you can sleep there." Kimberly blew out a breath, moving a stray strand of dark hair from her face as she dragged her suitcase and Michael's into the room.

Becca walked into the other bedroom that was connected to the small living room. The king-sized bed stared back at her, looming. She shoved her suitcase into the corner, mentally preparing for the next few days. Kimberly was there for work. Becca and Michael were there to explore.

The door to her room opened, and when she turned expecting Michael, she found Kimberly. Her honeyed gaze looked Becca up and down slowly, twice, before they connected.

"I thought I might take Michael to dinner tomorrow. I should be back for it and give you some free time to roam the town."

Becca grinned. "I would love that."

Michael pushed open the door all the way, slamming it into the wall. Kimberly called his name in a whine, but Becca caught him as he jumped onto the bed and sat him on the edge.

"Kiddo, you know better than to slam doors open, don't you?"

Michael nodded, sniffling in a clear attempt to make tears come. Becca closed her eyes and let out a sigh as she squatted to his level.

"You're not in trouble. Just don't slam the doors open or closed. We're in a hotel, and there are other people in other rooms, so we have to be respectful of that, okay?"

Michael nodded. "Yup. I'm going to listen."

"Good." When Becca stood up, the look on Kimberly's face shook her. She bit her lip as nerves tingled in the pit of her belly. "So sorry. I shouldn't have... That was overstepping."

"No, I appreciate it. I've already told him twice."

Becca gave a small smile, unsure if Kimberly had meant it or not. Michael jumped on the bed, distracting her. He was almost as excited as Becca. He jumped closer and closer to the edge. Becca took a step, bracing herself for what she knew was about to come. Sure enough, he jumped and shouted, "Catch me!" at the same time.

Flinging her arms out, Becca caught him mid-jump but underestimated the force of him landing in her arms. She stumbled as she tried to catch her footing. Suddenly, hands were on her arm and shoulder, steadying her until she could stand upright.

Letting go of Michael, she slid him down to the floor and pulled a funny face at him. Kimberly put both hands on her hips and stared down at him. "Let's not do that again. I don't need to be taking either of you to the emergency room tonight."

Giggling, Michael raced out of the room and left Becca and Kimberly alone. Kimberly sighed, and Becca chuckled lightly.

"He needs to burn some of that off," Kimberly stated, pointing her finger in his direction.

"I can take him down to the pool if you have something you need to do."

Kimberly's eyes lit up, and the little bubbles in Becca's stomach were back, but this time, it wasn't because of New York. She swallowed in attempt to wet her parched throat. She had to get this crush-thing under control if she was going to continue to work for Kimberly.

"That sounds like an excellent idea, but I think I'll join you."

Becca's throat constricted. Her heart pounded so loud in her ears that she could barely hear herself speak. "Right. I mean, if you want to just spend time with Michael, I can entertain myself for a while."

"I think Michael would miss you were you not to join. And I have a dinner meeting shortly, so this way he'll have more time with you."

Nodding, Becca drew in a deep breath and held it. "I guess we're going to the pool."

"Pool?" Michael's chipper voice resounded. "Yes!"

He bounced out of the room, Kimberly following him with a smile on her face. Becca moved to the door and shut it slowly, locking the handle then pressing her forehead to the cold metal of the frame. Being scantily clad in a pool with her boss had not been on her list of things to accomplish while in New York.

Before she knew it, she was in her bathing suit with a loose T-shirt pulled over her and Michael leading the way to the elevator in his board shorts. Kimberly followed behind. All of them had their bare feet padding on the carpet as they waited. Becca mentally checked through her plans for the few days they'd be there and tried her best to ignore the entire situation she found herself in.

Michael was bursting with energy. He fisted his hands as soon as they walked into the steaming warm indoor pool area and shook his arms back and forth in a sort of vibration in an attempt to contain his energy. Becca dropped her towel on one of the chairs and tugged her shirt over her head. She brushed her fingernails against the back of her short hair, trying to figure out exactly what she was supposed to do. Michael didn't wait. He held out his floatie for her and silently asked her to help him.

She held it open while he shoved his arms through the holes then snapped the clip together, tightening it. He was just about to take off when his mother's stern voice echoed through the empty pool area.

"Wait for me, Michael."

He humphed but did as he'd been told. Kimberly set the rest of her and Michael's things down on the chair next to the one Becca had claimed. When she grabbed Michael's hand and started toward the water, Becca sucked in a sharp breath and clenched her teeth. The one-piece did everything to accentuate Kimberly's curves perfectly. The zip bustier provided the perfect support and cleavage and the deep green color made her eyes appear brighter.

She swallowed hard then did the unexpected. Becca walked confidently to the edge of the deep end of the pool and jumped without hesitation. She stayed under the water as long as she thought possible, then pushed her feet against the floor, pistoning her body upward toward the surface. When she broke the water, Michael stared at her with awe.

"I wanna do that," he said with awe.

Kimberly chuckled and half-carried him as he half-doggie paddled to the edge. He pulled himself out and stood at the lip of the pool. Both Kimberly and Becca moved to catch him. He plugged his nose, grinned and jumped all the while shouting, "Cowabunga!"

Becca caught him, but he pushed away from her to float and swim on his own as much as he could. She stayed close to him, as did his mother. Becca focused all her attention on the four-year-old in front of her, thankful for the distraction as well as the cold water. All she had to do was focus on her work, focus on taking care of and teaching Michael and her school work, and she wouldn't get herself into any kind of trouble.

They spent nearly an hour in the pool before Kimberly begged off and headed for the room, leaving Becca alone with Michael. She taught him the basic tenet of floating on his back, but after another hour, he was bored of practicing and his teeth were chattering. Becca smiled gently at him and convinced him it was time to head to the room and perhaps get some food to eat.

At the mention of food, Michael's ears perked up, and he was out of the pool as quick as lightning. He struggled to get his towel wrapped around him, so Becca grabbed one end of it and helped him before wrapping her own towel around her middle. She didn't bother putting her shirt on, first because she didn't want to get it wet, but second because Kimberly was nowhere to be seen.

Kimberly had a work meeting over dinner and wouldn't be joining them, and Becca figured that by the time they got to the room, Kimberly would already be gone and on her way. When they rounded the last corner to their suite, Michael raced for the door, counting the numbers along the way until he found the room that ended in nine, which was theirs.

She pressed the key against the sensor and waited for the click and the light to turn green. As soon as it did, Michael gripped the handle and pushed with all his might. Becca helped a little above his head where he couldn't see.

"You're so strong. Thank you, kiddo," she said as he plowed into the room and held the door for her to enter fully. He beelined for his room, and as soon as Becca looked up, she saw Kimberly shifting out of the way of the toddler tornado while trying to press an earring into her ear.

"Careful!" she commented.

"Sorry, Mom," Michael called over his shoulder. "I take a shower. So cold."

Kimberly had a smile on her face as she turned to Becca. Becca's stomach flopped and then flipped. Kimberly looked gorgeous. Her tight black pants accentuated every curve, the tight shirt left no room for questioning and the deep maroon overcoat set off her eyes and dark locks perfectly.

"He said he was too cold to swim anymore," Becca managed. "I figured you would have left by now."

Kimberly checked her watch after finally sliding in her earring. "I'm running a bit later than I anticipated. It was worth it, though."

"He misses spending time with you like this at home." Immediately, Becca regretted her words. She was in no position to say anything about Kimberly's relationship with her son. She held her hand up with her palm open as she clutched her towel closer with the other one. "I'm sorry. I seem to be stepping over boundaries a lot today. Forget I said anything."

Kimberly's lips pursed then thinned. Becca wasn't sure how she was going to get out of this one, and she couldn't quite read Kimberly's look, which scared her even more. Kimberly said nothing, only took three steps forward with her hand extended. When Becca glanced down and saw the silver necklace between her fingers she was thoroughly confused.

"Would you help me with this? My publicist told me to wear it, but I can't for the life of me get it on. That's part of what's made me later than planned."

"Umm...sure."

Becca shook her head of the cobwebs as Kimberly turned around and lifted her hair to one side of her neck, exposing her skin to Becca in the process. Becca tucked the edge of the towel just above her breasts and prayed it would stay there as she gripped the thin silver chair with moist fingers.

It took her three tries to get the clasp to grab, and as soon as she was done, she stepped as far away from Kimberly as possible. Michael jolted out of the room buck naked, and Becca heard the shower running for the first time. "Where are the shower toys?"

Kimberly frowned, and Becca let out a breath as Kimberly's focus turned onto Michael and she bent down closer to him. "I'm sorry, baby. I forgot to pack them. You'll have to shower without them this trip."

Michael frowned and gave a small huff, but sauntered to the bathroom completely unabashed in his nudity. Becca was about to turn and get changed herself when Kimberly put a hand on her forearm to stop her from leaving.

"We'll talk about this later."

The pit in Becca's stomach grew. She swallowed and nodded in silence as Kimberly grabbed her purse and slung it over her shoulder while calling out her goodbyes to her child. She turned to Becca once at the door, eyeing her up and down again. Becca shuddered.

"I don't know when I'll be back, but it'll be late."

Becca nodded again, afraid to let her voice loose. With that, Kimberly left, but the tension in the room remained suffocating.

* * * *

Kimberly had spent the last twelve hours elbow-deep in the competition shoot she'd come to New York for. Her heart still raced a mile a minute as the taxi dropped her off outside the hotel. It was late, and she knew Michael would be sleeping, but there was no way she'd be able to fall asleep, not with the energy coursing through her veins.

This happened every time. Whether she won or lost, her adrenaline would keep her up through the rest of the night until she crashed sometime the next day, if she were lucky to have that opportunity. This time she had Michael with her, and she knew she wanted to spend at least a few hours with him in the city before they flew back to LA. They would have dinner for that tomorrow, but until then, she'd have to figure out how to stay awake for all her meetings in the morning when her adrenaline was no longer keeping her up.

The door snicked open, and surprisingly, there was a light on in the living area. Smiling at the thought that Becca must have left it on for her, she dropped her purse on the counter of the kitchen and toed off her tennis shoes. She was covered in food that had been tossed around, her chef's coat and pants a disaster, but she didn't care.

She grabbed an ice-cold bottle of water from the fridge, twisted the cap off and chugged nearly half of it before she realized she wasn't alone. Becca stared at her cautiously from the couch, her laptop and school book propped on the coffee table. Nearly choking, Kimberly sputtered and set the water down as she took a deep breath.

"Sorry! I didn't realize you were still up."

"Studying."

Kimberly raised her eyebrows, not sure Becca could even see her do it in the dim of the light. "Do you have a test coming up or something?"

"I always have a test, it seems. That or a paper."

"That last year of school is rough."

Becca didn't turn back to her schoolwork. Curious, Kimberly followed her instincts and moved toward Becca's perch, her water bottle in hand. She stood over her then bent down to read something highlighted.

"The multiple intelligences of learning... That sounds drab."

Becca snorted. "It's not all bad. Makes sense in a logical kind of way."

"Better you than me. College, while it was not so much my friend, also did not do me well in the long run."

"Oh?"

Kimberly rolled her eyes and sat next to Becca so she wasn't leaning awkwardly. Their knees touched, and Becca jerked away tensely. Ignoring the moment, she went on. "I told you that I majored in anthropology. A whole lot of good that degree is doing me."

Becca nodded. "Then why cooking? Why not use your degree?"

"Honestly?" Kimberly took another sip of her drink before setting it on the table. "It's the one thing I'm actually good at, because I'm not good at just about anything else, and in a weird way, I do use my degree on occasion. History of food, the culture of food, the evolution of food? It's all anthropology."

Becca bit her lip. Kimberly felt an urge to run her thumb over it but resisted by gripping her hands together tightly in her lap.

"How late are you planning to be up? I don't want to disturb your studying."

Becca closed over her book with a loud thump. "It's about time I stopped anyway. My mind is mush. Between being three hours ahead of where I normally am and after a long day of traipsing around the city, I'm pretty beat."

Kimberly moved her gaze down to her hands, trying to find something to say. As much as she wanted to stay up and talk to someone, she didn't want to intrude into Becca's personal time that she had very little of. Thankfully, Becca kept her talking.

"How did today go?"

Kimberly gave her a sly grin, her chin still pointed down toward the ground, but her eyes lighting with joy. "Wonderfully. Though this was quite a hindrance." She pointed to her still-broken wrist in its cast.

Becca stared at her with wide eyes, gave her an imploring look, then glanced side to side. "You can't tell me more, can you?"

"Tell you what?" Kimberly had no idea why she was dragging this out. They both knew what Becca was asking, and yes, they both knew that technically Kimberly wasn't allowed to say anything about the results of the competition. Normally, she would have called Bradley and shared the news with him, threatening to sue the socks off him if he told anyone — all in good jest, of course — but this time, she hadn't even thought of picking up her phone.

"Come on. Did you win?"

"You know I can't tell you that." Kimberly bit her lip and gave Becca another sly look. "It's in the contract they make me sign in a million and one spots."

"All right..." Becca licked her plump lower lip that Kimberly wanted to nibble. "So what can you tell me? Did you make it past the first round?"

Kimberly drew in a deep breath. She enjoyed teasing Becca and the banter they had. "I can tell you that I cooked some really damn good food."

Becca laughed. "Your food, I'm sure, is always pretty damn good."

Shaking her head, Kimberly laughed. "It's not, but thank you. I've burned chicken with the best of them — during a competition once, too. That was fun. I'm sure you can find the video if you try hard enough."

Becca leaned into the couch, still half-turned toward Kimberly. "I might take you up on that. What else can you tell me?"

"Twelve hours is a long time to be filming for only about two hours of actual cooking and judging time."

Becca shrugged.

Kimberly resisted the urge to reach out and play with Becca's fingers. "I can tell you that I made it into the final round. I mean — I think technically I'm not supposed to tell you that, so mum's the word."

"The final round? Wow! That's amazing." Becca tilted forward, captivated by every word Kimberly had to say.

Kimberly continued. "I can perhaps maybe not tell you that in the final round the other contestant had a complete breakdown."

"What?" Becca's eyes widened.

Grinning, Kimberly focused on the woman sitting next to her, leaning in closely to whisper. "She didn't, but it was fun to say. I've seen it happen, though. No, she was really good competition. Her style was a mix of French and Spanish with a Moroccan flair — go figure. I was pretty sure there was no way I could beat her."

"That sounds— Wait. What?"

Kimberly grinned broadly.

"Are you serious?" Becca jerked her head to the side as she tried to read between the lines.

"I never joke."

"You're serious. You won?"

"I didn't tell you that." Kimberly's eyes crinkled at the corners as the adrenaline pushed its way through and into her chest. "But I didn't tell you otherwise, either."

"Oh my God! That's fantastic! Congratulations!" Becca reached forward, reaching her arms around Kimberly.

Kimberly melted into the embrace. She clutched Becca's back and pressed her nose into her shoulder, breathing in the left-over chlorine from another trip to the pool, mixed in with some other fruity scent. Her stomach tightened and twisted. Something about this felt completely right and totally wrong in the same instant. But she didn't want to let go.

She didn't know how long they hugged, but it was over far more quickly than Kimberly had wanted. When Becca pulled away, Kimberly stopped her with warm fingers to her cheek. Becca closed her eyes, her long lashes covering the bright blue color. Kimberly licked her lips. Her heartbeat ratcheted up and fluttering started in her belly.

She wanted to kiss Becca.

Swallowing, Kimberly parted her lips, but she wasn't sure what she was planning on doing. Before she could make a decision, Becca's eyes popped open. Becca turned out of Kimberly's touch, slammed down the top to her computer and grabbed it and her book, pressing them against her chest.

"I should get to bed," Becca whispered.

Clearing her throat, Kimberly nodded. "Of course."

Becca was gone before she could say or think anything else. Cursing under her breath, Kimberly grabbed her half-empty water bottle harder than she intended and chugged the rest of it. She collapsed into the couch and cursed again. Now she'd be up all night, but instead of thinking about her win, she'd be thinking about the line she'd almost crossed.

Chapter Eight

The trip back had been tension-riddled, but Becca made the best of what she could. Kimberly had given her the opportunity to go to New York when she likely would never have had one. The night Kimberly had won her competition wouldn't leave Becca's mind. Becca'd almost crossed the line, the firm, thick line she had put out to the universe that she did *not* want to cross.

She couldn't jeopardize this job. She needed it in order to finish school, to not drag it out any longer — not to mention it was also a matter of pride. She'd never lost a job. Sighing, Becca flipped closed the book she was most definitely not reading or retaining and dropped it noisily on the coffee table in the living area. Michael was having his quiet time, and without him as an easy distraction, she was left with her own thoughts.

The flight home would have been glorious had it not been for the tension. It was the first time she and Kimberly had been able to sit in the same vicinity and not snap at each other since that night. Granted,

Michael had been pressed between them in the middle seat, talking animatedly about the entire trip in New York and how he couldn't wait to share with Bradley all he'd done and seen.

Groaning, Becca rubbed the bridge of her nose. She had an idea of how to distract herself even more and how to work with Michael on some of his fine motor skills and counting skills when he woke up, but until then, she was still left on her own. Her own thoughts. Her own dreams.

She bit her lip. She had almost kissed her boss. And for a brief second, when she'd opened her eyes, she'd thought her boss had almost kissed her. Whatever that was, it had to stop immediately. They both needed each other too much in their current capacities to even tangle with the possible what-ifs.

But Kimberly—sighing again, Becca relaxed—Kimberly was an enigma. Soft and gentle with Michael but hardened against anyone else in just about any other capacity. If Becca didn't know better, she'd say Kimberly was lonely, to the point where she almost didn't remember how to have a friendship.

Glancing down the hall toward Michael's room, Becca willed his quiet time to be up sooner rather than later. It was nearing late afternoon, and she had plans she wanted to complete—plans that would perhaps teach Kimberly that friendship was well worth the effort. Friends they could be, or at least friendly with each other. Anything else was off-limits.

Having given up on studying, Becca brought her books and computer to her room and tidied up there for a few minutes before she went to the kitchen. She pulled out the recipes she intended to try for dinner and took stock of what they would need to buy for the meal and what they already had. A chef's kitchen was like nothing she had ever seen.

Kimberly had jars upon jars upon jars in her refrigerator, mostly different kinds of mustards and various kinds of pickled vegetables. But the spice cabinet—yes, the whole cabinet was dedicated to spices—was beyond her wildest imagination. Kimberly had everything she could ever possibly need in there. Some of it was expired, but most of it was exotic.

For the distinct lack of cooking Kimberly did in her own home, Becca was surprised to find as many small jars of spices as she did. Locating everything she could on her list, Becca went down the rest of it double-checking. Just as she finished reading the last few items, she heard the click of Michael's door opening, indicating that he was finally awake.

She smiled and leaned against the counter as she waited for him to join her. He rubbed his eyes with a sleepy pout on his lips as he came around the corner and went face-first into her belly, wrapping his arms around her waist.

"Still tired, kiddo?"

Michael nodded.

"What do you say we cook your mom a feast tonight? Do you think she'd like that?"

Michael pulled back, his eyes alight with excitement. "I'm not allowed to cook."

"I think we can make an exception to that rule if you let me help you."

Thinking it over, Michael came around to the idea. "What are we gonna cook?"

Becca paused, making a big show of deciding, even though she already had an answer. She tapped a finger against her lip as she bent down to him. "Honey-glazed chicken, roasted veggies and maybe some jasmine rice."

Michael nodded his head enthusiastically. "I like honey."

"I thought you might. First though, you're going to have to help me at the store."

His eyes widened. "Okay, I think."

"You'll be good help, I promise. Want to grab a snack for the car ride?"

Michael headed for the pantry where he knew his snack basket was. He grabbed a small package of animal crackers then ran to the door to get his shoes on. Becca followed, tucking the list into her back pocket. She slipped on her sandals as he finished folding over the Velcro on his tennis shoes. He was ready to go just as she was and together they went out of the side door toward the driveway.

Becca waited to make sure he had his buckles done up right before she shut the door and slipped into the driver's seat. She had plans for him. The store would involve pushing the cart, but also be them talking about how to pick out good produce as well as how to read a price tag. She was excited to teach him, just as she knew he'd be excited to learn.

Turning the radio volume down, Becca pulled into the street and headed for the organic food store, the one she'd noted a lot of the items in Kimberly's pantry had come from. It took them about fifteen minutes to get there, and Michael had remained pleasantly quiet in the back, snacking on his animal crackers and occasionally asking questions about what they were cooking.

As soon as they arrived, Michael was ready to go. He held on to Becca's hand as he half-skipped half-walked toward the large automatic sliding doors. He continued to hold her hand as she grabbed a cart and turned down the first aisle.

"Okay, kiddo. We've got to find some vegetables."

"This way!" he practically shouted.

Becca didn't bother to correct him. She could tell he was excited to go somewhere new and do something nice for his mom. She steered the cart down to the side of the store toward the heavenly produce. It was her favorite part of any grocery store. The colors, the freshness of it all made her feel alive and healthy — which she knew was stupid, but it did.

Stopping by the front of the large produce area, she grabbed the list out of her pocket and bent down toward Michael. "All right. We need some bell peppers."

"What's that?"

She grinned. "Let's see if we can find some."

Walking a few more steps, she came to a stop. Michael diligently followed, his eyes lighting up. "These are bell peppers?"

Laughing, Becca nodded. "They come in different colors. My favorite is the red one. Could you grab two for me?"

Michael stepped forward and grabbed a big red bell pepper and brought it to her. She took it then waited to see if he would go back for another one. He hesitated, but Becca waited patiently.

"Can we try a yellow one?"

"Sure."

Michael bounced as he came over. "That's two!"

"Awesome job. We also need some shallots."

"What are those?"

"They're kind of like little onions."

Michael wrinkled his nose in a look of disgust. "Onions are gross."

"These ones are good. They're actually pretty sweet-tasting. Will you try one? After we cook it, of course."

Shrugging, Michael followed Becca as she headed to where she thought shallots might be. She grabbed a few of them, asked Michael to count them out then put them in the cart next to the peppers.

"What's next?" he asked.

"Chicken. Kind of need chicken for honey-glazed chicken, don't we?"

"Yeah. Where's the chicken?"

"I think it's this way."

They wandered through the rest of the store, Michael finding items and Becca asking him to count various things. When they got to the check-out line, Michael helped put everything on the belt and clapped his hands together excitedly as the cashier rang it up. He stood silently by Becca as she pulled out cash and paid the bill. As they left, Michael grabbed one handle of the reusable tote with all their goods in it and walked alongside her.

Upon arriving at the house, Michael was ready to cook. Becca barely had time to take her shoes off as she entered before he was already over at the kitchen sink, washing his hands. She laid everything out and pulled up the recipes on her phone. They started with the chicken, as that was going to take the longest. Michael measured and poured out all the ingredients for the glaze into the pot then backed away while Becca turned on the gas burner.

It took her longer than she expected to coax him into stirring the pot, and she had to convince him he wouldn't burn himself in any fashion so long as he was careful. Whipping out her phone, she pressed the camera button to record a video. She turned it to face Michael and herself.

"Michael, tell your mom what we're doing," she said into the camera with a smile on her face.

"Mom! We're cooking chicken! With honey. It's for you for dinner."

Becca expected him to stop there, but in typical Michael fashion, he went on.

"I put in the — the — "

"The lemon juice," Becca supplied.

"Yeah, the lemon juice and honey into the pot, and now I stir it." He made a big motion of stirring. "But I not get too close. It's hot." He wrinkled his nose slightly. "Becca turned the stove on, Mom. I didn't. Becca did it."

Chuckling, Becca popped into the camera frame. "He can't wait for you to eat his creation."

She ended the recording and sent the video. Without waiting for a response, because she knew this was prep time at the restaurant and Kimberly would be busy, she pulled up the recipe again and they continued to cook.

It wasn't until they were sitting down at the table that her phone rang. Rather than a normal call, it was a video call. Becca called Michael over and answered, handing it to him so he could talk with his mom.

"Mom! You almost home?"

"No, I'm so sorry, kiddo."

Becca heard the disappointment in Kimberly's tone as well as the stress and exasperation. It leaked through each word.

"I can't come home right now like I thought. Something happened at work, and I have to stay here.

But I'm really looking forward to the dinner you made me. That was so thoughtful of you."

Michael frowned, and his eyes watered with tears. Becca debated whether to comfort him or wait to see whether they were real tears or the fake ones he was prone to have as of late. As soon the first turtle-drop of salt water slipped down his cheek, she moved over to him and wrapped him in her arms.

Kimberly continued, "I'm so sorry, kiddo. I really wanted to be home. I can smell it from here, and it smells amazing."

Michael sniffed. "It'll be cold when you eat it."

"That's okay. It'll taste just as good. I promise. I loved watching the video of you cooking. I showed Uncle Maury and Uncle Zechariah, and they said you looked like a chef already."

Michael perked up at that.

"Kiddo, I've got to get going. It's a little crazy here. Can you give the phone to Becca so I can talk to her for a minute?"

Nodding, Michael handed the device over. Becca, sensing Kimberly didn't want Michael to necessarily hear what she had to say, started toward her room. As soon as she sat down on her bed, Kimberly closed her eyes and rubbed the bridge of her nose. It was odd to see her when normally this type of conversation would be done over a phone call or text message.

"The boiler is shot. I don't know what happened, but I've got a repair crew here. They're working as fast as they can to get it running. Meanwhile, dinner rush."

"I'm so sorry," Becca said, not sure why she was getting the explanation. "That must be rough."

"Of course it always happens on the nights I plan on being home early." Kimberly rolled her eyes. She looked stressed. Her hair was unkempt, sticking out from the pony she had shoved it into, and her cheeks were red with tension. "I don't know when I'll be home, honestly. I know tonight was supposed to be early for you. You didn't have any plans, did you?"

Becca shook her head.

"Would you be able to watch Michael then? I really don't want to call Bradley."

"It's no problem." Becca clenched her jaw as she worked through what to do next.

"Thanks." Kimberly took a deep breath and looked at something away from the camera. "Back into the fray, I guess."

"See you."

* * * *

Kimberly stopped short when she saw Becca bent over the laptop at the kitchen table, typing. It didn't take Becca much more than a few seconds to look up, and their gazes locked. She hadn't expected Becca to be up this late. It was well after midnight. Putting her purse and keys on the edge of the kitchen counter, she headed to Becca to once again thank her for saving her ass that night.

She plopped onto the chair and untied her tennis shoes that were covered in a fine layer of grease. "Thank you so much for watching him tonight. I don't know what I'd do without you."

Becca raised a single eyebrow curiously. "I think that might be the first compliment you have given me."

Kimberly was taken aback by the seemingly odd attack. Exhaustion had already taken over her and she didn't want to fight—and she certainly didn't want

Becca to quit. Bolstering herself, she popped her second shoe off and rubbed the arch of her foot.

"I know I can be a bitch sometimes." Rolling her eyes, she amended, "Most of the time. I'm sorry that I haven't been a good boss to you."

Something shifted in Becca's gaze. Kimberly wasn't quite sure what it was or where the hostility had come from, but she was glad to see it seemed to be gone.

"Thank you, I think." Becca bit her lip.

Kimberly switched feet. It had been a hellaciously long day, and her muscles ached from the exertion. Her stomach rumbled, reminding her that she hadn't eaten since prep. Becca must have heard it too, because the look she was now giving her was one of pity.

"Michael insisted on making you a plate. It's in the fridge. He tried to stay awake for you to come home but crashed at about nine. He really missed you today."

Kimberly's chest tightened and tears stung the backs of her eyes. She had missed him, too. Before she could even think about getting up, Becca was already on her feet and in the fridge. She pulled the plastic wrap from the plate and shoved it into the microwave. Cocking her head to the side, Kimberly became aware of her stomach twisting. Something about Becca doing this one thing that was so domestic and considerate had her stomach in knots.

When Becca set the plate in front of her, Kimberly risked a chance and pressed her fingers to Becca's wrist to get her attention. Smiling up at Becca towering over her, she flushed. "Thank you."

Becca shrugged and went to her seat, going nose-deep into her books again. Kimberly didn't wait a beat as she cut into the chicken, reveling at the steam that plumed up. Her stomach gave another growl, letting her know she shouldn't wait any longer. Shoving a forkful between her lips, she immediately regretted the decision not to wait. Her tongue burned like she'd just tasted fire.

Determined not to make an embarrassment of herself, she chewed through the pain until she thought the piece of chicken might be cool enough to swallow. Without attempting again, she got herself a bottle of cold water and sat down.

When she took her second bite, she got the flavors — the note of smokiness, the sweet glaze but with a hint of spice on the back of her tongue. Kimberly couldn't help herself. She moaned. Her eyes drifted shut as she savored every flavor exploding in her mouth. After the heat burned off, she was left with a sweet note lingering offset with a touch of sour.

"This is amazing," she said around a third bite. "Please tell me there's more than just this left."

Becca glanced up at her then down at her computer, unfazed. "There's more."

Kimberly practically bounced in her seat as she continued. Each bite brought her a new layer of flavor. When she finally tried the sautéed vegetables, she was blown away again. This time, she made sure to get Becca's full attention by grabbing her hand until their eyes were locked.

"Seriously, this is hands-down amazing. If I were judging this on a show, you'd win. No competition. I'd just hand you the prize."

A blush crept up Becca's cheeks.

"I'm not kidding. I eat a lot of really good food and a lot of bad food. This is beyond good. It's phenomenal."

Becca shook her head in rejection, but Kimberly stopped her.

"I'll stop. I promise. But really, this is go-od." Kimberly emphasized 'good' by dragging out the word before she popped another bite into her mouth.

"Thank you." Becca blushed fully now. "Maybe I should become a chef instead of a teacher."

Kimberly chuckled. "So you can deal with broken boilers, drunken dishwashers and twelve-to-fourteen-hour days?"

"You're right. Teaching is a better option."

Kimberly laughed again, her eyes scrunching in the corners. "You said you only have a few semesters left, right?"

Becca let out a heavy sigh and shut the laptop. Kimberly almost regretted asking the question, sure she was disrupting some deep study that she'd already forced Becca to push back because of the stupid boiler.

"I have been technically close to graduating for two years now. I've had to slow down taking classes so I could pay for them. But after this summer semester, I should be ready for student teaching. Then I'm done. That's all I have left."

"Wow. So close."

Becca hummed an affirmative. "Michael and I worked on counting today while we cooked, as well as fine motor skills with stirring and pouring. We also worked on learning different vegetables and colors, all while we were at the store."

"I never would have thought about that."

"The grocery store is an excellent place to learn, as is the kitchen."

Kimberly didn't miss the tone in Becca's voice, the slight of condescension and disapproval. It needled at

Kimberly. She set her fork down and leaned back in her chair. She'd meant to discuss it right after they got home from New York but had avoided the confrontation.

"I meant to talk about some things in New York before today, but I suppose now is as good a time as any." As soon as she'd finished speaking, the tension visibly tightened in Becca's shoulders. Instantly, she regretted the necessity of the conversation. "While I appreciate you and all you do for me, especially on nights like tonight, Michael is my son and I need to parent him, not you. I make the rules and you have to follow and enforce those rules, and I'd appreciate it if you would defer to me when I'm around in terms of discipline."

"I understand." Becca's jaw was clenched tight, the words barely audible.

Kimberly continued. "That said, what bothers me more is the judgment you seem to have about how I spend time—or don't spend time—with Michael."

"I know." Becca winced. "I've regretted it every time I've said it because I know I shouldn't have. I'm sorry. Truly I am."

Kimberly cocked her head to the side and gazed up and down Becca's form. She could see the remorse setting in her shoulders, the pain it took her to apologize. "I accept your apology, but that doesn't solve the issue that you're still thinking it."

"I know," Becca murmured. "I'm...I'm trying to work on that."

"I suppose that's something you'd have to deal with a lot of when teaching."

Becca nodded her agreement.

"But for now, for us, it needs to stop."

"I understand."

When Kimberly glanced over at Becca, she was digging her thumbnail into each of her cuticles, pushing them back. Pressing her warm fingers over Becca's to still the nervous gesture, Kimberly caught her attention again. "I'm not mad. I think you may perhaps be right, and I don't want to admit that, but I'm not mad."

Becca shifted her hand so she could entwine their fingers, giving a squeeze. "I need to learn to hold my tongue."

Kimberly chuckled. "Don't we both."

Her self-deprecating comment earned her a grin from Becca, and she squeezed her fingers again, enjoying the contact. It had been a long time since she'd spent time in relative peace doing normal domestic things with someone other than Michael, and it felt good. Smirking, Kimberly kept their fingers together, even though it would be far more appropriate if she broke the touch.

Becca smiled. "There's dessert, you know."

"There's…there's dessert?" Kimberly squealed. "Do tell!"

Grinning, Becca got up and headed for the kitchen. She came back with two bowls of sorbet, with a small mint-leaf garnish included.

"The recipe is a secret," Becca whispered.

Kimberly took a spoonful and burst out laughing as soon as it hit her tongue. "It's my recipe!"

"It's one of my favorites. I couldn't resist when I saw the raspberries in the fridge."

"This is perfect." Kimberly grabbed for Becca's hand again, but Becca pulled away. Put off, Kimberly focused on her dessert. "I think I forgot to tell you that

Bradley needed to switch weekends, so Michael will be headed over there tomorrow. You'll have the weekend to yourself. I have to film a competition tomorrow all day, so the house will be yours as soon as Bradley picks up Michael."

"Really?"

"Whatever shall you do with all that time?" Kimberly flirted.

"I'll probably be nose-deep in books. I have a paper due that I need to finish. Gotta ace this class."

"I have faith you can do it."

Becca snorted. "You might be the only one."

"Don't be so hard on yourself. You're brilliant. You taught my kid more today than I would have ever thought he needed to know."

Becca blushed again. "That was easy. This? This is hard."

"I think you can handle it."

They finished their sorbet, and Kimberly ordered Becca to bed while she cleaned the plates and tidied up. She would make sure to be up early to spend time with Michael before she had to go to work, no matter how exhausted she might be. Becca may have overstepped in her suggestions, but she had been far from wrong. Turning the lights off and making sure the doors were locked, Kimberly headed to her bedroom and blissful sleep.

Chapter Nine

She'd lost. She couldn't believe she'd lost. Well, she could, but still...it stung. Pulling into her driveway, Kimberly put her car in park and looked at her lonely house. She hated coming home when Michael wasn't there. It was cold and empty and way too quiet — even if he was asleep when she got home.

Sighing, she picked up her purse and made for the garage door. She was still in her chef's coat, still with gobs of makeup on that she normally wouldn't wear, including some odd magnetic eye lashes they had convinced her to try. It was close to midnight. She'd gone back to Gamma's to check in on everything before forcing herself to head home.

She'd wanted to wallow in despair, to beat herself up mentally, to go through the recipe over and over in her head in an attempt to perfect it, but nothing was working. Growling, she headed straight for the cabinet she kept her liquor in. One good stiff drink would help. After being heavy-handed with the vodka, she mixed it with some orange juice for a classic screwdriver and made her way to the couch.

Plopping down, Kimberly flipped on the television and sank into the cushions, rubbing her still-broken wrist. She couldn't wait to get the cast off, but at least she was now able to take it off for an hour here or there. Cooking with it was a chore in and of itself. Once she found her favorite station, she took a large gulp of her mixed drink, wincing as the alcohol hit the back of her throat and made her nose tingle. She took two more sips before she dared to wonder what Becca might be up to.

"Becca..." she said out loud, humming after the name left her lips. She seriously had to put up more walls around her. Every time they were together, Kimberly felt hers slipping away, the moat she had purposely built between her and pretty much every other adult in the world getting smaller — and it scared her.

She was just finishing her drink when the door clicked open. Kimberly stood, not swaying at all, and went to pour herself a second drink while Becca shoved herself through the door with a takeout bag hanging over her left wrist and her backpack over her shoulders. She was laughing.

Kimberly cocked her head to the side as she poured, not looking into the glass — one of the many benefits and skills she'd inherited from her years in the kitchen and behind a bar as she made ends meet. Becca was talking to someone through the doorway, but Kimberly couldn't quite make out who it was.

"I'll be fine."

Finishing mixing her second drink of the evening, Kimberly made a quick albeit influenced decision. "Is that you, Becca?"

"Yeah," Becca called over her shoulder.

"Who's with you?"

"Umm...my best friend, Drew. They were just dropping me off. Didn't want me to Uber by myself."

"Uber?" Kimberly asked, making her way toward the door, her bare toes pressing into the cold tile reminding her just how exhausted she was. "You took an Uber?"

Becca giggled. "We had one too many drinks."

Kimberly got to the door and opened it wide enough to see one of the most beautifully exotic people she had ever seen. They were dressed in bright colors, with glitter eyeliner, blue and purple hair that was cut short but styled so their bangs lay just right across their forehead. A black leather jacket was odd against the bright orange and yellow tie-dye crop top and short cut-off jeans.

"And you must be Becca's friend..." Kimberly said, extending her hand with a glint in her eye.

"Drew, ma'am."

Flushing, Kimberly took their fingers gingerly and squeezed lightly. "No need to call me ma'am. Call me Kim. Which, you should definitely do, if you're going to stay and share in some drinks. I've had a crappy day and would love some company if you're up for free booze and an old, crotchety bitch."

"You're not a bitch," Becca said.

"Of course!" Drew answered at the same time as Becca.

Drew plowed into the house while Becca waved off the Uber. Kimberly headed to her kitchen and pulled down a few more glasses. She took out every bottle of hard liquor she could find that she knew she had, along with anything she could figure to mix it with. Staring at it all set before her while she sipped at her own strong second drink of the evening, she finally decided what to make.

Becca had gone to her room and shoved her backpack in there, along with giving Drew a quick tour of the house. She came in with the takeout and shoved it into the fridge. Kimberly turned her nose toward it. "Is that Chinese?"

"Maybe..."

"I'll give you a raise if you share it with me."

Becca blanched. "I don't share my leftover Chinese. That's blasphemy."

Kimberly huffed. "Okay, but I'm not to blame if it magically disappears overnight."

Laughing, Becca grabbed the bag back out and pulled out two cartons, shoving them in Kimberly's direction. "These can be fair game. The rest is mine."

"You're a saint," Kimberly whispered, squeezing Becca's arm lightly.

Drew leaned against the opposite counter and took the drink Kimberly offered. Becca took hers, and Kimberly dipped into the chicken fried rice and crab Rangoon, humming in pleasure as the greasy, fatty, lukewarm food hit her tongue. It was just what she needed.

"I take it you lost," Becca commented as she took a sip of her drink.

Kimberly glanced from Becca to Drew and shrugged, not confirming or denying what Becca had said. "Comfort food is excellent after eating random weird concoctions all day." With that, she took another large bite.

Drew couldn't take their eyes off her. Kimberly finally leaned over the counter to stare back.

"I don't bite, you know."

"Might be nice if you did, just saying."

Kimberly's cheeks flushed hot, her chest constricting. She risked a quick glance at Becca and decided two could play at this game. "Why, is that what *you* like or *she* likes?"

Becca choked on her drink. Drew casually trailed one finger in a circle on the granite counter and sheepishly turned their eyes up to Kimberly. "You'd like to find out, wouldn't you?"

"All right!" Becca interjected. "Let's go to the couch, start over and take flirting off the table." Taking hold of Drew's shoulders, she steered them away from Kimberly, mouthing a 'sorry' over her shoulder.

Kimberly giggled. She actually giggled. Shaking her head, she took another bite of the Rangoon and grabbed her drink, following the clearly intoxicated duo. Drew and Becca sat on the couch together, and Kimberly made herself comfortable on one of the side chairs, balancing the Chinese food on one knee while she continued to eat and drink.

"What'd you guys do today?" she asked, conversationally.

"Becca studied," Drew answered with a bored expression. "Then I finally convinced her to go out for a bit and relax. God knows she needs to relax more." They pressed a hand on Becca's thigh and downed the rest of their drink.

"Where'd you go?"

"Nowhere you'd probably know," Becca said quickly.

Drew, on the other hand, didn't seem to be so standoffish toward Kimberly and elaborated. "It's this new gay techno club in downtown LA. This is their opening weekend."

"Yeah, so we had to wait in line for an hour before they let us in," Becca added.

Drew smiled and put their hands out in a hands-down gesture. "But it was amazing. Best club I've been to all year."

Kimberly hummed. "I had heard of a new place opening. Downtown LA isn't exactly where you want to be after dark, though."

Both Drew and Becca shrugged. Kimberly let it slide. She finished her drink, noticed both Becca and Drew had already finished theirs and went to refill everyone's. It might be unconventional to get drunk with her nanny and her nanny's best friend, but if she were honest with herself, she had no other friends to get drunk with.

As soon as she sat down again, the conversation flowed easily. She finished her Chinese — well, Becca's Chinese — and was feeling pleasantly dizzy when she went to throw away the empty cartons and make herself a fifth or sixth drink. Drew begged off for the bathroom, using the wall to balance as they went, and Becca stayed firmly in place on the couch.

When she returned, Kimberly sat next to Becca, their thighs touching as she settled onto the couch. She took a sip then commented, "I like them."

"Drew?"

Kimberly nodded.

"They've been my friend for many years. They get me out of my head space when I need it."

"Like tonight?" Kimberly asked.

"Yeah." Becca finished what was left of her drink and set it on the coffee table. She put her hands together and held them tightly, her body tense.

Kimberly was relaxed as she settled in even more. Silence took them over for a bit before she turned to Becca. "Do you think Drew's okay? They've been gone awhile."

"Probably passed out. I'll go check."

Becca's hips swayed from side to side as she walked away, which only made Kimberly smile. After a minute, she called to Kimberly.

"I may need your help for this one!"

Kimberly followed the path Becca had just taken. What she saw when she got to the door made her burst out laughing. Drew was passed out on the toilet, completely dressed. The water was running in the sink, and their head was pressed against the shower door. Becca moved into the small room, turned off the water and lifted Drew as much as she could.

"They're too heavy," Becca whined.

"Hold on." Kimberly moved into the room, the walls spinning as the bright light hit her eyes. She grabbed Drew's other arm to steady them before tapping their face lightly. They semi-woke up, and between her and Becca, they got them into Becca's bed after what seemed like a mile-long walk down the hall.

Kimberly waited for Becca to get back after making sure Drew was settled. When Becca plopped down next to her, she giggled and put her head on Becca's shoulder. "I think they're going to have the world's worst hangover in the morning."

"Probably," Becca responded.

Kimberly sighed and relaxed into Becca's side as she finished her own drink. She could smell Becca's light, fruity shampoo, even through the scent of alcohol and body sweat she'd accumulated at the club. Rubbing her lips back and forth, Kimberly closed her eyes. Becca didn't move.

It was some time before Kimberly dared to shift. She checked her watch, noted it was nearly three in the morning and moved to sit up. Her head rushed. Moaning and leaning down, she blinked until she could mostly see clear. Becca also shifted. Kimberly wasn't sure if they had fallen asleep or if they'd just fallen into a quiet lapse of comfortable silence.

When she moved to sit, she remained close to Becca. Before she knew what she was doing, Kimberly turned her head up and pressed her mouth to Becca's lips. Pleasure coursed through her chest and down into her groin. Becca parted her lips, and Kimberly reached up and cupped her smooth cheek with her fingers, caressing her soft skin. Becca drew in a sharp breath.

Kimberly didn't hesitate as she swept her tongue out against Becca's lower lip, tasting the salt from rim of the glass Becca had been drinking from and the sourness from the lemon juice Kimberly had added to the mix. Kimberly sighed again and wrapped her hand behind Becca's neck, pulling her impossibly closer. Becca melted.

Lying on the couch, Becca's body covered hers, and Kimberly kept kissing her. She didn't want it to end. Tingles moved in waves throughout her body every time Becca shifted and touched her accidentally in a new place. Their tongues entwined. Their breathing became quick. She lost count of how long they spent making out, but when she finally pulled away, she knew she wanted more.

"I want you," Kimberly whispered as she trailed a hand down Becca's back.

Becca moaned softly in an answer, but it wasn't good enough. Kimberly kissed her again, but this time she pulled away and made sure she had Becca's attention.

"I want you," she repeated. "Will you let me have you?"

Letting out a groan, Becca put her forehead to Kimberly's chest and calmed her breathing. Kimberly barely heard Becca's response as she whispered, "Yes…" into her breast.

Lifting Becca's chin with two fingers, Kimberly shook her head. "Say it like you mean it *if* you mean it. I'm not doing this if you don't want me to."

"Yes," Becca answered firmly. "Please, Kimberly."

Her name coming from Becca's lips was her undoing. Crashing their lips together, Kimberly tugged Becca's shirt up and over her head, dropping it somewhere on the floor. She didn't care. All she wanted was to get her hands on Becca's body, her mouth on her, wanted to tease her into orgasm after orgasm.

Kimberly scraped her nails lightly down Becca's sides until she reached the waistband of her jeans. They were still locked together in a deep kiss, and Becca was shifting again. Breaking away, Kimberly pushed lightly at Becca's shoulder and ordered, "Sit up."

Becca complied. Kimberly followed and unclasped Becca's bra deftly. With one single finger, she ran a feather-light touch over the exposed skin before she shoved Becca into the couch and loomed over her.

"It's time to get these off."

Plucking at the button of her jeans, Kimberly began to pull them off. Becca shimmied her hips to help. Kimberly ignored them as she dropped them to join Becca's wayward shirt. Pressing Becca's knee up against the back of the couch and her other down along the edge, she dropped a delicate kiss against Becca's thigh.

"May I touch you?"

Becca's eyes fluttered shut as she nodded, a blush creeping up her chest to her cheeks.

"Say it or I won't do it," Kimberly's voice rang out in the still room.

Her eyes flew open. Becca reached forward and ran her fingers through Kimberly's hair, scraping her nails against her scalp before she held her hand in position. "Touch me, Kimberly. Taste me. I want your mouth on me."

Growling, Kimberly nipped the tender skin of Becca's inner thigh lightly before she leaned down and nuzzled her nose against Becca. The scent was glorious—musky, dark, wet. Moaning, she dared herself to dash her tongue out for just one taste, one blissful flavor of Becca to wipe away everything she had had that day, wash away the sting of her loss, the ache of her deep-seated isolation, the pain of being so alone.

Becca's sharp intake of breath spurred her on. She used her tongue, she used her lips, she used her teeth—lightly, of course—and she used her fingers. She took Becca on a ride up and down, feeling her muscles tense and relax as she pulled back then amped her up again. When Becca finally gripped her hair, tugging hard, Kimberly tilted her head up to make eye contact.

"Stop teasing," Becca ground out between clenched teeth.

Chuckling, Kimberly went to work, this time not playing games and pushing Becca straight over the edge. When she came, Becca cried out, her fingers still tightly wound in Kimberly's long locks, her ankles crossed behind Kimberly's back. Her stomach rippled as the orgasm shook through her body.

She came down from her high, and Kimberly continued to slow her movements, enjoying the last lingering flavor. When Becca finally moved her legs to allow Kimberly up, Kimberly stretched herself over Becca's prone form and pressed her lips quickly to Becca's mouth. "Was that enough? Or do you want more?"

Becca whimpered.

"I need words, my friend. Sounds do nothing to tell me what you want."

Becca popped her eyes open, and their vibrant blue about knocked Kimberly on her butt. Becca was beautiful in the throes of sex. Still not speaking, Becca cupped both hands around Kimberly's cheeks and drew her down for a long and deep kiss. When she broke away, she had a sly grin on her face.

"Again," Becca demanded.

"At your command," Kimberly whispered and kissed her way from Becca's jaw to her neck and down over her breasts. Even through her drunkenness, she formulated a plan for exactly how she would have Becca this time. Just as she got between Becca's legs, Becca stopped her with a palm to her forehead. Slightly miffed, Kimberly pulled away a bit, waiting to see what Becca had to say for herself.

"Take it off. It's got too many buttons for my drunk fingers to handle. I want to see you."

Cocking her head to the side, Kimberly laughed before she started in on her chef's coat. Underneath she had on a thin tank. She tugged that over her head as soon as she could and dropped it with the rest of their clothes. Not hesitating again, she reached behind her and flicked the hook on her bra, dragging that over her arms until she was bare. Becca sat up, her lower lip pulled between her teeth as she reached for Kimberly's chest.

"You can touch," Kimberly stated matter-of-factly, but her voice was raspy from drinking and exhaustion.

Becca brushed her fingers over Kimberly, grinning at Kimberly's vocal response. Kimberly let her have her way for a few minutes before she leaned forward again and pressed their mouths together in one more kiss. "I thought you wanted my way again."

Humming, Becca smiled. "I do."

"Then get on your knees."

Kimberly waited while Becca shifted, her knees pressed firmly into the cushions while her elbows and arms hung on the arm of the couch. Kimberly licked slowly but firmly, reveling in Becca's shudder. She explored as slow as she could, knowing Becca would likely be very sensitive.

"Do you mind," Kimberly began, swallowing as she slid her finger farther up Becca's ass, "if I taste here?"

Becca tensed. She turned her head to look at Kimberly, and Kimberly smiled, trying to be as gentle as possible. She waited patiently for an answer, not wanting to pressure Becca in any way. If she said no, then she said no, and Kimberly would move on to plan

B, but if she said yes... She shuddered at the thought, her nipples hardening.

"I'd rather not, not this ti— I'd rather not."

Kimberly's heart skipped at beat at the words Becca had almost said. Guilt seeped into her chest as she sobered, but she was in as far as this. She would go the rest of the way. "Okay," she answered. "New plan then."

Standing straight up, Kimberly shucked her own pants and underwear. Becca awkwardly sat up, one leg curled under her body as she waited for directions. Bending down, Kimberly kissed her senseless, trying to rid the guilt from the corner of her mind as they continued. She grabbed Becca's hand as she continued to kiss her and pressed it between her legs so Becca could feel just how wanted she was.

Becca moaned and tickled her fingers back and forth, sliding them through Kimberly's slick heat. "I want us to do this together."

Nodding, Becca shifted out of the way so Kimberly could lie down with her legs spread. Becca climbed over Kimberly going the opposite direction, her ass once again in the air. With one longing look at Kimberly, Becca bent her neck. Kimberly jerked at the first touch and willed her body to calm.

When Becca repeated the movement, Kimberly's breath left her. "God, that feels so good."

Humming, Becca continued. Kimberly let Becca work until she was beginning to lose her control. Not wanting to waste another second, she shifted her arms around Becca's thighs and pulled her hips to her mouth. Together they moved in sync, using everything they had at their disposal in the position they were in.

It wasn't long before Kimberly burst over the edge of orgasm.

She breathed heavily on Becca's body as she collected herself, but she didn't want to waste time. As soon as she had her wits about her, she continued until Becca shuddered under her touch again. Once they were both calmed, Becca shifted around until she could lay alongside a sweaty Kimberly.

They kissed again, their lips slowing with the time of night and weariness. Kimberly drifted to sleep, her fingers in Becca's hair and her other arm wrapped around her back, holding her tight.

Chapter Ten

The sound of retching reached Becca's ears. Shifting her head, Becca tamped down her own nausea as it threatened to surface. The retching noise continued. She rubbed her eyes and tried to go back to sleep. Light filtered through the windows dimly, but it was there. Groaning, Becca shifted. She was on something soft, very warm and comfortable.

A chill ran over her, and she forced her hungover brain to focus. When she turned and pushed up, she panicked. She wasn't sleeping on something. She was sleeping on some*one*. Fear welled up in her chest, the nausea this time not coming from the amount of alcohol she had consumed.

"Fuck," she muttered.

As slowly as she could, she extracted herself from between Kimberly's legs and stood up, wobbling from side to side. She braced a hand on the coffee table, bent down and gathered her clothes. She barely remembered what had happened, but she did remember pleasure and a general sense of peace.

Clutching her clothes to her chest, she headed for her bedroom.

She changed into clean clothes and moved to the bathroom. Drew was sprawled on the floor, their eyes closed and their face pale. She ordered an Uber and went to work at sobering Drew up enough to get in the vehicle and to their apartment. It didn't take long before she and Drew were sliding into the car, her backpack with extra clothes and her schoolwork shoved down by her feet as she gave the driver directions.

Once they got into Drew's small apartment, Becca put them to sleep with two bottles of water. She chugged her own water and lay carefully down on the couch to stare up at the ceiling. She'd covered Kimberly with a warm blanket before she'd left, but her boss hadn't even stirred. Becca put a hand to her eyes. Her *boss*.

I slept with my boss.

While it had been glorious from what she remembered and something she most definitely had wanted, she'd had sex with her boss. Fear clenched around her heart as she stayed motionless on the couch. Nothing good could come from this. Briefly, she wondered if that was why all the other previous nannies had been fired or quit — sleeping with the boss, sexual advancements from the boss, sexual harassment.

The thought lingered in her brain for at least an hour before she mostly dismissed it. She had wanted to have sex with Kimberly. She'd wanted it for almost as long as she had known the woman. Unsure of what to do and knowing she couldn't make rational decisions yet, Becca turned on her side to face the back of the couch and willed her body into sleep. She needed more time, and luckily, she had all weekend.

* * * *

Kimberly stirred awake with the sun shining bright on her face. Her mouth was dry and cottony, the leftover alcohol lingering in the center back of her tongue. Swallowing to try and rid herself of the awful flavor, she sat up. The blanket covering her fell around her waist, and a cool breeze touched her chest. She was naked. Blinking to clear her eyes, she noticed that she was on her couch with a thin, fluffy blanket half-covering her form. Her clothes were strewn about on the floor, but only her clothes were there. The house felt overwhelmingly empty.

Rubbing sleep from her eyes, Kimberly steadied herself on the edge of the couch as she attempted to figure out what had happened. She was sore. And she was sore in places she hadn't been in years. Pursing her lips, she gripped the blanket in her hand, balling it in her fist.

"Oh. My. God."

Guilt pummeled her and almost knocked her flat. She covered her face with her hands, her hair cascading around her as she tried to hide from the world. She'd had sex with her nanny, with a woman she employed, with her son's caretaker, with someone she truly admired. While she didn't think it had been coerced in any form, the boundaries she had crossed were immeasurable.

She'd been told by Kiddie Academy that if Becca were to quit or if she were to fire her, they wouldn't work with Kimberly any longer. This was her last chance before having to start all over again from scratch. She was sure the color had drained from her cheeks as the realization hit.

She very well had just screwed herself over — and Michael. *God, Michael.* He loved Becca. She was the first caretaker he had clung to and seemed to get along with. Becca, while she had her quirks, was excellent for teaching Michael, for taking care of him like Kimberly would have done had she been home each day.

"Fuck," she muttered.

She had really just screwed herself over — and perhaps even Becca — all because she couldn't control herself when she was drinking, all because she couldn't make herself stop, all because she just had to have Becca and couldn't think about what was best for both of them.

Sighing, she shoved the blanket to the floor and stood up, her muscles protesting as she stretched. Her back ached from sleeping on the couch, but her thighs ached from sex, from the ripples of pleasure Becca had brought her in the wee hours of the night in a drunken haze. She remembered most of it — Becca's taste, her smile, the flush in her cheeks as she came.

She groaned and leaned against the bathroom door. Kimberly took two deep breaths before she flipped the water on in the shower as hot as she dared to make it then she stepped under the spray while the water was still cold and heating up. The droplets sluiced over her skin. She had to find a solution. She had to figure out how to make this all okay, how to fix anything she had broken, because she knew she had just broken it.

The water turned cold again before she got out. When she stepped into the steamed bathroom, another wave of guilt crushed her. Knowing that was going to be her norm for the next while, she ignored it and wrapped herself in a large towel sheet. She headed for her room, dressed in loose shorts and a tank and crawled into her bed. She needed to focus on something other than Becca for a few hours. They could talk when Becca woke up and was sober enough to have a conversation.

With her laptop resting on her legs, Kimberly stared at the screen and the half-dozen starts to the cookbook she had already attempted to make. Biting her lip, she took a risk and opened a new file. Maybe there was something to what Becca had been saying all along. Time with her son... That was what not only he wanted, but that was what most people wanted.

She typed, the words flying from her fingers as she outlined how she would work up her cookbook. She would focus it around cooking with her kid, cooking easy at-home recipes anyone could make, recipes that didn't take a long time but that small hands would have no issue helping out with.

Before she knew it, hours had passed. Her very rough outline was near done, and she felt as though her plan was able to come to fruition. Dying for more water, she set her laptop aside and decided a break would be useful. She headed for the kitchen and grabbed herself a water bottle. As she drank, she stared down the hallway toward Becca's room. Checking the time, she decided she couldn't wait any longer to repair all the damage she'd done the night before — or rather, that morning.

Knocking on Becca's door, she waited patiently. When there was no answer, she knocked again. After the third time, Kimberly gently opened the door and peeked inside. The room was mostly clean, everything put away. The blankets were ruffled, but as she opened the door wider, Kimberly could clearly see the bed was empty. No Becca. No Drew.

That empty feeling she'd had when she'd first woken up pounded into the forefront of her mind. She was alone. She was desperately alone in a giant house with no one to fill it, no one to talk to, no one to share it with. Shutting the door a little harder than she'd planned, Kimberly stalked to the kitchen and pulled out the rest of the cake Becca had made a few days before. She didn't even bother to slice it as she took it and a fork, along with two more water bottles, to her bedroom so she could gorge herself in peace.

* * * *

By the time Drew woke up, Becca had already been to work on her plan. She wasn't going to waste any more time. If anything, working for Kim Burns the television personality of a chef had shown her that she was done with nannying. She wanted to teach. That was what she enjoyed the most about being with Michael, seeing him learn something new every day. While she liked her job, it wasn't what she wanted to do any longer than necessary...especially now.

The applications for her student teaching had been sitting on her computer just waiting. She'd spent the last few hours researching which schools to apply for, which would best suit what she wanted to learn and how and which were the most supportive. She made a checklist, adding to it as she went about her research.

Drew slipped into the chair next to her at the table and pressed their forehead to the cool metal. They groaned. Becca slid her gaze over to them and patted their head gently. She shut her laptop and rubbed her eyes, still not feeling the greatest, but definitely more with it than she had been hours before.

"How did we get here?" Drew asked.

Chuckling, Becca answered, "We took an Uber at about seven this morning."

Drew grunted. "Why in God's glorious and all-loving name did we do that?"

Becca rubbed her lips together, trying to figure out how to answer.

"Did we drink with *the* Kim Burns?"

"Yes."

"Good. At least I remember that right." Sitting up a bit, Drew chugged some water and some pain killers before laying their head down. Becca bet the cool of the table felt good against their heated skin. "Do I remember right that I saw *the* Kim Burns naked?"

Becca blanched. Heat raced to her cheeks, and she knew she was blushing. She opened her computer again in an attempt to hide, hoping Drew wouldn't notice. But her luck was out.

"Oh my God! Is that why we left at seven in the goddamned morning?"

"Yes…" Becca hissed. Tears stung at her eyes as she tried to tamp the feeling of hurt down. She didn't really want to feel right now — or at all — about this particular situation. She wanted to let it go and move on with her life, to push through in her job until she could start her student teaching and fly under the radar. That was her MO, after all, out of the spotlight.

"Becca, sugar." The sympathy in Drew's tone of voice set her on edge. She rolled her eyes and went back to her list, even though she struggled to focus on it. "Was the sex at least good?"

"What I remember of it was amazing," Becca murmured.

"Oh, honey!"

Becca held her hand up. "Stop. I don't want to hear it."

The pout on Drew's lips was almost her undoing. She loved them deeply, but in times like this, she wanted to smack them upside the head then run away. Sometimes she hated that they knew her so well. Cringing, Becca made to get up, but Drew's hand on her wrist stopped her.

"Talk to me, sugar. Spill it all."

"Do you think this is why she's been through so many nannies?"

Drew's jaw dropped then slowly, hesitantly, they shook their head in the negative. "No, I don't. But that doesn't really tell you much. I just met her last night, while drunk, and high."

"High?" Becca's eyes widened, and she jerked.

Grinning from ear to ear, Drew tottered their head back and forth. They took their finger and thumb and put them close together. "I may have had a little."

"You didn't." Becca's stomach dropped again for the second time that day. "You know — I just... I don't even know what to say to you right now."

Slamming her laptop lid down, Becca stood up and went to the kitchen. She felt displaced for the first time in her life with nowhere to go. Becca knew Drew sometimes imbibed, but they had never done it in her presence before, and she certainly didn't approve. Beginning dishes, she cleaned the kitchen while she cleared her mind. Perhaps it really was time for her to grow up and truly live on her own. She'd been on the right track that morning, but she'd need more time to finalize her plans.

"Drew?" she called from the kitchen.

They came in and grabbed some leftovers from the fridge. "What's up, sugar?"

"I'm going to stay the night, but after that? I'm not so sure I'm going to be spending as much time with you if you continue to do drugs. You know how I feel about it."

"Come on, honey. It was just a little E. One small pill."

"One small pill too many. I'd appreciate it if you didn't take any more while I'm here."

Drew dropped the food in the microwave and leaned against the counter. "What's gotten into you? You never would have minded before."

"Before what?"

"I don't know," they said. "Before now."

Pursing her lips again, Becca put her hands on her hips. "They why haven't you done it in front of me before? Hmm?"

Caught in the trap, Drew rolled their shoulders and turned to the microwave, pulling their food before the beep indicated it was done. The tension that filled the small kitchen was almost too much to bear, but it was the first time in years that Becca felt she was truly making the right decision.

"I need to think about my future. My future as a teacher. I don't want to be caught with you with drugs, and I don't really want to be associated with people who do drugs. I have more to life than that to think about."

After a few seconds, Drew nodded slowly. "Okay. I think I understand. I won't do them anymore."

Becca narrowed her eyes, not sure she believed Drew but willing to at least take the declaration as enough for the rest of the weekend until she was able to go back to Kimberly's and figure out her plans in detail. Kimberly had said Michael would be starting kindergarten in the fall, so that meant she only needed a nanny for the next three months. They could easily push through the mess they had made of things until then, so long as Kimberly didn't fire her in the meantime.

Nodding to herself, she grabbed some food and sat down at the table with her computer in front of her. With her mind made up, Becca was ready to focus on her future and not her past. She wanted to be a teacher, and it was time to make her dreams come true.

* * * *

Kimberly headed to Bradley's a few hours early, no longer able to stand being in her house alone. Becca hadn't come back. She'd opened her phone more times than she cared to admit or count, ready to call her and beg her to come back so they could talk, but she'd chickened out every time.

Bradley would be someone to talk to, and his door was always open. Pulling into the parking garage of his high-rise condominium, she got out and locked her car door. Even at their worst, they could talk to each other. She looked a mess. It had taken her the rest of Saturday to feel sober and most of Sunday to feel anywhere near decent. Her stomach was still queasy, and she had to remind herself over and over again that she was not twenty-eight like Becca. She was fast approaching forty-one—next month—and she did not rebound like she had when she was younger.

Bradley opened the door with a surprised look on his face, but he let her inside. When she sat on the couch instead of grabbing Michael's things and heading out, he seemed curious but went with it. She rested her head.

"He napping?"

"Yes. Care to share what's going on?"

She sent him a sideways look.

"You didn't!" His eyes narrowed. When she didn't respond, they grew wide. "Oh, you did!" Sitting next to her on the couch, he gripped her hand and squeezed. "That good, huh?"

"Amazing," Kimberly sighed. "But now what? She's our nanny! Michael adores her. For the first time ever, he adores a nanny. I can't take that away from him."

"Not to mention you'll be SOL for finding a replacement."

"Don't remind me," she said, giving him a sideways glare. "I fucked this up, B. I really did."

He smiled and kissed her knuckles before setting her hand down. "Stay for dinner. You can cook," he added before she could decline. "Let's talk about it."

"You don't think it's weird to talk to my ex-husband about sleeping with the hired help?"

Bradley burst out laughing. "Heavens, no. I wouldn't have given her such a hard time when I met her if I didn't think you'd be attracted to her. She's gorgeous and just your type."

"My type?"

He hummed. "Tall, smart—really smart, like me."

Kimberly snorted.

"She's in love with Michael, which, let's face it, is step one into getting into your heart nowadays. I'm lucky I didn't have that problem to work around."

"Yeah, you are," Kimberly readily agreed.

"Ouch!" He feigned injury by pressing a hand over his heart. "Nonetheless, let's try to figure something out, all right? Have you talked to her yet?"

"No. She disappeared before I even woke up and hasn't been back since."

"Have you called her?"

Kimberly flushed and looked down at his thousand-dollar carpet. "No."

Bradley rolled his eyes. "Talking to her might help in figuring out where to go from here — and if you'll be looking for new help or not."

Kimberly dragged her hands through her fluffy hair, still not sure what she would even say to Becca when they did finally talk. *"Hello, I know I fucked up, but I really liked fucking you. Let's do it again?"* just didn't sound like it would go over all that well.

When she glanced at Bradley, he was giving her a look of curiosity. "What?"

"You like her."

"Of course, I like her. She loves Michael, she's amazing with Michael and — "

"And nothing." He poked a finger to her chest. "You, Kimberly Thompson, mother of Michael, yes, but you as Kimberly? You like her."

Ignoring him, Kimberly went into the kitchen to figure out what Bradley even had for her to cook, since she'd been voluntold. He tried to pull her into the conversation, but she continued to ignore him, something she had perfected over their ten years of marriage. When she popped out of the fridge, he was standing right there.

"What?" she said accusingly.

"Just know I'm here to talk when you want to."

"I'll remember that," she said, narrowing her eyes at him.

It still felt a bit odd, talking to her ex about her one-night stand, but she did feel much better confessing it to someone. Before she began prepping their meal, Michael woke up and raced out of the room when he heard her voice. He wrapped his arms around her waist and buried his face into her belly.

She gave him a strong hug and closed her eyes as she breathed in his scent. No matter what she did or what she and Becca did, Michael had to come first and be first in their minds. They couldn't hurt him or confuse him in any way. And she wasn't ready to start that conversation with a four-year-old. Bradley hadn't even done that with all his dates and boyfriends since they had divorced—or before. No, Michael deserved her best, and she was determined to give it to him.

Chapter Eleven

Becca came home late Sunday night, knowing she wouldn't have to work until morning but also knowing she needed the extra time away from Kimberly to sort out her thoughts and feelings. When she arrived at the house, she had to convince herself to go inside. Most of the house was dark, save for one light she knew was Kimberly's bedroom, and the kitchen, which wasn't a surprise to her.

Forcing her legs to move, Becca walked inside with her backpack over one shoulder. She put her key in the lock and twisted. Everything moved in slow motion, daring her to run away. She wanted to on one hand, but on the other, she wanted to march straight into Kimberly's bedroom and pick up where they'd left off. She might regret sleeping with her boss, but after two days of deep soul-searching and listening to her emotions, she did not feel negative about what she'd done with Kimberly.

When she entered, she was pushed back with a flood of scent. Her heart raced as she shut the door behind her and moved toward the kitchen, which she'd have to walk through in order to get to her bedroom. Kimberly was knocking pans around, shuffling one against the gas stove top, undoubtedly mixing something in it so it didn't burn and was evenly cooked.

She tried to skirt around the edge of the room unseen but was stopped in her tracks at the sound of Kimberly's confident voice, although it still had a hint of huskiness to it.

"Glad you finally came back," she said.

Biting her lip, Becca turned on her heel and faced her boss. Kimberly's cheeks were red from the heat of cooking, a thin sheen of sweat riddled her forehead like she'd been hard at work for some time, and if the dishes upon dishes of food littering the counter were anything to say about that, Becca was right. Kimberly had been cooking up a storm.

"I remembered you liked Chinese, so I started there."

"You... I'm sorry, what?" That had been the last thing Becca had thought she would say, and confusion rained down on her like a monsoon.

Rolling her eyes, Kimberly walked around the counter and toward Becca. Becca stayed firmly where she was, scared to take a step forward. Her heart raced even more than it had before, and she wasn't sure what was up Kimberly's chef's sleeves.

"I started with Chinese. I've been wanting to write a cookbook for years. Everyone keeps telling me to, but no matter how many times I started it, I never got more than a few recipes in. You said something to me, and it put everything in perspective."

"I did?" Becca's forehead furrowed, and she dared herself to step forward.

"You did." Wrinkles appeared at the corner of Kimberly's eyes as she stayed at least two feet away from Becca so they couldn't touch each other. The chasm between them was easily noticeable, but Becca was curious nonetheless about what Kimberly had said. "You said Michael wanted to spend time with me in the kitchen, a place I love to be, but a family place."

"Right. I did," Becca started, still not quite sure where the conversation was going.

Kimberly spun around when she heard something sizzle on the stove. She raced in that direction, forcing Becca to follow her, even if she wasn't sure she wanted to. She really just wanted to disappear into her room until morning then put on a brave and calm and serene face for Michael when he woke up and do her job.

After shifting a pan off the stove top onto a cold burner, Kimberly turned around. "Anyway, it got me thinking. People don't want just another cookbook with a bunch of fancy recipes in it that they don't actually have ingredients for or that they'll cook once and never again because it's so complicated. They want a cookbook they can use, that their kids can use, that they can use together."

"Oh." Becca formed a soft smile on her lips. She hadn't anticipated her crossing the boundary line of telling Kimberly to be a better parent would somehow miraculously turn into her being a better chef and even better at her job. Pursing her lips, she still wasn't sure that had been the best course of action. "Wasn't quite what I meant."

"I know." Kimberly grinned again. "But it's how my brain works. Anyway, I remember from the other night that you like Chinese, so I started with those recipes. Here."

She shoved a bowl toward Becca, insisting she take it, even when she hesitated. The heat from the food inside warmed the ceramic and seeped into Becca's cold fingers. When she dared to look down, she saw fried rice with ground meat on top and an over-easy egg on top of that, with scallions sliced on the angle and sprinkled with a few black sesame seeds.

"What's this?"

Kimberly shrugged. "Egg roll in a bowl. Mostly healthy, somewhat not, but still needs perfecting."

"Oh." Awkwardly, Becca continued to hold the bowl, realizing she didn't have a fork and wasn't really hungry. Kimberly must have noticed because she was about to say something, but Becca cut her off. "It looks delicious."

"Still not perfect."

Becca stood stock-still, not sure where to go from there. Kimberly was being overly bubbly, excessively friendly and very uncharacteristic of the woman Becca had come to know in the last two-and-a-half months. She wasn't quite sure what to make of it except they had slept together and neither of them were talking about the consequences of their actions or having had sex at all.

Giving in to the smell, Becca shifted her backpack on her shoulder and rounded the kitchen to grab a fork. When Kimberly gave her a questioning gaze with one thick dark-brown eyebrow raised, Becca raised the fork into the air and wagged it back and forth.

"I'll just eat this in my room."

She didn't wait for an answer as she scooted down the hall toward her sanctuary. She shut the door behind her, locked it and collapsed onto her bed, glad the initial conversation was done and over with but confused that they hadn't actually talked about anything. No matter what she did, she would have to find a way to focus on Michael, teach him and push through until she could start her student teaching in the fall. She had to make this work. Moving to a whole new house, starting up with a whole new family, was not an option at this point. Three months and two weeks. That was all she had to get through.

* * * *

When morning came, Becca dressed carefully and modestly, then she plastered a smile on her face. If Kimberly could play bubbly, so could she. Becca left her room, ready to see Michael again for the first time in days. She had spent the night planning how to teach him to read — mostly through play and phonics — and planning her own future.

As soon as she reached the living area, Michael bounded out of his seat and wrapped his arms around her waist, shouting her name. Becca hugged him and smiled. "Did you have fun at your daddy's?"

He shrugged and pulled her toward the kitchen table. "Mama cooked! Look!"

Placed on the table were plates of food — eggs, waffles, sausage, breakfast casserole. It looked as if Kimberly had been up all night cooking. Becca had heard her in the kitchen until very late, but she'd drowned out the sound with her television and gone to sleep.

Kimberly popped up from somewhere in the kitchen, startling Becca. "I did cook."

Michael's eyes were wide. "Mama never cooks breakfast."

Becca gripped Michael's hand and sat next to him at the table. He was already halfway through his plate. She took one of her own and piled it high with a little bit of everything. Michael grinned around the maple-syrup-covered waffle in his mouth as he stared at her.

"It's so good." His eyes widened.

She took one small bite and nodded, agreeing with him. "It really is. Did you tell your mom that?"

"Mama! You're the best cooker *ever*."

Kimberly blushed and came over to join them. She ate in silence while Michael chatted with Becca, telling her tall tales of his weekend with his dad. It wasn't until Becca was grabbing seconds of the casserole that she realized Kimberly was more pushing her food around her plate rather than eating it. Normally she would have said something, but in light of everything, she kept her mouth shut and focused on Michael.

It wasn't long until Kimberly begged away from the table, saying she had to get ready for work. It was early yet, but she claimed she had paperwork needing to be done at the restaurant that couldn't be done at home. After she'd left and Michael and Becca had cleaned up and miraculously found a place for all the food in the suddenly overcrowded fridge, she got him dressed and they started on his reading lessons for the day.

He picked up on the individual sounds rather quickly but struggled a bit with how to put them together into a full word. It wasn't unexpected, and when his frustration level rose, Becca decided it might be a good time to switch gears. She finished out the lesson and put the book away.

"Do you want to build something with Legos?"

Michael's eyes lit up. "Yes!" he shouted before running toward his bedroom. He came back dragging behind him a large plastic tote filled to the brim with the plastic bricks. Becca had discovered that Legos were one of his favorite things to play with, and he particularly liked to build all different kinds of robots. They spent the next hour building and destroying, building and destroying.

It wasn't much longer until Becca realized Michael needed to burn even more energy. She grabbed his hand and asked, "Want to clean this up after we go for a walk?"

"A walk?"

"Yeah, we can go around the neighborhood and look for bugs."

"Bugs?" He pulled a disgusted face. "Bugs are gross."

"No, they're not. Bugs are very good for the earth."

He gave her a look like he didn't believe her.

"Wanna go for a walk or not, kiddo?"

"Yes. I get my tennis shoes."

They both slipped their shoes on and headed for the front door. Becca made sure to lock it behind her and set the alarm. They spent over an hour walking through the neighborhood, looking at the different kinds of plants and flowers, and yes, bugs, much to Michael's disgust. Soon enough his stomach rumbled, as did hers, and they headed to the house for lunch. They spent the rest of the day playing, practicing writing, prepping dinner and taking naps.

* * * *

Kimberly enjoyed the quiet of Gamma's for hours before anyone else joined her. But it wasn't long until her head chef and sous chefs showed up to prep for lunch, and her still quiet was displaced into the chatter and joyous jokes of the crew. She hid away in her office until Zechariah knocked on her door. Turning to face him with a glum look, she didn't even pretend to be pleasant.

"What do you need?" Her tone was sharp and harsh, but she didn't feel the need to explain herself. She wanted her peace and quiet, the focus that was her paperwork and the joy that was her restaurant. Instead, all she could think about was Becca and the conversation they hadn't yet had. The one they *needed* to have.

"Carter called out. Stomach bug."

Cursing under her breath, Kimberly rolled her eyes. "That's the fifth time this month."

"I know. I told him as much when he called."

She glanced at the paperwork, then went back to the computer. "I told him if he didn't work well with you and the crew, he wasn't going to last. What do you think?"

Zechariah shrugged nonchalantly. That was why she was the boss, she supposed. He never wanted to make these decisions, and she always had to. She was pretty strict when it came to attendance, although illness was something she'd always let slide, but someone having the stomach bug this often proved to her they really didn't want to be there.

"I'll deal with it," she muttered, knowing the conversation would end in a firing. Luckily, private non-chain restaurants had a bit more autonomy than a lot of other retail places. She wasn't going to put up with someone who didn't want to be there, and she certainly wasn't in the mood to deal with anyone's funny business.

Zechariah hadn't left, though. He stayed by the door, staring at her. It didn't take her long to look at him with a scathing glare, daring him to say something. He put both his hands up and straightened his back. "You okay, Chef?"

She scrunched her nose in a sneer. "Could be better."

On one hand, she felt kind of bad about treating him poorly, especially since he wasn't anywhere near the person who she was really mad at. On the other hand, they had worked together for twelve years, and by this point, he knew when to give her a wide berth and when not to, and he probably knew she wasn't mad at him.

"You want on the line this afternoon?" he asked.

Her heart jumped. Being on the line would be her best distraction. When she was upset or unsure, it was best for her to bury herself in the kitchen and the oven—literally—and get to cooking. It made her feel that much better. She leaned in her rolling chair in her tiny office filled with piles of papers and crossed her arms, debating. Being on the line would make her feel better, but being on the line would also make her crew *not* feel better, especially with the mood she was in, and she was still technically on light duty because of her wrist.

"Lunch only," she answered, finally. "I need to be home tonight for the kid."

"Gotcha, Chef. We've got you."

She smiled sweetly as he left. Twelve years was a long time to work with anyone, and they had formed some sort of pseudo-friendship in the process. He had been there through her divorce. He had been there when Michael was born. He had been there when she'd caught the kitchen on fire. Grinning at the last memory, Kimberly turned to the work at hand. She would let them do the prep then show up for cooking.

With her paperwork almost done, she joined Zechariah in the back of the kitchen and waited for the first order to come in. She'd already run through the rest of the restaurant and double-checked that everything was ready for service. She didn't have to. Her team was well-oiled, her front-of-house managers did their jobs and did them well, as did her back-of-house managers and her head chef, Zechariah. But sometimes she couldn't help herself as she double-checked. It was, after all, her name on the line if they did mess something up.

The ovens were already going, the stoves were hot and pans were warming as they waited until an hour before noon for the first ticket to come in. The sous chefs chatted amicably as they chopped vegetables and broke down the chicken. They told joke after joke until Kimberly's head spun.

She wasn't there for the conversation. She was there for the distraction. Sneering, she heated up some oil in a pan for no reason because she didn't have anything to cook and tried to push the waiting game to the next level. She slid some onions into the pan, shifting them back and forth with small flicks on her non-injured wrist until they became translucent. Then she took some garlic greens and slipped them in. Soon enough, she heard Zechariah call out orders for appetizers. She'd guessed correctly, and the order was coming in for the very thing she was making.

Kimberly continued to sauté the garlic greens and onions until she put in the sliced chicken and bell peppers. This was one of the newest items on her menu, with a bit of a Mexican flair—'build your own fajita' as an appetizer. She wasn't sure how well it would go over, but it seemed to be doing okay for now. It'd only been on the menu for all of one week, so it was hard to tell if it was going to flop or succeed.

Either way, she was determined to make the dish look perfect. When she finished plating, she put it on the warmer and called out to Zechariah, letting him know the dish was done and perfect. Even still, when he grabbed the plate, he checked it over to make sure. If she'd been in a better mood, she would have teased him about it, but in her foul demeanor, she gave him a death glare. Rightfully so, Zechariah ignored her.

As the afternoon and lunch rush wore on, she became more and more petty in her responses. It was only two hours in when Zechariah took her by the arm and pushed her into her office. He towered over her, his added height a bonus in some situations, but in this one, it was to her disadvantage. She crossed her arms as she waited to see exactly what he was going to say.

She'd just made a snarky comment to one of the busboys who was rather new to the job and had dumped—rather loudly—the dirty plates into the sink. She'd told him quite shortly that he didn't need to be so loud that the President could hear it all the way at the White House.

Zechariah's temperament softened. "Look... I don't know what's going on, Kim, but I think it's better if you just work in your office and not on the line. I'd like to still have a team tomorrow."

Huffing, she nodded. "You're right. I'll apologize before they leave."

He lifted one singular eyebrow at her. "What crawled up your butt?"

Staring at him, she sighed in resignation. "You don't even want to know. I'll apologize later."

Zechariah jerked his head up at her in agreement and went to his station, leaving her alone. Now not only did she feel guilty for everything she had done to Becca, but she was alienating her crew, something she most certainly didn't want to do. Her restaurant was her life outside of Michael, and she had to keep it. It was what gave her the most joy, and she would need it to rely on for the next few months while she waited out kindergarten.

After washing her hands of the grease that had spat back at her and the food she'd cooked, Kimberly went to her office and sat in her chair. Whatever mood she was in, it was not good for anyone, least of all her.

Finishing out her paperwork, she helped prep for dinner, made her apologies then headed home to hopefully a much calmer house. At the very least, she would be able to entice Michael to help her cook dinner, give her a few more ideas for her cookbook and spend some quality time with her leading person. She just needed to find a way to keep Becca employed and happy until Michael went to school. Then she could deal with whatever it was she was feeling. Until then, she had to play nice.

Chapter Twelve

Four semi-awkward weeks had passed, but Kimberly had managed to tame her anger. Everyone at Gamma's clearly appreciated it and probably so did Becca. Michael had taken a better attitude as well, not fighting her on cleaning his room or anything she asked him to do.

She'd felt torn between spending time at home, which meant being in Becca's vicinity or spending time at Gamma's, which meant time away from Michael. While Becca wasn't in every moment of her day when she was there, Kimberly felt her presence in the house, the energy she had that Kimberly seemed to lack most days. Spending a lot of her nights up well past when she should be, she worked tirelessly on her cookbook. It came together wonderfully. She'd pulled back on the home cooking and tried not to overwhelm their fridge, and she had even tried to teach Michael how to cook, which was an adventure in and of itself.

Four-year-olds simply did not have long attention spans. After trial and error, she realized most of the recipes she ended up doing with him that were very successful were in up-front prep. He enjoyed that. He loved mixing anything together and dumping the different spices and ingredients into the bowls. When it came to the actual cooking part, he was less enthused by the task and the waiting—not to mention she really didn't want a preschooler near an open flame.

She was home for the day. It was Becca's designated day off, as it was hers. She hadn't seen much of Becca, but she had also tried to avoid her at almost any cost. She and Michael had driven to the grocery store and spent an hour there. Kimberly could have stayed longer—grocery shopping being one of her favorite things to do—but Michael was hungry.

Then they drove to the farmer's market. They ate until they could eat no more, stopping at nearly every booth that had snacks, but also toting around a wagon full of fresh vegetables, as well as some meats. The meat producers were new that year at the market, and Kimberly thoroughly enjoyed getting as much local food as she could. Farm-to-table was certainly a popular trend, but for her, it meant the cleanest, best cuts and supporting the little guy—just like she had been when she'd started up at Gamma's.

When they got to the house, Michael fell asleep on the couch while he tried to avoid taking a nap in his room. Eventually, Kimberly covered him with a blanket and went to the kitchen to debate what to make for dinner while putting away the majority of their finds from earlier in the day, as well as separating out what she was going to take to the restaurant.

She was in the midst of sorting when Becca came out. Her hair was mussed, sticking up in the back, and she wore thin sleep shorts and a baggy and obviously very old T-shirt with the Pink Floyd logo on the front. Smiling to herself, Kimberly focused on her work. Becca rummaged in the fridge then in the pantry for a few minutes before turning to the counter that was completely covered in fresh produce.

"Guess I'll take this to the table," Becca muttered.

"Sorry!" Kimberly called, a little louder than she'd expected, but being alone with Becca without Michael as a buffer ratcheted up her nerves. "I'll have most of this gone as soon as he wakes up. I'll have to take it in tonight so they can use it for dinner."

Becca shrugged and plopped down at the table with the chips and dip she'd chosen for her snack. Kimberly moved around a few more pieces of yellow-neck squash before she turned to Becca. They had to make amends somehow, figure out how to exist in the same room without all the tension. It had been weeks that they hadn't talked about what had happened, but they had to work through it.

Rolling her eyes, Kimberly knew that if she said what she was thinking she'd be labeled as crazy. Michael was due at Bradley's for the weekend, which meant forty-eight hours without her main distraction and buffer. Confrontation was not something she was normally fearful of. That was what usually got her into so much hot water in the first place.

Dropping the squash onto the counter, she wiped her suddenly sweaty palms on her thighs and headed for the table. She glanced at Michael to make sure he was still sleeping, then she sat right next to Becca, pulling out her chair at an angle so she could see Becca fully.

Becca paused, skimming her gaze up and down Kimberly's form. Kimberly begged for the flush starting in her toes not to reach her cheeks, but she was fairly certain her body had betrayed her and that she was outed. Biting her lip, she started. "Look... I want you to be comfortable here. I don't want this" — she waved a hand between them — "whatever this is, which is really nothing, I guess, to be an issue. Michael loves you, and I want you to stay on as his nanny."

Popping another chip in her mouth, Becca chomped down. Kimberly squelched her nerves when she was unable to read Becca's mannerisms. Was she angry? In disbelief? Concerned still? Or...what? Kimberly had no idea. She sighed and leaned back in her chair. That move seemed to have caught Becca's attention, as she raked her gaze up and down Kimberly's form again.

Kimberly shivered. She stared directly at Becca until their eyes locked in a silent battle. Kimberly dared Becca to say something, anything. Becca shrugged and turned back to her chips. The indifference in Becca was infuriating. Kimberly gave in and grabbed her hand, wrapping her fingers around Becca's.

"I don't want this to be hard, and I don't want either of us to be walking on eggshells."

"Okay," Becca answered.

Kimberly nearly rolled her eyes at the one-word answer, but she stopped herself in time. She didn't understand why Becca was being so childish. It seemed very out of the norm for her. Giving up, Kimberly released Becca's hand and decided she would have to be the one to make the concerted effort.

Plastering a smile on her face, Kimberly shifted in her seat as if she were about to get up. Becca followed her every move. "I'm just going to go chop, and chop, and chop some more for prepping dinner tonight because this" — she held up her finally brace-free wrist — "is no longer hindering my mastery."

Becca snorted. Kimberly, pleased to have finally gotten a more normal response from Becca, pushed herself to stand and went to the kitchen. She finished sorting far more quickly than she had anticipated. As Becca was headed to her room, Michael woke up. He jumped off the couch when he saw her and gave her a hug like he hadn't seen her in weeks.

Kimberly furrowed her forehead at him when he waved his hand down to whisper in Becca's ear. She turned her head to him and asked, "Are you sure?"

"Yeah!" he replied, excitedly, his voice going up in pitch as he barely stayed flat on his feet. "I think I'm ready."

"Okay, go get it."

Michael ran off, and Becca turned on her toes and headed for the couch, putting herself on one side of it. She raised her chin toward Kimberly, who was watching carefully, and beckoned her over.

"You'll want to see this," Becca called. "Come grab a seat."

Kimberly was about to sit on the far end of the couch when Michael came bounding back. As soon as he got to the couch, he pointed to the spot next to Becca. "You sit there."

"All right, then." Kimberly sat down, her thigh brushing against Becca's. Shots of electricity went through her that she tried her best to ignore. Michael sat next to her and curled slightly in her lap. He placed a book on her legs and opened the first page.

Kimberly waited, curious as to what he was going to do next. He glanced at Becca, who gave an encouraging nod and smile.

"One word at a time, kiddo," she whispered.

He nodded and put his finger down on the thick-board book, tracking it from left to right. "Mama wakes me up. Mommy cooks me food."

Kimberly jerked in surprise. Michael continued, turning from page to page, stumbling here and there, but then sounding out each word carefully and precisely until he got it. Becca only helped him twice. Kimberly wisely kept silent as she listened to her little boy read. She was all-out impressed with what he'd been able to learn in such a short period of time.

When he finished, Kimberly grabbed him by the cheeks and pulled him in for a big kiss on each one. Then she put her forehead to his and held in the tears threatening to spill over. "That was amazing, kiddo. Beautiful, even. When did you learn all that?"

"Becca taught me," he answered, grinning up at both of them as wide as he could. "She's a good teacher."

"That she is," Kimberly answered, turning her gaze onto Becca and smiling at her. She was completely warm inside, a feeling she hadn't felt in years, since very early on with Bradley. Closing her eyes and pressing her nose into Michael's hair, Kimberly smiled again and shook her head. "Thank you, Becca. Really. I never could have taught him to do that and really never in that short period of time. You've been amazing for him."

Becca blushed, her cheeks reddening as she looked down at her hands in her lap. Kimberly wanted to keep praising her but got the sense that it might fall on deaf ears. Becca wasn't the sort to take praise well, and she wanted to make sure Becca heard her when she spoke.

Turning to Michael, Kimberly told him to put his book away and that when they got back from the restaurant, he could read to her all he wanted while they cooked. Grinning again, Michael ran to his room. Kimberly got up and slipped her shoes on as Becca disappeared into her bedroom.

* * * *

Becca pulled up her email once again and opened one of the more recent ones she had gotten that morning. She read every word again, her heart breaking at the words. She was not accepted for student teaching at her top-choice school. Perhaps she had waited too long to really look and apply, seeing as how most applications had needed to be in before the end of spring semester, which had already passed.

Rubbing her eyes, she leaned against her headboard and dropped her head back with her eyes closed. She'd read the email over a dozen times that day. It had put her in such a sour mood that she was glad Kimberly was home to watch Michael, so she could wallow alone in her ocean of self-pity.

She had scurried into the kitchen for dinner then holed up in her room. It was dark. She'd heard the argument between Kimberly and Michael over first bath then bed. She'd ignored it as she attempted to study. She might be reading the text, but she certainly wasn't retaining any of the information.

Groaning, Becca gave up and tossed her book on the floor in a fit of frustration. Leaning back on the comfortable bed, she turned on her television and zoned out to whatever was on. If asked, she probably couldn't even tell anyone what had happened.

The knock on her door was a surprise. She checked her watch, noting it was late. Furrowing her forehead, she muted the television and sat up, trying to make herself look a bit more presentable. She finally called, "Come in."

Kimberly opened the door, her wider stature almost filling the frame as she dared to take a step in. "Got a minute?"

Nodding, Becca curled her legs under her to sit cross-legged and invited Kimberly all the way in with a wave of her hand. Kimberly shut the door behind her, and Becca immediately regretted it. She had been trying her best over the last few weeks to stay as far away from Kimberly as possible. She worried that if they were to get too close—like that afternoon reading session—she wouldn't be able to help herself.

Kimberly sat on the bed.

With only the blanket, their clothes and not enough space separating them, Becca's heartbeat turned up a few notches. She was sure Kimberly would be able to hear it if she listened close enough. Swallowing, Becca turned her head to the side and tried to will Kimberly to get on with whatever it was.

"I wanted to thank you again for teaching Michael to read. I really appreciate all you do with him."

"Oh?" Becca hadn't expected the conversation to take that turn. "It's no problem. I enjoy teaching, obviously."

"Yes."

Kimberly smiled, but it looked more like a grimace. Her beautiful warm-honeyed eyes stared straight through Becca, and Becca was sure she could read everything racing through her thick brain.

"You're very good at teaching. I've tried to teach him to read a few words here and there, but he never could quite get it. He'd just get frustrated and quit after the second try."

Becca chuckled. "Well, he wanted to quit plenty of times when I was teaching him, too."

"Really?"

"Yeah. But we worked on it for small chunks multiple times throughout the day. I'd tell him he'd have to work on it for ten minutes each time, and when the timer went off, we could do something he wanted to do. That seemed to work well. When he figured out he could read books, that's when he really got interested in learning."

"Interesting," Kimberly answered.

Becca let loose. "The trick of it is to find what works for now and keep going with it. Michael responds really well to verbal praise, so I made sure to keep that up. He also really just wants attention. He feels he can get that one-on-one attention with this."

"Hmmm..."

Scrunching her nose, Becca shook her head. "Sorry... I'm rambling."

"No, you're not. I love hearing you talk about teaching in this way. It shows how passionate you are about it."

"Like you and cooking."

Kimberly bopped her head from side to side as she debated. "Most days."

Chuckling, Becca grabbed Kimberly's hand and twined their fingers together. "I see it every day."

When Becca looked up, Kimberly was biting her lower lip and staring at their joined hands. She had a flush to her cheeks. Giving in to the urge, Becca reached forward with her free hand and tilted Kimberly's chin up with the crook of her finger. She said nothing as they looked at each other.

Her breathing hitched and her heart was in her throat. As Kimberly continued to look at her with honeyed eyes, all she wanted to do and more tumbled through her brain. *Kiss. Touch. Sex.* Blinking, Becca gave in to temptation and leaned forward until she pressed their mouths together.

Kimberly gasped at the contact then pulled away, closed her eyes and pressed their foreheads together, much like she had done with Michael earlier in the day. Becca closed her eyes, too, listening to Kimberly's breathing, allowing her spicy scent to reach her nostrils and letting their hearts beat together.

"Only if you want to," Kimberly whispered.

Without hesitating, Becca locked their lips together again and cupped Kimberly's cheek with her thin fingers. They tangled their tongues before Becca pulled Kimberly's lip between her own teeth, scraping lightly — something she had been wanting to do all day.

"Oh, I want to," Becca answered, enthusiasm lacing her tone. "I have wanted to…"

She trailed off, distracted by Kimberly's neck as she kissed her way down it, sliding her fluffy dark brown hair behind her back. Thanking whatever God was out there that Kimberly did not have her chef's jacket on for once in her life, Becca slipped her hand up the thin T-shirt until she cupped Kimberly's breast.

Kimberly moaned and tilted her head just as she listed her body forward. Becca skillfully flipped the shirt up farther and the cup of Kimberly's bra down so she could latch on with her mouth. Swirling her tongue, she giggled. She had pushed herself to wait four awful weeks for this, and she wasn't about to waste any time. Kimberly would figure that out soon enough.

Using her other hand to guide Kimberly backward, Becca pulled down both sides of Kimberly's bra and feasted on the newly exposed skin. Kimberly hissed as Becca left one side and went to the other. When Becca looked up, Kimberly's eyes were completely closed, pleasure written all over her face.

She didn't dare speak. Normally she would talk throughout sex, but with Kimberly, she didn't. She loved listening to the deep and precise tones that left Kimberly's throat. She'd imagined them over the past four weeks, masturbated to them, dreamed about them.

Sliding Kimberly's pants down, Becca shoved them to the ground, not caring where they landed. When she moved up, Kimberly already had her legs opened and ready. Becca nuzzled her, slid her tongue in circles agonizingly slow and missing the one spot she knew Kimberly wanted her to give some attention.

Kimberly pressed her hands above her head, stretching and relaxing, unabashed in her nakedness. Becca marveled at her confidence, wishing she could somehow gain only a small portion of that for herself. Pushing the thought from her head, she focused on what they both wanted. At her first touch, Kimberly's voice broke the silence of the room. Then Kimberly's rhythmic keening kept up the whole time Becca had her under her control.

Finally breathing out a word, Becca heard a simple 'yes' float through the air. That one word rejuvenated her. The second word 'more' reached her, and she doubled her efforts. Kimberly was ready and waiting. Becca took her up, high on her orgasm then walked with her down as she eased Kimberly through the heat and flush and pleasure.

Once Kimberly was finally with it, she grinned and pulled Becca up so they could kiss. "I wish you could do that every day. I'd probably be in a much better mood."

Becca smiled, but she wasn't sure how she felt about Kimberly's sentiment. Before she could think on it further, Kimberly sat up and pulled her shirt and bra the rest of the way off. She reached for Becca's and made eye contact. "May I take this off for you?"

"Ye—yes..." Becca answered.

Kimberly cocked her head as she seemed to debate something. She took in a deep breath and smiled. "I think I need a more definitive answer than that."

"Yes, take it off," Becca responded, giddy at the thought of having so much control.

Kimberly repeated the process with each article of clothing she removed from Becca's body, then beckoned her to climb upward on her hands and knees. "Right here," Kimberly said, pointing to her lips as she pressed her head into Becca's pillow. "I want to be able to see your face."

Shuddering, Becca complied and moved to straddle Kimberly's face as she had been told. Her stomach flipped and flopped with nerves and excitement in a way it hadn't in their previous encounter. Perhaps that was one of the joys of being sober this time around. Better decisions meant better sex.

When Becca lowered herself, Kimberly started with her fingers. Becca gripped the headboard to keep herself steady. As Kimberly continued to work her, Becca found her knuckles white as she clung to the wood to keep herself upright and in the perfect position as pleasure coursed through her over and over again. When she came, she ground down hard onto Kimberly's face.

Kimberly eased her hands up and down Becca's thighs, gently using her nails to half-tickle, half-scrape. Becca stayed put until she thought she could move without falling over, then slipped beside Kimberly to curl into her side. Kimberly turned and pressed their mouths together, sighing and closing her eyes at the same time.

Becca felt her withdrawing, felt her putting up those walls again, and she desperately wanted it to stop. When she moved her hand down between Kimberly's legs, Kimberly stopped her with a gentle hand to her wrist. "We have to talk about this."

Panicking, Becca moved to sit up, but Kimberly opened her eyes. Sadness echoed at Becca, and she wasn't sure what to make of it. Kimberly licked her lips, and Becca waited patiently for Kimberly to share her thoughts, because she had so many racing through her mind that she wasn't even sure where to begin.

Once again, they were back at the start. Kimberly was her boss. She was the hired help. Kimberly was rich. Becca had twenty cents and a beat-up Toyota to her name. Kimberly owned the house she lived in. Becca wasn't even going to have a job in the next two months. But she wanted this. God, she wanted this.

"I want this," Kimberly said.

Becca's eyes widened in fear, thinking she had spoken out loud. After staring at Kimberly, she realized they only shared the same thoughts, but Kimberly was willing to speak them out loud.

"I want to be with you like this. I think we're good at this. Is this something you want?"

Suddenly afraid, Becca nodded her answer. She normally wasn't one to be at such a loss for words, but it seemed that any time Kimberly wanted to have a serious conversation, she would pull back and hide, withdraw from the what-ifs.

"Good." Kimberly grabbed Becca's hand. "I don't want Michael, or really anyone else, to know. I—I'm not ready to explain that to him yet, and I don't want him to be confused when I do explain it to him."

"I don't think he'll be confused," Becca finally spoke. "He's a very smart little boy."

"I know." Kimberly's lips quirked up in a smile. "But this...? His mom in this kind of relationship? I think it's too much for him to handle."

"You're his parent. I won't tell him if you don't want me to."

"I don't. But that's where this gets hard."

"What do you mean?" Becca snuggled in closer to Kimberly's side and pressed her nose into the crook of Kimberly's neck, breathing in her scent and basking in it.

Kimberly took her time to answer, but when she did, Becca knew she wasn't going to like it. "He can't see or know anything. So that means when he's around, we can't do this. We can't act like a couple. We can't hold hands, or touch, or kiss."

Becca wrinkled her nose at the list Kimberly continued to put out there of all the things they couldn't do together. She finally stopped Kimberly from talking with a deep kiss. When they broke apart, she gave a gentle but sad smile. "Then we'll do that. It'll suck, but we'll keep our distance when he is around."

Kimberly nodded. "The good news, though, is he's at Bradley's this weekend."

"Well, that is *very* good news." Becca laughed and kissed Kimberly again, hoping against hope to start their night over again. This time, when she reached her hand between Kimberly's legs, she wasn't denied. Instead, with Kimberly's hand atop hers, Becca was encouraged.

Chapter Thirteen

Kimberly hated not being able to touch Becca when she wanted, and she could only hope the longing looks she sent helped. It'd been two days since their talk, Michael was finally back under the roof and their separate-but-together lives had begun. She *hated* it.

Putting much of her energy and focus into her cookbook and cooking with Michael, she once again cooked dish after dish. Michael would typically tire out after the first round unless she was baking something sugary and sweet, like a cake. Then he wanted to be involved from the first minute she started until the end.

They had spent what time they'd been in the same room that day avoiding each other and keeping a wide berth. Michael, hopefully, hadn't noticed, but if they didn't start acting more normal around each other, he would certainly pick up on a few of the clues.

They had spent the weekend together, gloriously together, then when Kimberly had gone to pick up Michael, a war had waged within her. *Becca or Michael.*

It was a near-impossible decision. She wanted more time with Becca, but she missed her son dearly.

When they had returned home in the evening, Becca had been nowhere to be found. Once Kimberly had gotten Michael down for the night, she went to Becca's room. Hearing the shower running, she decided to take her chance and join in.

It wasn't long before they were both naked and wet on Becca's bed, spending most of the rest of the night together. But when everything had calmed down and Becca had drifted off to sleep, Kimberly slipped from the warm covers and smooth skin she was becoming obsessed with and headed for her own bed, with cold sheets.

She hadn't been able to sleep for the rest of the night and, instead, found herself wide awake and glued to her computer screen when Michael shuffled his tired feet into her room and cuddled under her blankets. She *hated* it. That was the best explanation she could give. For once she wanted to be in a normal relationship, one where the other person was just as interested in her as she was them, where they could openly and freely be together without fear of consequences, where she could be herself.

Groaning, Kimberly shut her computer. She curled around Michael's sleeping form and closed her eyes, begging her mind to shut off so she could go to sleep and catch at least a few hours before she had to take on a twelve-hour day at work and even more of this upset she'd brought on herself.

* * * *

Becca woke by herself and sighed as she felt the emptiness of the bed next to her. This had not been what she'd wanted to sign up for. She turned onto her back and stared at the ceiling, trying to make sense of everything running through her brain.

Did she like Kimberly? Yes. That was a fact. She'd had a crush on her since before she'd met her in person and only watched her on television. Coming into the house had only amplified that crush until she couldn't resist it any longer.

Did Kimberly like her? That one stumped her. Becca clenched her jaw tightly. Kimberly certainly liked sex with her, and it was good sex, but her? She liked her with Michael—how she interacted with him, loved him, praised him, taught him—but her?

Shaking her head, Becca turned onto her side and buried her face in the pillow, screaming into it. She didn't know the answer to her own question—and she had very little idea about who Kimberly was—if this was something that happened with all the nannies who came through the house or if it just happened with her. She couldn't get a sense of it one way or the other. All she knew was that there had been a myriad of nannies in the door and out, almost a rotating list every month. Was it that when Michael was gone Kimberly would pounce on them like a hungry cougar then fire them the next week or month?

If so, she'd already lasted longer than the best of them. Groaning, Becca shoved her hair out of her eyes and forced herself out of bed. She wasn't going to get any answer from speculating. She would have to ask Kimberly, but asking her would seem to cross one of the many boundaries and lines the two of them had set up and agreed to—or rather Kimberly had insisted on in order for any kind of a relationship to continue.

There was barely any time the two of them had alone together without Michael around, and if they did have it, they were usually fucking like rabbits, putting their hands anywhere they could on each other, then drifting apart as was pre-destined.

She hopped into the shower and turned the water on cold. She needed the wakeup call, in more than one sense. Bowing her head under the spray with both hands plastered against the shower wall, Becca tried not to cry. She was caught between a rock and a hard place—her boss and the girlfriend she wanted that she couldn't have.

After a few more seconds, Becca turned the water on hot and showered, since her shower the previous night had been interrupted, albeit nicely. She took her time washing her hair and her body, knowing Kimberly wouldn't dare interrupt her at this time of day, not in the morning when Michael was very likely to wake up and find them.

When she was done, she dressed, towel-dried her hair and headed for the kitchen for some food. The kitchen and living area were dead silent. Curiously, Becca glanced at the clock on the stove. It was nearing ten in the morning. Kimberly would need to be leaving soon, and she should be in charge of Michael. They were going to work on more reading and some writing that afternoon, but there was no sign of either of them.

She grabbed herself a bowl of the cereal she had stashed way in the back of the pantry and sat at the kitchen table, eating. When thirty minutes had passed and there was still no sign of either of them, she bit her lip and debated. She wasn't Kimberly's keeper, but she certainly was the reason she was probably still sleeping.

Sighing, Becca headed down the hall for Kimberly's room. The door was ajar, and when she peeped her head in, she could see the dark forms of Kimberly and Michael both sleeping soundlessly. Kimberly lay on her back with her arm tossed above her head. It was only the second time Becca had ever caught Kimberly sleeping, and she looked beyond peaceful, something she had never seen before on her.

Michael was lying sideways in the bed, his head on his mom's chest and turned toward her face, his stomach on the mattress and his feet spread out behind him. Chuckling quietly, Becca shook her head. She was glad it was Kimberly and not her who got to sleep with those acrobatics. Deciding she needed to wake them, she closed her fist and knocked on the door.

Neither moved. This time knocking more loudly, she got Michael to stir, but Kimberly remained motionless. Rolling her eyes, Becca walked into the room. The feeling that she was violating a sacred space hit her hard, but she pushed it to the side as she moved to Michael's side of the bed. She rubbed circles on his back with care. He rustled some more, then his eyes popped open like he was wide awake all of a sudden.

He grinned at her. "Is it wake-up time?"

"It's well past wake-up time, kiddo. You need to wake up your mom."

He turned to look at her. "Okay."

While he went to town on waking his mom up, Becca slipped from the bedroom and headed to the living room. When she heard the curse echo down the hall, she knew Kimberly was awake and had looked at her clock to see the time. Michael headed down the hall toward Becca, but she stopped him with her hand held out and sent him to his room to change into day clothes before he could come back.

She would take each day one at a time until she could figure out exactly what Kimberly had up her sleeve. But she'd be watching and waiting for an answer to her many questions in the next few short weeks, because until she had them, she wasn't sure why she'd agreed to Kimberly's terms at all.

* * * *

Kimberly got home late that night. The entire day had been stressful, mostly because she was so tired that she was struggling to focus and remember anything anyone told her. Poor Maury had needed to repeat everything to her at least four times until she gave up and just wrote it down on a sticky note so she could maybe remember it for more than twenty seconds.

Coming through the door to the house, she about collapsed on the couch to fall asleep. But Becca was there, sitting quietly on her computer, no doubt studying some more. The girl never stopped, and Kimberly had no idea where she found the energy to keep going every day.

She sat down wordlessly and waited for Becca to look up and make eye contact. It seemed to take forever, but Becca finally glanced in her direction, and Kimberly smiled. "How was your day?"

Becca nodded. "Good. We did some reading, worked on writing, went on a walk. Michael helped make dinner and insisted on taking the world's longest bath."

"He loves his baths."

"He does."

Kimberly's feet ached and exhaustion seeped through her bones. She leaned back into the couch even more and closed her eyes. "Thank you for waking me this morning."

"I—I didn't."

Giving Becca a sideways glance, Kimberly shrugged. "Guess it was your twin who came into the room then. Didn't know you had one."

Becca remained silent, but when Kimberly looked her over again, she knew she'd hit some sort of nerve she hadn't meant to. Reaching out, she covered Becca's hand with her own and gave a gentle squeeze. Becca didn't return the embrace.

"Michael told me you woke him up."

"Oh."

Taking in a deep breath, Kimberly debated what to say next. Becca was acting odd, giving her the cold shoulder, and she could not figure out why, or what she had done to cause her to react that way. Perhaps it had been leaving her bed in the middle of the night, but that had been what they'd agreed to, so she certainly couldn't be mad about it.

"I appreciate you teaching him to write. He's shown me some of the letters and written them for me. He absolutely loves it."

"I'm glad he does," Becca answered, still giving short, non-committal responses.

Kimberly spun her brain in circles, trying to get Becca to talk, to even just entertain a conversation with her. The tension in the room continued to grow until Becca gathered her things and stood. Kimberly was quick to follow her move, her aching feet protesting, as she pushed to stand and gripped Becca's arm tightly in fear.

"Don't go," Kimberly whispered.

Becca's gaze was downcast, her lips slightly parted as her breath rushed from her lungs.

"I don't want you to go."

At that, Becca locked her eyes on Kimberly's face. The swirling emotions Kimberly saw frightened her even more than she had been before, and she stepped forward, attempting to lessen them, to take them from Becca, to ease her discomfort. Becca drew in a deep breath and closed her eyes slowly, tilting her face back toward the ground.

"Are you all right?" Kimberly asked, sliding her hand up and down Becca's arm in a comforting move.

Becca nodded. "Yeah. I am. Just tired like you are, I suppose."

"I meant what I said. I don't want you to go."

Licking her lips, Becca set her things on the table and stepped into Kimberly's circle. When their lips touched, Kimberly moaned. She kept the contact as much as she could, her chin tilted up as she parted her lips to accept Becca's exploring tongue. Becca cupped her cheek and neck, tilting her farther until she had complete control. Kimberly gripped Becca's waist to hold on as she let Becca do as she wanted.

They stayed that way for minutes. There was no way Kimberly could count them. When Becca finally released her, Kimberly knew exactly what she wanted to happen, if only Becca would be amenable. She wanted it slow — slow and sensual. She wanted to savor every piece of Becca she could.

"Come with me." Kimberly took Becca's hand in her own and moved backward away from the couch and the coffee table. Becca hesitated, not taking more than two steps before she stopped sharply. Kimberly came back to her and looked up at her. "Come only if you want. I don't want to pressure you. I promise this time will be slow."

Becca seemed to contemplate her options for a few short seconds before she nodded and followed Kimberly, visibly surprised when instead of heading down Becca's hallway, they headed down Kimberly's. Kimberly took her into her own room, shutting the door as soon as they entered and locking it with a firm click. Immediately, she started undoing the buttons on her chef's coat, knowing Becca did not enjoy that part of their lovemaking.

When Becca didn't budge, Kimberly took her by the hands again and settled her on the edge of the bed. She finished removing her chef's coat and threw it toward the hamper. She pressed one hand firmly to Becca's shoulder and pushed her back as she climbed on top of her and straddled her hips. Becca skimmed a hand down Kimberly's arm to her elbow then stopped as their mouths joined again.

Kimberly wanted this slow, and she was determined to make it as unhurried as possible. She wanted to pull up Becca's shirt but resisted the temptation and instead pressed kisses to her cheeks, her forehead, her neck and her collarbones she could just make out through the neckline of the T-shirt she wore. Becca hummed in satisfaction, and it spurred Kimberly to keep going.

She kissed over Becca's clothes, her breasts heaving with each breath as Kimberly pressed her mouth to the cotton. She moved down until she got to the hemline then back up. She desperately wanted to feel Becca's bare skin against hers, but she didn't dare. She wanted to draw this out.

Becca raked her fingers through Kimberly's hair, tugging at one point to redirect Kimberly's wandering mouth to Becca's neck. Kimberly happily complied with the subtle demand and this time used her tongue. Becca moaned and arched her back off the bed, keeping Kimberly's head in place, so Kimberly continued.

It wasn't much longer when Becca lightened her touch and drew Kimberly back to her mouth, kissing her senseless. Heat rose in Kimberly's chest, settling there as she dared herself to breathe and break the moment. When she did, Becca's words sent another surge of pleasure through her.

"Take my shirt off now."

"Yes, ma'am," Kimberly answered with a quirk to her lips.

Instead of responding immediately, though, she kissed her way down Becca's body through the fabric, teasing her even more until Becca writhed under her touch. When she reached for the hem of the shirt, Kimberly only raised it a few inches, feasting on the newly exposed skin with her tongue and teeth, lightly scraping. Becca let out a guttural sound of surprise and bucked her hips with Kimberly still on top of her. Smiling to herself, Kimberly continued to tease, slowly moving Becca's shirt up inch by inch then making sure none of the newly exposed skin was left untouched by her tongue.

Reaching Becca's breasts left Kimberly's chest heaving and her underwear dampening. She ignored her body and sat back enough to skim her fingers carefully over Becca's tender and sensitive skin. Becca whimpered and shut her eyes. Kimberly did it again, this time pleased when Becca's nipple hardened under her bra. Keeping up the slow pace, Kimberly moved her mouth along the top edge of Becca's beige-colored bra, peeking her tongue under the fabric then pulling away.

This time, when Becca arched her back, Kimberly was ready for her and reached behind Becca to unhook the clasp of her bra then removed her hand and put it back against Becca's side. When she looked up, Becca's bright blue eyes were glued on her.

"Take it off," Becca ordered, her voice firm and resolute.

Kimberly ignored her, pretending she hadn't heard the command. She continued to tease and torture Becca's breasts with her tongue and fingers until Becca's hand in her hair, pulling sharply, forced her to stop.

"I *said* take it off."

Unable to resist, Kimberly passionately locked their mouths together in a heated kiss, the complete opposite of what she'd intended, but the pain Becca had caused, plus the command and confidence in her tone, had gotten hold of her, and she couldn't help herself.

Growling when she pulled back, Kimberly grinned. "I love it when you talk that way."

She listened to what Becca had said and tugged the shirt and bra over Becca's head and arms, clearing them from their vicinity with a flick of her wrist. Before she could go back to her exploration of Becca's body, Becca pressed her own hands to her chest, rubbing herself and flicking her nipples. Kimberly whimpered at the sight and bit her lip as she forced herself to stay put and watch the beautiful woman below her take control.

She became lost in Becca—not just her body, but in her mind, in who she was, in how she loved. Distracting herself from those thoughts, Kimberly shed her own bra and kissed Becca senseless again. They explored with their hands while their mouths remained connected. She wasn't sure when, but at some point, Becca moved her hands downward and rubbed Kimberly firmly through her clothes. Kimberly ground her hips, pleasure shooting through her core each time Becca brushed over her.

If she wasn't careful, she would come before they were both naked, and she certainly didn't want that to happen, but at the same time, she couldn't stop herself. She broke the kiss long enough to whisper, "More."

Kimberly closed her eyes, pressing her forehead to Becca's as she tried to steady her breathing and get control of her body, but Becca didn't stop her movements. Within seconds, Kimberly rocked her hips back and forth against Becca's hand, her cheeks heating as she got closer and closer to orgasming.

"Come for me." Becca's voice rang clearly through the room.

The firm command was her undoing. Kimberly's hips jerked unevenly as she tried to continue the motion and keep up the friction. Her nipples peaked, and she called out Becca's name as she attempted to prevent herself from collapsing on top of her. Kimberly barely had control of her wobbly body, and Becca took advantage of that, flipping Kimberly onto her back.

She shucked Kimberly's pants, spread her legs and licked straight up her, humming against her. Kimberly whimpered and moved her hand down to caress the top of Becca's head, smoothing her hair to one side. Without warning, Becca took her up again, a second orgasm washing over her before she even knew what was happening.

This time, she turned on her side, closing her legs so Becca couldn't touch her oversensitive skin anymore. She breathed deeply until her chest stopped heaving and she could focus on what exactly was happening. Becca ran a gentle hand up and down her back in a comforting motion, and she almost broke.

When Kimberly dared to turn her head and look at Becca over her shoulder, Becca grinned broadly and laughed. "Good?"

"Do I really need to answer that?"

"Yes."

Shuddering once again at Becca's command, Kimberly turned on her back and grinned. "It was better than good. You've got a wicked tongue there. It may need some tempering, you know."

"Hmmm," Becca answered. "It's more your tongue I'm interested in right now."

"Oh?" Kimberly asked, curious as to where this was going.

Becca stood up and shucked her pants in one swift movement before getting back on the bed but staying on her hands and knees, popping her butt in the air. Kimberly raised one eyebrow as she waited for directions, not quite sure where this was going.

"I did some thinking, and if you ask again, I will say yes."

"Ask—ask what?" Kimberly sat up and curved her hand down Becca's butt to her thigh, admiring the slope when it hit her. "Oh...ask that."

"Yes. I want you to use your tongue on me."

Kimberly situated herself carefully on her knees and massaged Becca's butt tenderly, sliding her thumb over her anus. "Just to be very clear here, you want me to use my tongue right here." She pushed in slightly.

Becca shivered but moved against Kimberly, forcing her thumb in even more. "Yesss..." she hissed out. "Do it *now*."

Grinning cockily, Kimberly kissed Becca's skin, but not where she wanted. Then she scraped with her teeth, once again slowing down the process until she could make Becca burn with pleasure. Torture. Well, torture through pleasure—that was what she wanted Becca to experience. Becca pressed backward, but Kimberly didn't give in. She ran her hands up and down the outside of Becca's thighs, then ran her nails lightly on the insides. She giggled when Becca cursed under her breath.

Sliding her thumb against Becca, she pressed it in just as she reached out her tongue and took a quick taste exactly where Becca wanted. Since this was clearly Becca's first time in this position, Kimberly wanted to give her time to get used to what was happening. Slowly, she took her tongue in a circle around the edge of Becca's anus, knowing the skin was insanely sensitive and wanton for touch.

Becca shuddered and bent lower to the bed. Kimberly pressed down a bit farther into her, spreading her cheeks with one hand so she could have better access while keeping her thumb and forefinger moving on the other. Becca rocked her hips in a timeless rhythm. Kimberly focused her efforts, increasing her speed and pressure until she was sure Becca wouldn't be able to stand it.

As soon as Becca moaned, Kimberly pulled back. *Slow...* She had to keep reminding herself that this was supposed to be slow. She poured everything she had into making Becca feel pleasure, feel Kimberly's care and concern for her when she couldn't so easily say the words. Kimberly gave her everything she could in that moment, her entire focus and all of her control.

"Don't stop," Becca breathed the words out. "Don't stop," she repeated, turning her face against the sheets as she tried to catch her breath.

Kimberly had no intention of stopping, but she did want to drag it out longer. She didn't want the night to end. She changed her pattern, forcing Becca to catch her ground again. Becca's words became a chant as Kimberly found a new and better pattern. Giving in to the command, Kimberly picked up the pace and pressure once more, not letting up until she got the sweet squeeze of Becca's muscles around her thumb and her breathing hitched a few times.

Slowing down, she eased away as Becca flopped onto the bed. Kimberly pressed kisses into Becca's skin as she worked her way up Becca's body until their lips connected. Her heart felt content as she lay against Becca's still form. Satisfaction flowed through her, and hope for something new followed on its tail.

She grinned when she pulled away from Becca and rested her head. Gingerly, she traced her fingers over the side of Becca's hair and behind her ear, pulling her in for one more sweet and tender kiss. Emotions flooded her as Becca's gaze locked with hers, and she found herself at a loss for words.

Saying the first thing that came to mind, Kimberly asked, "Good?"

Becca blushed, her face so red Kimberly was worried she'd completely embarrassed her. She ran a soothing hand down her arm and rested it on her hip, trying to convey that there was no reason for embarrassment.

Becca finally nodded and rolled her eyes at the same time. "Yeah, it was good, to say the least."

"I like you being bossy. It's a nice change."

Becca snorted and fiddled with the ends of Kimberly's hair. "You must just bring it out in me."

Kimberly put their foreheads together. "As much as I would love to continue this, I am not as young as you are, and while the past few nights have been exhilarating, I need to sleep."

Nodding, Becca sat up stiffly and looked around the floor. She grabbed her clothes, dressed rapidly and made a silent exit. She hadn't even dared to look at Kimberly again. Unease settled in the pit of Kimberly's belly. She wasn't sure where it was coming from, but she was sure that whatever had just happened was going to come back to bite her in the ass.

Chapter Fourteen

Kimberly left for two days to film yet another television episode. Becca watched Michael during the day with modified hours while Bradley took him at night. He hadn't said much to her but had nodded and smiled in her direction the first time he'd shown up at the house to collect Michael. In that instant, she knew that he knew.

Kimberly hadn't been able to keep the secret from everyone, much like she hadn't been able to either. Drew had texted her almost daily to check in and make sure she was doing all right. She skirted around truly answering them with how she felt, unsure of what to say.

As each day passed, she felt more and more torn. The sex might have been wonderful, and she might have certainly enjoyed the last evening they had shared together, but the way she'd been forced to leave the room had created a bitter taste in the back of her throat.

Try as she might, the house no longer felt comfortable. She was either walking on the eggshells of their pseudo-relationship or she was running on the fumes of worrying about her future. She couldn't take it any longer. Knowing for certain she would have a student teaching position come fall — no matter where that position was — she made the decision to hand in her resignation as soon as Kimberly returned from New York.

Drew showed up as their shift ended and plopped on the couch with their bag thrown haphazardly on the floor. "Feed me," they begged.

Becca chuckled and went to the kitchen to grab some of the many leftovers Kimberly had made for them to eat. Bradley had taken Michael hours ago, and Becca had felt the loneliness of the house creep under her skin inch by inch to the point she had called Drew and begged relentlessly for them to come over and stay the night.

She made two plates then sat down next to her best friend. She put her head on their shoulder and ate wordlessly as they stared at the television. It wasn't much longer until Drew nudged her off and wrinkled their nose. "When are you going to tell me what's really going on?"

"I don't know what you're talking about," Becca answered defensively. "There's nothing going on."

"Come on. I know you better than that, and frankly, you know me better than that. Tell me what's wrong."

Becca sighed. "It's so quiet when she's gone."

Drew waited in the silence for Becca to continue.

"I don't know. It's... I just don't know."

"Well, start with what you do know. Maybe that will help."

"All right." Becca thought long and hard before she spoke again. "I think I might... I think I might be able to fall in love with her, but I'm ninety percent sure that feeling is not reciprocated."

"Oh, sugar," Drew whispered, "your heart is breaking, and it hasn't even had time to be happy yet."

Tears sprang to Becca's eyes and caught her off-guard. She wiped them away and scoffed when her nose stopped up. "It's not just that. I'm pretty sure this is just about sex for her, and that when she's done with me, she'll toss me aside like she does everyone else. I'll not only be left without her, but I'll be left jobless and homeless. I mean, I live here, for Christ's sake. Where am I supposed to go if she fires me?"

"Becca, I don't think she's going to fire you."

"She's fired other nannies before. I'm sure she'd have no qualms about firing me."

Drew, for once, did not speak. Becca wiped her eyes again and shook her head.

"No, I need to protect myself in this."

Confused, Drew asked, "What does that mean?"

"I need to be on the offense and not on the defense. I need to take charge here and stop letting her be the one to push me around."

Still unsure, Drew sat back. "Is she making you do things you don't want to do? Is she threatening your job if you don't sleep with her?"

Becca shook her head sharply. "No, not that. But I need to rely on me and me alone. I can't keep hoping for the best and taking what little crumbs she offers me. I need to look out for myself."

"Okay, so what are you going to do then?"

"I'm going to quit. It's a done thing. When she gets back, I'm going to quit, hand in my notice. I had been waffling on it, back and forth, because I love Michael so much, but I can't. I just can't. I have to do something."

She looked at Drew with fear and frustration written all over her features. "I have to take control."

"Got it." Drew pressed a hand to her thigh. "You know if she fires you, even if you want to stay all summer and she fires you, you are always welcome to crash at my apartment. You know the standard fee for overnights."

Smirking, Becca nodded. "Thanks. I may take you up on that offer."

"You'll get a student teaching spot soon enough," Drew insisted. "Then all your dreams will come true."

Becca laid her head on Drew's shoulder and calmed herself. Now that her decision was made, she felt better, confident for the first time in months. She knew she had her life in her own hands. Brushing the final fleeting tears from her cheeks, she vowed to not let her emotions get the better of their evening. They spent the rest of the night chatting about life and boys.

* * * *

When Kimberly walked through the door in the late evening, she had a plan formed. She wanted to share with Becca all about her cookbook, everything. She wanted to bare her soul and lay it all out on the table. If she was sure about how Becca felt, then she was sure she wanted to take the next step soon.

Becca leaving the last night they'd slept together had been the tipping point. She hadn't wanted to have to kick Becca out of her bed before the night was over. She wanted her to stay there, relax, perhaps even call it her own. Michael was no doubt already asleep. She'd video chatted with him during her layover, and Becca was supposed to put him to bed since her flight was landing too late for her to see him, but she would certainly do so in the morning.

Just as she dragged her stuff down the hall and plopped it into the corner of her bedroom, she sighed. It felt good to be home. Hotels were one thing, but her own bed was something else completely. She pulled off her shoes and tossed them into the corner, along with her unopened suitcase, then made her way out into the kitchen.

Becca had left everything clean and pristine as she normally did. In some ways, it was odd and set Kimberly on edge, because there was barely any sign of her in the house. In other ways, it was nice that Becca cared so much to clean up after not only herself but Michael when she didn't have to.

Rummaging through the fridge, Kimberly moaned when she saw the leftover cake still sitting on the shelf. She grabbed a fork, put the cake on the counter, popped the lid of the container off and shoved a bite into her mouth, moaning once again around the food. The sweet German chocolate cake was one of her favorites, and she had hoped there would be some left when she returned.

She was halfway through the slice when Becca came down the hallway. She stopped short at the entrance to the living area then started slowly toward Kimberly. Standing straight up, Kimberly set her fork down and stared at the soft sway of Becca's hips.

"I didn't think you were back yet," Becca said.

"Not a lot of traffic, surprisingly."

This was her chance, and as much as she wanted to take it, she couldn't force herself to say the words. She couldn't make them exit her throat or her mouth.

Swallowing hard, Kimberly waited patiently to see what Becca would do.

"I wanted to talk to you," Kimberly finally made out after Becca said nothing. She twisted the fork on the countertop as nerves continued to flow through her. She hadn't been this nervous when she'd played out the conversation in her head a half-dozen times on the flight back.

"Oh?" Becca answered, coming to sit at the stool on the other side of the counter. "What about?"

Kimberly dropped her fork in the sink and moved around to sit next to Becca, deciding that would be the better option for this type of conversation. As soon as she sat down, Becca visibly tensed in every way — her shoulders, her chest, her jaw, her eyes as she focused in on Kimberly.

Pushing forward because she wasn't sure what else to do at that point, Kimberly leaned one arm on the counter for balance and tried to remember one of the dozen-and-a-half scenarios she had practiced en route — but promptly forgot them all.

"I wanted to tell you something more about what I was doing, have been doing — what I've been working on," Kimberly corrected herself.

Becca relaxed in the slightest, but Kimberly was sure she still hadn't convinced her the world wasn't going to explode into nothing yet.

"You had talked to me awhile back about how I spend my time with Michael."

"I didn't mean to upset you."

"I know. I know." Kimberly raised a hand in an attempt to wave off Becca's concerns. She lowered her gaze, staring at Becca's knees, not sure she could even look her in the eye. "I'd told you that I've been trying to write a cookbook for decades. Honestly, it's the number one question I get when I have interviews. *'When are you going to write a cookbook? We all want to see a cookbook by Kim Burns. When will that happen?'"*

Kimberly rolled her eyes. Becca waited silently. Kimberly was sure it was because she was rambling and Becca likely had no idea where the conversation was even remotely headed.

"Anyway, to make a long story short and because I shared with you at one point, it wasn't until you brought up my interactions with Michael that it hit me. I needed to write a cookbook for normal people who do normal things, like try to cook with their toddlers underfoot. People who want easy meals that don't take a lot of effort, because let's face it, who doesn't have an insanely busy life as of late?"

"Sounds like you have a good plan," Becca interjected before Kimberly could finish.

Becca's seeming lack of interest in the conversation put Kimberly on edge. She wasn't quite sure where it was coming from, but it bothered her deeply. The dismissive tone in Becca's voice left her reeling, grasping for strings. "I thought it might interest you, since you had such an influence in it."

"It doesn't really."

Taken aback, Kimberly sat up straighter. "I'm sorry, then. I won't bother you with it anymore."

Becca made to move, but Kimberly grabbed her wrist and tugged her back around. She had a sinking feeling that there was something else going on, much like the other night. There was a disconnect between the two of them, a chasm rapidly widening. She'd thought a few days away would clear both their minds. She knew it certainly had done her wonders.

"Did I do something to tick you off?" Kimberly asked, anger lacing her own tone, as much as she tried to keep it out and keep herself grounded. "Because you're treating me like dirt."

"I'm treating *you* like dirt? That's lofty coming from you."

Shaking her head in confusion, Kimberly tried to backtrack. "I—I'm sorry. I don't understand."

"Michael had a good weekend. Bradley was here on time every evening. We worked more on reading and writing. He can write all his letters now in upper case. Next, we'll work on lower case."

"I don't need a list of the shit you did with my son," Kimberly spat, pulling her eyebrows tightly together in anger. Her jaw tensed as she planned for another attack. "I know you take good care of him. I wouldn't have hired you otherwise."

"You didn't hire me. Kiddie Academy sent me. You didn't have a choice in the matter."

Coming to stand, Kimberly crossed her arms and kept her distance from Becca. "Excuse me?"

"You didn't hire me because you had a choice. You hired me because I was your last resort."

"How do you even know that?"

"They told me. You think they'd really send me to a house that has had someone new in here at least once a month for two years and not tell me something was going on? I've worked with them for years, longer than almost any other nanny. I am the one they send to their problem children."

"Problem children?" Offense rang through tone as her head jerked in surprise. "I'm a problem child."

"Apparently. I don't dictate that. I just come in and fix the problem."

"Fix the problem. Good Lord." Kimberly ran her hands over her face and through her hair. She spun around to face the counter, bracing her hands on the cool granite to keep her centered. She didn't want to say anything she regretted. She had wanted this to be a time when she shared something good with Becca, something Becca had done that she may not have fully realized her impact about. Struggling to hold her tongue, Kimberly turned back around. "What's gotten into you?"

"Nothing has gotten into me, except maybe some self-worth for the first time since stepping into this house."

"What are you talking about?"

Becca was visibly furious. Her cheeks were red, her eyes wide, her shoulders once again tense and rigid as she stood before Kimberly, not budging one step in any direction.

"I quit."

"I— You *what*?" Kimberly's eyes about popped out of her head. She took one step toward Becca, and Becca stepped back, putting her hand up in front of her and forcing Kimberly to stop in her tracks.

"I'm quitting. I can't do this any longer. You may think this is okay, but it's not. I can't. I can't keep living this way."

"Living *what* way?"

"Like *this*!" Becca's voice took on a dangerous level.

Kimberly again put her hands out, trying to understand what was going through Becca's mind and heart, but she was left lost in the dust. She repeated as calmly as she could but knowing her tone was full of anger, "Like *what*?"

"This. This...all of this." Becca put her hands out between them. "I can't do it."

Kimberly's heart ached. "I don't know what to say."

"You don't have to say anything. I quit. I'll be gone in the morning. I can't keep doing this."

"What?" Rage brimmed in Kimberly's chest this time. Questions of logistics with Michael raced through her mind, but she was stumped by only one of them.

What will I tell him?

Becca stepped away from Kimberly and nodded her head. "I'm leaving. I would appreciate not hearing from you again except in the form of my last paycheck. I need to live my own life."

Becca turned on her toes and made for her room. Kimberly stared after her, still not quite sure what had just happened or how they had gotten from point A to point who-knew-where so quickly. She still wasn't processing what Becca had said. She plopped her butt on the stool and sat in the silence of the room, working through everything each of them had said.

Becca had been on the defense from the moment they'd started talking. She'd clearly already made up her mind about what was going to happen before they'd even talked that evening, but how on earth had she gotten there? This time apart was supposed to have put everything in perspective, but obviously they had different viewpoints. After sitting in the quiet for ten minutes, Kimberly got up, put the lid back on the cake and shoved it a little too hard into the fridge.

When she turned around, the house felt emptier than it ever had before. She was lost without Becca there, and even though she was still physically in the house, she had clearly left mentally and emotionally some time when Kimberly had been gone to New York.

Adrian J. Smith

Maybe it wasn't a great fit, then. If the two of them couldn't even handle one work trip away, then they certainly wouldn't pass the test of time. If Becca was this upset over something she had done and wasn't even willing to talk to her about it, to compromise, to discuss, to work it out, then there was no way a relationship would ever happen.

Hitting the lights, Kimberly stared down Becca's hallway, silently begging her to come back out and talk to her. After seconds ticked by and there was no movement, she headed to her own room and shut the door behind her. She collapsed on her bed, rolled onto her side with her pillow shoved under her for support and buried her head.

A general sense of unease settled over her as she continued to sort through the explosion of emotion that had happened in her kitchen. Normally the kitchen was a place for jokes, laughter, fun and good food. Suddenly, her kitchen had been turned against her, and she wasn't sure how she felt about it. 'Violated' was a word that came to mind.

Lying awake in the dark, she listened as Becca made trip after trip from her room to her car. After a period of awkward silence, she looked up when there was a gentle and quiet knock on her bedroom door. When she got up to open it, Becca stood in the doorway, dimly lit by the lights in the living room that barely reached all the way down the hall.

"The keys," Becca said, handing over the lanyard.

Kimberly hesitated before putting her hand out and accepting them, not wanting to touch Becca's fingers for fear of what she might feel. The conversation was clearly over. There was no opening it back up to talk about anything. She fisted the keys hard, the metal

203

biting into her skin as she looked up, maybe for the last time, at Becca.

"You don't want to talk?"

Becca shook her head.

Kimberly sighed and moved her gaze down to Becca's shoes. "He's going to miss you."

"And I will miss him."

This time Kimberly made sure she had Becca's full attention when she spoke. "*I'm* going to miss you."

Becca said nothing as she turned and left. The door shutting behind her was the last sound Kimberly wanted to hear. She stayed rooted to her spot for a good five minutes before she went to her bed and hid under the covers, wishing she could start the evening over again and change everything that had happened.

Chapter Fifteen

Becca hadn't slept in nearly three days. She had been focusing all her energy on her schoolwork and trying to find some kind of job to help her pay for food and maybe even pitch in a little bit on Drew's rent. She had an interview later that day to be a cashier at a grocery store down the road from Drew's. It wasn't ideal, but it would do in the pinch she found herself in.

She needed something to get her through the next eight weeks. Eight weeks, and she still wasn't sure where she'd be student teaching. Groaning, Becca pressed her head down onto Drew's very small two-person kitchen table. She'd thrown away her life, and all for what? Morals? Fear? Frustration?

None of it seemed worth it now. Drew slid into the seat next to her and patted her head gently as they applied a fresh coat of makeup before heading off to work. Becca still couldn't believe the situation she found herself in. Drew's semi-gravelly morning voice broke her pity-party line. "It'll all be okay, sugar."

Becca snorted.

"Just go on a date, any date. Get her out of your head."

Looking up at Drew, she shook her head. "I don't know. That doesn't seem like the greatest plan in the world."

Drew raised on delicate and thin eyebrow in question. "What about that Jessica girl?"

"Jessica?"

"You know, the one you met that day with she-who-shall-not-be-mentioned. The one who gave you her number — pretty, cute, flirty — at the school or whatever when she-who-shall-not-be-mentioned was teaching."

"Oh...that Jessica. I don't even know if I still have her number."

"Well, I have the text picture you sent me of the piece of paper with her number on it, so I do."

Becca blanched. She hadn't really thought about Jessica since she'd left that day, after telling Drew about her adventures of the week with Michael and Kimberly. On the other hand, she had enjoyed flirting with Jessica while it had lasted. She'd felt free of pressure or stresses.

"Maybe I will," Becca muttered and turned to her computer.

An email popped up on her open laptop, and Becca's stomach clenched when she saw who it was from. 'Student Teaching Position Available' was in the subject line. She scooted the computer over so Drew could see and held her breath.

"Open it already! I want to see what it says." Drew tried to move Becca's hands away so they could click the email.

Becca pushed their hands right back. "No matter what it is, I'm going to take it. I have to have a position somewhere to graduate in the winter."

"Open it!" Drew repeated, egging her on.

Rolling her eyes, Becca clicked the email and about fell out of her chair. It was her second-choice school, one of the best in the county. Her heart ratcheted up a few notches until she struggled to catch her breath. Skimming the email, she saw she would be placed in the kindergarten class. As soon as she read that word, bile tried to come up her throat full force. Her stomach churned, and she had to leave the table.

She ran to the bathroom and splashed freezing-cold water on her face. It wouldn't happen. There were two kindergarten classes at the school. It couldn't happen. When Drew came into the doorway to check on her, she blinked back tears masked with water.

"That's the school Michael will be going to."

"Oh... Oh!" Drew said. "But he won't be in your class, will he?"

"I can only hope not. I'm not sure I could handle that after everything, but I probably won't know until I get the class roster."

Drew hummed. "You have eight weeks. Maybe another school will pop up with a position for you."

Becca rolled her eyes and drew in a deep breath. "Maybe, but it's my second-choice school."

"You're going to have to make a decision."

"I know." Becca wallowed some more, really not wanting to dwell on it. "I know. I'll figure it out. I just need a bit more time than I have right now. I have to get dressed for my interview."

"That's right! You knock 'em dead. I gotta get to work, but text me if you need something, and to tell me how the interview goes."

"I will."

Drew left, meaning Becca was alone in the small one-bedroom apartment. Drew would be gone for easily the next ten hours, between commute and work time, but that was okay. She was getting used to being by herself, something she rarely had the privilege of since she'd mostly nannied.

Rummaging through several boxes and two suitcases, Becca finally found a pair of slacks and a nice button-down shirt she could wear. It wasn't fancy, but it was nice enough for a grocery store interview. She got dressed, spritzed one of Drew's perfumes over her so her clothes didn't smell musty and made for the front door. A text rang through her phone, and she stared down at it. It was the picture of Jessica's phone number. Rolling her eyes again, Becca cursed under her breath and locked the door behind her as she headed for her car. Stress be damned... She was going to rock her interview.

* * * *

She landed the job. Getting back to her car and throwing out a cheerful whoop, Becca immediately texted Drew the outcome. She started the next week. She'd be making minimum wage, but anything was better than zero. She drove to Drew's apartment and did one more happy dance as soon as she got in the door.

The rest of the afternoon, she spent organizing her things to make the space seem less messy and roomier in the tiny five-hundred-square-foot apartment. There was barely room for two people in there, especially one with as many clothes as Drew owned. Chuckling, she headed to the laundry room to start a load. When she came back, she found herself sitting once again at the tiny table and reading over the student teaching email.

Biting her lip, she closed her eyes and thought. Would the pain of potentially being Michael's teacher — which wouldn't actually be the hard part — be worth it to teach there? Would seeing Kimberly again be worth it? Her stomach spun with nerves and anxiety, threatening to make her puke.

Eight weeks. Would she feel different in eight weeks? With all that time between their argument and her quitting, would she be able to find some sort of calm and peace when she saw her again? Becca sighed. She wanted the job more than anything. She wanted to be a teacher. This was her calling. Just like Kimberly found such passion in cooking, she found all her passion in teaching, in watching young minds grow and expand and learn.

Following the directions in the email, she went through the portal to the school's website and accepted the student teaching position. Kindergarten was what she wanted to teach — that or first grade. The offer could not have been more perfect. As soon as she clicked 'submit', a sense of peace washed over her. She wasn't going to do anything because of Kimberly again.

This was for her and her alone. This was for her future, her career, her happiness. Smiling, Becca closed her laptop and picked up her phone again. She opened it to the photo Drew had sent her and bit her lip. Why not? She was on a roll. She was taking charge of her life, making the changes she wanted and would benefit her and no one else. She was tired of holding back and waiting and living on someone else's time.

After putting the number into her phone, she typed the message in hopes she wouldn't chicken out before she sent it.

Hi. I don't know if you remember me, but it's Becca. I worked for Kim Burns and met you when she did a cooking demo at the school. Anyway, just thought I'd text and see if the offer still stood for getting together sometime.

She pressed 'send' then set her phone down. Once again, her heart was in her throat. She flicked her gaze back and forth to the phone several times before she gave up and went to take a shower to distract herself. A date would be something new, something she hadn't done in years. She'd never paid too much attention to her love life. Honestly, Drew paid more attention to it than she did. She'd had her flings, usually one every couple of months, but a tried-and-true date where she intended to see if the relationship would last? That was something rare for her.

When she got out of the shower, she checked her phone before she fully dried off. There was one text message waiting for her.

Yes. When?

* * * *

Kimberly had flown back to New York. Bradley was in charge of Michael and finding care for him while she was gone. Since Becca had quit, he'd really stepped up his game in helping with Michael's daily care. For some reason, he felt the need to suddenly embrace his father-role and take it on in full force. He'd actually started before Becca had quit, but since then, he'd been a perfect gentleman.

The show she was filming was one on which she made guest appearances regularly. She'd signed the contract the day she and Becca had fought. It had been one of the things she'd wanted to share but had never gotten an opportunity. This was her dream, something she'd been working toward since she'd first seen that it might be a real possibility. Most of the filming was in New York, but the network had plans to expand into southern California and were working on hiring and building up some more chefs who resided there before truly moving out to the coast.

It was one of the reasons she knew she could do this. It was only temporary — a year or two tops — then she'd be able to film a whole lot closer to home. As much as her life was coming together professionally, it was falling apart personally. She and Bradley might have been on better terms, but she hadn't been able to get Becca out of her mind since she'd handed her the key and left.

She sat down on the sofa in her hotel room and relaxed. It was late. Filming hadn't lasted long, but she'd stayed then gone out with a few of her friends to enjoy the evening. When she got back, her hair was still up in the tight pony with a braid down the side that the hair artist had done up for her, and her makeup was still heavy from filming.

She always hated getting it on and taking it off, but she liked wearing it. It made her feel strong, confident and beautiful, and that was exactly what she needed. She needed to know she would be okay, that Becca leaving wasn't her fault and that it would all turn out for the better...because it had to.

Pulling bobby pins and thin rubber bands from her hair, Kimberly sighed. It *had* been all her fault. She should never have slept with Becca. Well, she should never have slept with her employee. If they hadn't been in that situation, she was pretty sure everything might have turned out different. But they also were likely to have never met.

She ran her fingers through her hair, pulling out a few tangles and untwisting the braid. Eventually, she set everything to the side and grabbed her laptop, ready to focus on her cookbook. She was nearing completion of the first draft. Once she went back through it, she'd start contacting publishers to see if any wanted to take her up on the project.

Then they could cook, take pictures of the results and really start putting the book together. She typed away at her keyboard until the clock told her it was nearly four in the morning. Deciding it would be better if she had a few hours of sleep before a second day of filming, she stripped down and put on a loose pair of shorts and tank top, then slid under the cold covers.

The bed felt empty. The entire room felt empty. *She* felt empty. Professional life aside, she had very little to live for personally except Michael, and her little boy would eventually grow up, leave her house and go on to shape his own life. And where would that leave her? Alone with an amazing career and nothing else.

She didn't want it that way. She wanted something else, something for her, someone to come home to, who enjoyed her as much as she enjoyed them. Someone like Becca. Sighing, she forced herself to lie still and get comfortable, then begged her brain to shut down and allow her some rest.

* * * *

Becca's first date with Jessica was awkward. Something about their flair for flirting had vanished in the interim, and they spent most of the night just trying to get conversation going. At the end of the meal, Becca paid for her half of the bill and wanted to escape as quickly as she could, but Jessica stopped her at her car.

"I'm sorry. I don't know what's with me tonight," Jessica stated. "That was not a great date."

Becca frowned and gave her a sad look. "Yeah, I wasn't at my greatest either. I've had a lot of changes going on lately, and I think it's probably all catching up with me."

"What kind of changes?"

Sighing, Becca leaned against the trunk of her car, half-sitting on it as she debated how much to share with Jessica. While she wanted to talk about quitting her job and why she'd done it, she also respected Kimberly's privacy and did not want to add any stress to that.

"I quit my job kind of suddenly. Lost my place to live, so I'm couch surfing at my best friend's tiny-ass apartment. I start a new job next week at a grocery store. Not ideal, but it's something. And I'm waiting for all my student teaching paperwork to go through so I can teach in the fall and graduate in the winter."

Jessica smiled, her full pink lips coming to a curve. "It sounds rough, but it also sounds like you're headed in a direction."

"Yeah. What about you? What's got you so off tonight?"

Pulling herself up on Becca's trunk, Jessica crossed her ankles and leaned back with a big smile on her lips. "My divorce finalized."

Becca did a double take. "Wait...! You were *married*?"

"Yeah, very briefly. It did not last long. We'd been engaged for a long time, three years. He was in the military, so he's been moved three or four times in that time span. I forget how many for sure. Anyway, he was about to be moved again, and we decided to just go get hitched, because why else should we wait? But two weeks before he was supposed to fly back here, I got a very interesting phone call from his girlfriend."

"His *what*?"

"Uh-huh. His girlfriend. They'd been seeing each other for months. She had a son who was about five who had gotten into his phone one afternoon and had seen some texts from me, some...not-safe-for-work texts, if you know what I mean."

"I know what you mean." Becca, intrigued, pulled up to sit straight on the trunk of her car next to Jessica, fascinated at how this story was playing out. "So if he was cheating, why did you get married?"

"Stupidity? I don't know. Once a cheater, always a cheater, right?"

"True, for the most part." Becca thought of Bradley, wondering if he would ever attempt to settle down with someone and stay with them rather than jumping from man to man as a way to avoid cheating. She shook the thought from her head and focused on Jessica.

"Anyway, she and I decided to confront him together, because she didn't know he had a fiancée. That was not a fun phone call, by the way — the first one when she'd figured it out. She cussed me out for a good ten minutes before I could even get a word in edgewise. Eventually, I flew out there, met up with her and when he showed up at her house for a booty call, there we both were."

"You're kidding." Becca's eyes widened.

"I'm not. This sounds ridiculous, though. She broke up with him. I broke up with him. But the next day he was back here, begging me to give him a second chance. You know, all that drama. I caved. We eloped a week later in an attempt to prove we could do it, and three weeks later, I found out he was cheating again. We were only married six months. Trust me. I'm better off."

"Sounds like it. So, you're…bi then?"

Jessica nodded. "You could call me that. I really just like to think I don't discriminate."

"Ah." Becca licked her lips and stared at the restaurant they had eaten at.

"So, I signed the papers this morning, unexpectedly. I didn't think I'd get them for another week or so, but my lawyer called and said she had them for me. That's what threw me off tonight. I'm sorry I made for not good company." Jessica covered Becca's hand with her own and gave a light squeeze.

In a fit of brevity, Becca picked up their hands and kissed Jessica's knuckles. "Maybe we could try again sometime next week."

"I'd like that very much. I probably should have rescheduled to begin with, but since it took you months to call, I didn't want to wait."

Scrunching her nose, Becca nodded her agreement. "I can understand that. Try again next week? I'll have to let you know what day, though, since I don't have my new work schedule yet."

"Oh yes, the new job." Jessica wiggled her eyebrows up and down. "That definitely takes priority. Can't have you jobless again. Wouldn't be good."

"For sure," Becca agreed. She didn't want to get off the trunk of her car now that they had finally seemed to find their flirty rhythm again. Jessica had yet to let go of her hand, so she got the sense the feeling was mutual.

When she turned back to face Jessica, she connected with her in a brief and awkward kiss. Jessica pulled away and let out a sweet giggle. Becca smiled and took the chance to try again. Kissing Jessica deeply this time, she closed her eyes. Every thought she had was of Kimberly — their last kisses, their first kisses, heated kisses, quick kisses, stolen kisses.

Forcing herself to continue, Becca reeled from unrequited emotions. Kimberly had never shared how she felt with her, which had left her in the dark the entire time. Jessica, however, seemed to be the complete opposite. Becca opened her eyes and stared into Jessica's beautifully rounded face and her long blonde curls that moved in the gentle breeze. This was where she needed to focus her attention. Like she'd decided earlier, it was time for her to move on and take charge of her own life.

Chapter Sixteen

Kimberly rode the elevator up the high-rise to Bradley's apartment. When she got to his door, Michael, on the other side, yelled and screamed. She knocked, and it wasn't long before the door popped open and an exasperated Bradley looked at her like she was a knight in shining armor.

"I don't know what to do with him," he confessed.

"What's wrong?" Kimberly entered the apartment and set her keys on the counter. Michael ran up to her, stopped short of her and let out a wild scream before running to his room and slamming the door. Shaking her head in shock, Kimberly looked to Bradley for some answers.

"He's been like this all day. I don't know how you do it."

"Well, what's he so upset about?"

"I told him he had to pack up because you were coming, and he had to clean up the toys so he could go back to your house. He didn't like that. Told me he never wanted to go back to your house, then this all started and hasn't stopped. It's been nearly an hour now."

"Oh, boy. Did he say why he didn't want to go?"

Bradley grimaced and crossed his arms. "I'll give you one guess."

"I'm gone too much?" she posited, not sure where to begin.

Shaking his head, Bradley looked her up and down. "Becca."

"Oh." Kimberly's face fell. She let out a breath and looked to Michael's door, really not sure how to deal with his sudden dislike of her house and him missing Becca so completely.

Michael had been through so many changes since the stability Becca had brought, and she was sure this was all a reaction to that. He'd started daycare proper and was only expected to be there for a short period of time before starting a brand-new school. Kimberly had been gone more frequently than she had in the past, and Bradley was attempting to parent in ways he hadn't before.

"I'm sure he's struggling with everything that's going on. I'll go talk with him."

"Please do, but then you and I need to have a chat."

The tone of his voice set her on edge, but she ignored it as she made for Michael's room and knocked on the door. "Can I come in, kiddo?"

"Don't call me that!" he shouted through the door.

"Okay, may I come in, Michael?"

"No."

"Well, I need to talk to you, so maybe when you are calm and ready to talk, you can come out here and talk to me and Daddy, okay?" He didn't answer. She knocked again and pressed closer to the door to make sure she didn't miss anything he might have said. "I need you to acknowledge what I said."

"Fine!" he shouted, nearly knocking Kimberly back a step with its forcefulness.

"Okay, Michael. I will check back in a few minutes to see if you're calm, but if you decide you are, you can come out and talk to me and Daddy when you feel ready."

She walked to Bradley and sat at his counter next to him. She rolled her eyes and shrugged. "Guess I'm going to be here for a bit. Did you have somewhere to be?"

He shook his head. "But since he's holed up in there, that gives us time to talk."

"Great," Kimberly muttered. That was exactly what she wanted to do, talk to her ex-husband, because she was pretty sure — once again — where this conversation was going, and she'd much rather talk to a friend, if she'd had any.

Bradley gave her a hard stare. "Tell me why she really quit."

"She quit because she didn't want to work for me anymore, like all the rest of them."

"Not like the rest of them. Becca lasted months, almost five months if I remember correctly. None of the others made it anywhere near that long."

Rolling her eyes, Kimberly stared at Michael's door, silently willing him to leave the room to end this conversation between her and Bradley.

"Come on, Kimmie. Why did she quit?"

She peeked her tongue out of her mouth before she clenched her jaw, determined not to talk about it.

"It's affecting Michael. I deserve to know."

"I don't know why she quit, okay? She just up and quit one night after an argument that I certainly did not see coming. I didn't expect it. I didn't think she would do it, but she did. I don't know why. Stop asking."

Bradley softened. He relaxed his posture and ran a hand up and down her arm. "Tell me what happened."

Grunting, Kimberly stared at the floor but started anyway. "We started a relationship, of some sort, I don't know what you'd call it. We had sex, a lot." Her cheeks heated. "Then she just up and quit one night."

"Okay, whoa, slow down. Something else happened."

"I don't know." Kimberly tossed her hands in the air, really wishing Michael would decide he was calm enough to come out of his room.

"Kimmie, think about it. What happened?"

"I don't know," she repeated. "We had talked about making sure Michael didn't see anything that was going on, so it was awkward, and of course, I paid her because I was her boss and that was awkward, but..."

"Did you tell her how you felt about her?"

Kimberly balked. Heat ran from her face, and she turned to look at him with wide eyes and fear in her heart. "What do you mean how I felt about her?"

"Kimmie." He whispered her name with a sigh. "You didn't just fuck the girl senseless every night and not tell her how you felt, did you?"

"I don't know what you're talking about."

"Oh, yes, you do."

"I don't love her." Kimberly pouted, crossing her arms as if to protect herself from anything else that could break through her hard exterior.

Bradley raised an eyebrow in disbelief. "First, I don't believe that. Second, I don't think *you* believe that."

She squinted at him, still avoiding answering as best she could. Michael opened the door, and she thanked the heavens she now had a proper distraction. He popped his head out and stared at her. She opened her arms to him, and he ran to give her a hug. Kimberly dragged him up to sit in her lap and pressed kisses into the side of his head.

"Wanna tell me what's going on?"

"I'm mad," Michael stated, matter-of-factly.

"Mad about what?" Kimberly asked, softening her tone of voice.

"Becca left without saying goodbye."

"Yeah. I know. That really hurts, huh, bud?"

He nodded then buried his face in Kimberly's neck. She curled her arms around him in a hug and held him close. She felt the same way. He didn't know, but she hadn't even gotten a proper goodbye, and her heart ached the same if not more than Michael's. Blinking back sudden tears, Kimberly looked over at Bradley, who watched quietly from his stool.

He mouthed the word 'love' to her, and she rolled her eyes at him. Perhaps there was something to what he was saying. Maybe it wasn't love but the fact that she hadn't actually told Becca how she felt. She thought she had, but they hadn't spent much time talking. They'd spent most of it wrapped up in each other.

Kissing Michael's head again, Kimberly waited for him to decide cuddles were enough and to leave her embrace. He was never one to sit still that long, and definitely not when snuggles were involved. He was beyond independent, and her heart broke that she had in essence caused him any pain through her own stupid and very selfish decisions.

He didn't need to get dragged into anything of the sort. Sighing into his hair, Kimberly looked over at Bradley and shrugged. He probably was right. She hadn't told Becca how she felt because she'd never analyzed how she felt.

Michael shoved off her lap and stood next to her. "Can we stay for dinner?"

"It's up to your dad, but I'm not cooking." She said the last with a glance at her ex, making sure he understood she was exhausted and did not want to be thrown under the bus again with making them all dinner.

"We can order in," he supplied. "My date for tonight canceled anyway."

"Oh goodie," Kimberly answered sarcastically. "I'm your back-up date."

"Never my back-up, always my first." He kissed the top of her head as he went for his drawer of menus. "Chinese?"

"Indian."

"Indian it is."

Michael went to play on the floor with whatever toys he'd left there that Bradley had attempted to get him to clean up, leaving Kimberly to her own devices. After Bradley ordered the food, he leaned over the counter and planted a kiss on her cheek.

"For what it's worth, Kimmie, I really liked Becca. She held her ground with me. I appreciated that."

"You're an asshole."

"Maybe, but I liked her."

"I don't think you're the only one." She risked a glance at their son. "I think you may be right."

"Of course, I'm right. I'm always right when it comes to matters of the heart. That's why I'm a cardiologist."

Snorting, Kimberly rolled her eyes at his antics. "How long until the food gets here?"

"Thirty minutes."

"Fine. Enough talk about this. Let's focus on him." She nodded in Michael's direction. Bradley got the hint, and they both went over to spend some quality time with their son.

* * * *

Becca's new job had entertained her for thirty-six hours a week, and she spent the rest of the time completing her summer courses. With two weeks to spare between summer classes and student teaching, Becca was giddy. She was already planning and in communication with her host teacher about who would be doing what, when and where. She wrote out her first official lesson plan then laughed because she wouldn't even get to teach for two months into the school year, until she had sufficient learning from her host teacher.

Deciding to keep her part-time job at the grocer, Becca changed her availability to evenings and weekends only, knowing it would drop her hours and money would become even more sparse than it was before. Drew was still letting her stay at the apartment, but it was certainly cramped, not to mention Becca would have a forty-five-minute commute one way without traffic to contend with.

Sighing, she put the final touches on her lesson plan then checked her new campus email she'd been assigned to use while she taught there. The email flashed with the subject line 'Roster', and her stomach dropped. This was going to be it. This would tell her how difficult her semester was going to be.

Licking her lips and straightening her shoulders, she prepared herself to read through the email. With one last deep breath, she opened the list up and skimmed it. Right there, toward the end of the names, was Michael's. *Michael Thompson. Age five. Birthday, July 18.*

She'd missed his birthday. Her heart sank. Tears stung the backs of her eyes. It was stupid. She shouldn't be so put out by the fact that she'd missed his birthday. He had only been talking about it for months, but still, to have missed something so special weighed on her heart.

Then it hit her. She'd have to see Kimberly. She'd have to deal with Kimberly. And most likely, Kimberly wouldn't even know she was Michael's teacher until she showed up one day and saw her, because her name wouldn't be given to the students—maybe even the first day of school. Knowing Kimberly, she'd make sure she was there.

Groaning, Becca rubbed the bridge of her nose. What would she even say to her? *"Hey, how's it going? Mess up anyone else's job lately?"* Bitterness left a lingering taste on her tongue.

Letting out a grunt, she dropped her head to the table and banged it lightly twice before sitting up again. She would have to come up with something better than that, but she had almost two full weeks. She had time to prepare. Kimberly would probably be caught totally unawares. That did give Becca a distinct advantage.

She closed her laptop and put together everything she would need for her meeting with Miss Knorr the next day. They were going to start the detail planning and set up the classroom in the next week. The wait time was finally over, and she was so close to the end of school she could taste it. This was all she had left. She only had to take one other class while she taught, so she could spend more time in the classroom than a normal student if she wanted.

That was it. Her focus had to be on the class and on Michael, not on her past whatever-relationship with Kimberly. That was how she'd get through the semester and make it to graduation. Becca got dressed for her date with Jessica, changing her focus to something positive rather than negative.

She put on a light coat of makeup, some red lip gloss and spiked up the back of her short red hair until it sat perfectly against her head. She was ready to be her new self. Jessica pulled up outside the apartment to pick her up on time, and Becca ran out to the car, slipping into the passenger seat.

"Where to?" Becca asked as soon as she buckled her seatbelt.

"Do you want to go anywhere? Or would you rather just hang out here for a while?" Jessica asked, glancing back up at the second-floor apartment. "I mean, I'm not really wanting to go to the movies tonight."

"We could stay here. My roommate is out and won't be back until late, if at all, depending on how their night goes."

"Let's do that." Jessica grinned. She parked the car, and they both got out and headed up to the apartment.

Becca opened the door and dropped her purse onto the table and spun in a circle. "Well, this is it. Not much to it. It's pretty small."

Jessica glanced around and scrunched her nose. "Where do you sleep?"

"For now, the couch."

"Oh."

Jessica grabbed Becca's hand and tugged her closer until their lips touched. Becca leaned into the kiss, delighted that she felt free to do so. It was only their fourth date in the last few weeks, but they seemed to get along well enough. Jessica moved her hands to Becca's hips and guided her backward until she found the couch against the backs of her knees. With one sharp shove, Jessica pushed her down onto it. Becca bounced slightly, and when she looked up, she saw the desire in Jessica's eyes.

She hadn't intended on sleeping with her any time soon, but it was clear Jessica had other thoughts. Jessica straddled her, cupping her cheeks to kiss her again. Their few make-out sessions, starting with the one on their first date on the trunk of her car, had gone well enough, but something was missing, something not quite aligning.

Pressing her hands to Jessica's sides, Becca moved her fingers until she could pull up Jessica's shirt and feel her hot skin underneath. With her mouth occupied, she trailed her hands up until she cupped Jessica's breasts and squeezed. Jessica moaned, and Becca did it again, hoping it was a good moan and not fake.

Jessica kissed her way down Becca's neck, and Becca took the opportunity to drag Jessica's shirt off and over her head. She marveled at the red and black lacy bra she wore underneath. Jessica had planned this. Slightly put off, Becca ignored it. She had to get over Kimberly and move on. This could only bring her one step closer to that.

Fingering the delicate fabric, Becca pulled it away from Jessica's body, unhooking the catch and dropping it to the floor. She skimmed her thumbs across Jessica's nipples then gripped her, pulling them together so they could kiss again. Kissing was good. Kissing distracted her from the fact that she wasn't sure this was what she wanted to be doing, but she wasn't going to stop either way.

When Jessica pulled away to breathe and smile, Becca took her chance and shifted so Jessica was flat on her back and she had the upper hand. Becca pushed Jessica's maxi skirt up to her waist, pulled down her underwear and didn't tease. She went straight for what she knew Jessica wanted.

With her mouth, she brought Jessica up, using her fingers to take her over the edge. She inched away, but Jessica gripped her hair hard and tugged her down. "Do it again," she demanded.

Becca once more brought her to orgasm, Jessica's legs shaking as she held them tightly with her hands against her chest. This time, Becca moved away before Jessica could pull her down again. Jessica walked backward on her elbows until she could sit up and lean against the armrest on the couch. She grinned wickedly in Becca's direction, her golden locks falling around her breasts.

"Are you wet for me?"

The pit in Becca's stomach hardened. She nodded, though she wasn't sure it was true. The stark contrast from the way Kimberly talked to her while they had sex and the way Jessica did could not have been more prevalent. If Jessica hadn't been in charge, they most likely never would have gotten this far, because Becca didn't know if she wanted it.

Jessica shoved her hand between Becca's legs and rubbed hard, almost uncomfortably. Becca listed forward and widened her stance so Jessica would have better access. Without thinking, she undid the button and zipper on her jeans and shoved them open and down her hips enough that Jessica could wiggle her hand in.

Doing just that, Jessica plunged two fingers in, forcing a guttural gasp from Becca's lips. Jessica put one foot on the floor, giving her more stability and force to push as she thrust her fingers in and out. Becca gripped the top of the couch, leaning forward with each jerk of Jessica's wrist. Jessica used her free hand to shove Becca's shirt up and over her breasts, pulling down the cups of her bra.

The next time Becca jerked forward, Jessica took one of Becca's nipples into her mouth and sucked hard, letting it pop as she moved back. Becca groaned, begging her body to start feeling pleasure faster, to end this quicker. Becca rocked her hips, trying to offer a better rhythm for Jessica to use, but she must not have noticed because she continued in her own pace.

Eventually, Becca leaned down next to Jessica's ear and harshly said, "You have to rub it."

Jessica let out a squeak then a growl. "I love it when you talk dirty."

Shivering, Becca focused on her body, closing her eyes and listening to the sensations flowing through her nerves and over her skin. This was far more like a one-night stand than anything she and Kimberly had done. It felt raw and selfish. Neither of them cared if the other got off, just themselves.

Grunting, Becca drew in short breaths as her orgasm built, finally. She willed herself over the burst of pleasure, begging her body to answer her call for it. As soon as her muscles clenched, Jessica ripped her hand from Becca's pants and left her clenching at nothing. Slowing her breathing, Becca finally opened her eyes as she steadied herself and saw Jessica happily licking her fingers one at a time, like she thought it was sexy.

Biting back the curse under her breath, Becca sat on her butt on the opposite side of the couch and released a long sigh. She brushed her hand over her hair and massaged the back of her neck lightly. Jessica was already redressing. Becca was lucky she'd hardly been undressed at all. She rolled her eyes, fixed her bra and tugged down her shirt before standing to button up her pants.

It was awkward as she turned to look at Jessica, wondering if they were just going to shake hands, say 'thank you for the time' and go their separate ways. Instead, Jessica tugged Becca down onto the couch and leaned her back against Becca's front like they were long-time lovers.

"Let's watch something," Jessica said.

Not quite sure what had happened, Becca picked up the television remote and turned it on, cringing when it popped up to the food station she and Drew routinely watched, and lo and behold, none other than Chef Kim Burns was on, judging some sort of competition.

"Oh, I love her. Let's watch this."

Becca rolled her eyes, thankful Jessica couldn't see her, and left the station on, staring at her old boss and ex-lover for the next three hours until Jessica finally admitted exhaustion and left with one soft sweet peck to Becca's lips. As soon as Jessica had left, Becca changed the channel and went to take a shower.

Chapter Seventeen

When Becca's first day of school finally arrived, her stomach was a bundle of nerves. She had gotten to her classroom insanely early that morning, making sure everything was in perfect order before the kids arrived. She'd gone on a walk through the campus, circling each of the buildings that housed four classrooms total as she tried to calm herself.

Miss Knorr laughed when she walked onto campus and grabbed Becca by the arm. "I was this nervous my first day, too."

"Student teaching or as a full-time teacher?"

Grinning, Miss Knorr answered, "Both. Honestly, being fully in charge might have been worse."

"Great," Becca muttered. "Just what I have to look forward to next year."

"That confident I'm going to pass you?" she teased.

Becca shrugged and grinned. "If I fail, I just wasted ten years of my life getting to this point."

"You'll do great." Miss Knorr pressed a hand to Becca's forearm and gave a gentle squeeze. "First day jitters are completely normal for everyone, teachers included."

"I know. I guess I didn't expect it to be this bad, seeing as I'm not the student anymore."

Grinning, Miss Knorr shook her head, her dark afro moving slightly but popping back into place immediately. "I wish it worked that way too, but it doesn't."

Becca shrugged. "I told you I used to nanny, right?" At Miss Knorr's nod, Becca continued, "Well, one of the kids I used to nanny is in the class. He's really smart, but it's going to be so weird to hear him call me 'Miss Kline'. Won't seem right for a while."

"You'll get used to it, and he'll probably go right back to calling you Becca as soon as you're not his teacher anymore."

"You're probably right."

"I know I'm right. Come on. Let's get to the classroom and get everything set to go for this morning."

"Right."

Becca followed Miss Knorr to the room and propped the door open, allowing the cool breeze to flow into it. Their classroom was toward the front of the campus, where the younger kids' classes were. The older kids were farther away from the administration building. Their classroom was shaded by large trees, covering the sidewalks that led to the retaining wall out of the back door, which was rather secluded for a school.

Becca had only gone out there a handful of times, but Miss Knorr had shared that they would often put crafts out there to dry faster in good weather. They left that door closed the rest of the time to discourage children from heading in that direction, especially —

according to Miss Knorr—for the first month or so of school when they were all getting used to the rules.

Becca busied herself making sure all the kids' nametags were at the tables and the chairs were pushed in properly. Miss Knorr gave her a few more pitying stares before she looked up brightly as the first student showed up. She came around her desk to greet the student and parent. Becca stayed quietly in the back corner, not quite sure what she was supposed to do.

When Miss Knorr introduced her, she balked. Her mouth dried and all she could do was nod her head and wave at the tiny little girl who stood close to her dad. She heard her name again and had to refocus her attention. "Miss Kline will help you find your cubby and your seat, okay?"

"Okay," the girl squeaked.

Becca walked over and bent down low so she was eye to eye with the blonde-haired, blue-eyed girl. "What's your name?"

"Victoria Sampson," she said triumphantly.

"Well, Victoria, I'm Miss Kline. It's so good to meet you and have you here today." Becca stood up. "Let's find your cubby for your lunch box and backpack then find your seat. I think there might be some crayons and paper there, so you can color until the rest of the class gets here."

"Oh, good!" Victoria answered. She dutifully followed Becca until they'd found her things.

Becca stood up from the table after making sure Victoria was settled and turned back to the door to see what she could do next. Immediately, she froze. There was Kimberly, as beautiful as ever. Her hair was down around her shoulders. She'd obviously had gotten it cut recently. Her eyes were bright as she exchanged words with Miss Knorr.

Her heart was in her throat. Becca swallowed hard, trying to make herself move, make herself breathe. Eventually she drew air into her lungs and lowered her gaze, realizing suddenly that it was a mistake. Becca's gaze caught the shiny necklace that rested between Kimberly's breasts and the dark, sweater-y fabric of her shirt. Lowering her gaze farther, Becca followed the curve of her hips down to her toes.

When she looked back up, Kimberly's hazel eyes were staring straight back at her with her lips slightly ajar. Becca swallowed hard and stayed rooted on her spot. She didn't break their eye contact until Michael saw her and ran straight for her, giving her the world's biggest hug.

She wrapped her arms around him and clung on tightly, closing her eyes and breathing in his clean scent. Oh, how she'd missed him. Her heart broke as she continued to hold on to him, knowing this would likely be one of the last times she was allowed to. Eventually, she pulled back and held him by his shoulders to put some distance between them.

With a huge smile on her face, Becca looked him over again, making a big show of it. "I think you've grown a whole foot since I've seen you last, kiddo!"

"Don't be silly, Becca."

Turning her head to the side, Becca tsked him. "I'm one of your teachers now, Michael, so you'll need to call me 'Miss Kline' while we're in this room, okay?"

"Okay, Miss Kline." He tried out her name, sliding the vowel of her last name out as long as he dared before grinning. "Mama's here. You should go see her."

He grinned then leaned in close to Becca again. "I think she missed you a lot, too."

"Aww, kiddo, that's so sweet. Why don't you go find your cubby and your desk, okay?"

"Okay." Michael waltzed off in the opposite direction.

More students and parents filed in then out, but Kimberly stayed in the room, staring straight at Becca. It wasn't until Miss Knorr got her attention and asked if she had any other questions that Kimberly jerked out of whatever trance she was in. Becca stayed with the children, preferring to avoid Kimberly at all costs.

Her voice was clear when she spoke, the brusque, raspy sound sending shivers up Becca's spine. "Could I have a word with Becca for a minute?"

Miss Knorr looked back at Becca for confirmation before nodding. "She's all yours."

"Outside?"

"Your choice."

Kimberly curled a finger at Becca, and Becca walked in her direction, not quite sure if she was in control of her own faculties or if Kimberly was pulling the strings like she was a marionette. When she reached Kimberly, they left the classroom and turned the corner to the back of the building between the class and the retaining wall.

With both hands on her hips and her chin jutted forward in anger, Kimberly grimaced. "Why didn't you tell me?"

"You knew I was looking for a student teaching position."

"Yes, but here?" Kimberly drew in a deep breath. "Why didn't you tell me? Don't you think I deserved to know?"

Becca shook her head. "No. You're not a part of my life anymore."

"Clearly, I am." Kimberly rolled her eyes and turned as if she were leaving, but she stopped short and moved back toward Becca. "You can't tell me you didn't want to see my reaction, didn't want to see the shock on my face when I dropped him off today."

"I didn't know they would put me in his classroom. I have no control over that."

"You could have chosen another school."

"There was no other option." Becca kept her face stone cold. Her heart and stomach told a different story, but she didn't want to let Kimberly in on how truly hurt she felt. She didn't want this space between them.

"Bullshit."

"Language. This is an elementary school, and there are students all around us." Becca's lips thinned as she raised her chin.

Kimberly drew in a deep breath and let it out slowly. Then she licked her lips and looked Becca up and down twice. "I'm glad Michael will have a familiar face around here. He's been very nervous about school starting, especially with all the sudden changes he had recently."

"It's not like you didn't keep the instability around before me," Becca shot back. "I was the only one willing to put up with you long enough to give him some semblance of normalcy."

Kimberly's mouth opened, but then she shut it. She clenched her jaw and closed her eyes, rubbing them before she stepped away from Becca. "I should let you get back."

"You should," Becca answered. "I have a job to do, and I won't have you impeding on my work any longer."

As Becca went to step past and go to the classroom, Kimberly grabbed her hand and laced their fingers. She brushed her thumb over the top of Becca's hand until Becca turned to look down at Kimberly. "What happened?"

"Now is not the time to talk about this."

"I know, but...I want to know what happened. You just left."

"You were my boss."

"I know." Tears brimmed in Kimberly's eyes. "I know, and I crossed way too many boundaries to even be worthy of that title, but I never got the sense from you that you didn't want it to happen."

"I did," Becca confessed. "I did want it. But if you'll excuse me, I have students to teach, including your son."

Without another word, Becca broke the connection of their hands and went into the classroom, leaving Kimberly to fend for herself. She didn't look back, no matter how much she wanted to, and when she got inside, she dared herself not to look out of the window and see if Kimberly was still standing there, watching and waiting.

Miss Knorr clapped her hands together to get the kids' attention. She started with one clap, then said, "If you can hear me, clap once."

Only one or two students listened. She then clapped twice, saying, "If you can hear me, clap twice."

She went all the way up until five before she had every students' attention. When they were all looking at her, she smiled. "I'm Miss Knorr, and I'm going to be your teacher for the year. It's so good to meet all of you. We're going to play some games later to get to know one another better, but for right now, I want to introduce you to Miss Kline. Miss Kline is a student too, just like you, and she's learning how to be a teacher, just like me. So, she's going to be with us for a few months to learn. Isn't that awesome?"

The kids responded with excitement, and Becca waved nervously at them. She smiled then waited for Miss Knorr to continue her lesson for the day, which was really mostly an introduction of rules and names. She'd mentioned it would be that for the better part of two weeks while they all adjusted to everything in the classroom.

When Becca gave in and looked up, Kimberly was gone.

Kimberly watched and listened through the window as the teacher made her introductions. She could barely see Becca standing in the corner of the classroom, her beige slacks clinging to her slight hips and her button-up shirt not hiding what she knew was underneath.

Her heart had done a full stop when she'd looked up and seen Becca standing there, staring straight at her. She'd felt betrayed once again, as Becca had clearly had all the control and all the knowledge of what was happening, and she had been left completely in the dark. She'd wanted to take Michael and run but knew that as soon as he'd seen her, the game was over.

Kimberly brushed her fingers over her lips and sighed, remembering the last time Becca had kissed her, the last time Becca had spoken to her. So much had gone unsaid, so much untold. It seemed as if Becca didn't want Kimberly to talk to her or pry into what had happened. For Kimberly, at least, the last thing Becca wanted was Kimberly back in her life.

Shuddering, Kimberly turned and headed toward her car. She slid behind the driver's seat and headed to her house. When she walked inside, she was hit with how empty it was. Michael was at school and Becca was gone, with very little hope of ever returning. She dropped her keys onto the kitchen counter and sat, her eyes pooling with water as she pressed her head to the cold granite and begged for the ache in her chest to disappear.

She had eight hours until Michael was done — to try to distract herself, to try not to think about Becca — Becca, who was spending the same eight glorious hours with her son. Becca, who could have sent a text forewarning that she was Michael's student teacher. Becca, who wouldn't answer the simple question of why she'd left.

Closing her eyes, Kimberly sobbed. She cried. She ached. She let it all out, as much as she could, before she was cried dry. When she looked up at the clock, it had been over an hour. She wiped her cheeks, still sniffling. She'd sworn she'd cried enough over Becca and she wouldn't do it again, yet here she was, sitting at her kitchen counter bawling.

With teeth clenched, Kimberly straightened her back. She could do so much better than this. She *would* do better. Leaving the kitchen, she headed to her office and sat down. She slid the proof of her cookbook in front of her and spent the next six hours painstakingly going over every page to make sure it was exactly as she wanted it. She looked for typos, she checked photos and she looked at flow and consistency.

When the clock hit two-thirty, she leaned back in her rolling chair and stretched her aching muscles. Bradley was supposed to meet her at the house to go pick up Michael from his first day of school together, as he'd only been able to change his schedule enough for a half-day off work. She set the cookbook to the side, flipping it open to the front dedication page. She'd written a brief thanks to certain people in it but had left off the one she truly needed to thank. Taking her pen, she scrawled across it then closed the book for good. She'd mail it the next day, and her book would be out in a few months.

The front door opening brought a small smile to her lips. She plastered a look of general annoyance on her face as she turned to meet Bradley. He was late, and she certainly didn't want to ruin the surprise of who Michael's new teacher was.

He came around the corner to her office and knocked. "Ready?"

"More than ever," she answered.

"Did you finish?"

"Hmm?" She glanced over her shoulder at the proof text on her desk. "I did. I'll mail it tomorrow. When I get the final proof before I get the first bound copy, I'll let you look."

"Can't hardly wait," he answered, holding his elbow out for her. "My lady."

"Such a gentleman. What's gotten into you?"

As they headed down the hall to her car, he leaned down to press his lips to her ear. "I have a date tomorrow."

Kimberly rolled her eyes. "You always have a date tomorrow."

"True, true, but this one is different."

"Oh?"

"Yup."

"Care to share?" Kimberly got into the driver's seat and waited for Bradley to walk around the car and get into the passenger side.

"Nope. Not yet."

"Okay." Kimberly made her eyes go with fake surprise before she pulled out of the driveway. "To school it is."

When she pulled up to the school, the kids were playing on the small equipment up front. It was where the little kids killed time while waiting for their parents to pick them up. The big kids were either already walking home, waiting to get on the bus—along with some littles—or playing inside the school playground area.

Bradley got out of the car and held his arms open as Michael ran in his direction. Kimberly looked around, waiting for Becca to show up. When she didn't, she turned to Michael. She gave him a big hug and got down on one knee to be on his level.

"Did you have a good day?" she asked.

"I did!" he answered. "I had so much fun."

"Good, I'm glad. Let's get in. We're going to have pizza for dinner as a special treat to celebrate your first day."

"Pizza! I love pizza!"

Michael clambered over to the side of the car and tugged at the door handle until Bradley moved over to help him. Kimberly was back to looking for Becca with her arms crossed. She wanted to finish their conversation, even if she knew in some ways it would never be finished. When the door shut behind her, she turned and went back to the driver's seat to head home.

As soon as she sat in the car, Michael jabbered about school. "I made so many friends today, Daddy. There's Lauren, and Liam, and Wyatt, and Grace, and Toria."

"I'm glad you made so many friends," Bradley added, obviously not fully paying attention.

"And my teacher is Becca. She played a name game with me today. That was after we drawed."

"Drew, not 'drawed'," Kimberly corrected.

"Becca?" Bradley asked with wide eyes, more to Kimberly than to Michael.

Kimberly almost didn't dare look at him, but she turned as Michael spoke.

"I'm sorry. Miss Kline. I have to call her Miss Kline now."

"Becca is Miss Kline?" Bradley asked again.

When Kimberly risked one more glance to him, she gave him a slight nod and blinked back the sudden tears. Bradley reached over and covered her thigh with his hand, giving it a gentle and affectionate squeeze. "Why didn't you tell me?" he whispered.

"I didn't know," she whispered back. "Trust me. I was just as surprised this morning when I dropped him off."

"We can talk about it later."

"I don't want to."

"Then we ate lunch. Mama packed me my favorite! Peanut butter and jelly. Mmm. It's so good." Michael smacked his lips together like he was eating his lunch again.

Kimberly avoided Bradley's gaze as best she could, even after they got home. She truly did *not* want to talk about it, and he, thankfully, seemed to get that hint. Every time Michael mentioned Becca's name, or rather, Miss Kline's name, Kimberly's heart twisted a little more. She focused on the fact that he'd enjoyed his first day at school and was excited for his second day, that she knew Becca was a good teacher and Michael would no doubt learn a lot in this coming year — anything other than her own self-pity and anguish.

And it worked until it was dark, the house was quiet, Bradley was gone, Michael was asleep and she ran out of distractions. Climbing into her bed, Kimberly pulled the covers over her head and let herself sob once again as all the pain of the last few months came rushing back.

Chapter Eighteen

Six weeks into Kimberly completely avoiding drop-off and pick-up as much as she humanly could, she ran into a problem. It was open house. She would have to spend the next hour in Michael's classroom, looking at what the kids had done so far in the school year and hearing about all that they would continue to do. Michael was thriving, but every day she saw Becca standing solitary in the classroom or outside, her soul crushed even more.

She'd done as well at avoiding everything as she possibly could, but in those moments of drop-off and pick-up at school, she allowed herself to open to the hurt and to the pain she was feeling. An hour of it would be nearly impossible for her to handle. Thankfully, Bradley would be with her, but he was only so much help in that department, especially when he kept pushing Kimberly to admit she loved Becca, which she didn't. She just wanted answers as to why Becca'd left so suddenly and without talking about it.

Pouting, Kimberly sat in her tiny office at Gamma's, attempting to do some paperwork. She was so distracted by what that night was going to hold that she struggled to stay focused on the computer screen in front of her. Zechariah had even made comments about it for the last two hours, teasing that she had love on the brain. She'd rolled her eyes at him and kicked him out of the room.

But he was right. She was distracted. For the last few months, she had been so focused on work, growing the restaurant, advancing her television career and her cookbook that she'd done everything. There was no late paperwork. There was no late planning. Everything was set and ready to go through the Christmas season and perhaps even a little after.

She knew who she needed to hire and who she needed to fire. She knew how many pages to the exact number her cookbook was going to be, along with how many advanced copies were going to be printed and exactly where they were going to be sent. Her publisher had reassured her that she didn't need to know that information, but she had insisted. Her entire life had been consumed by work and Michael, and for one hour that night, she was going to be forced to look at the one thing she didn't want to.

Becca.

No matter how much she wanted to, there was no longer any avoiding it. That night she was going to have to face her fears, her doubts and her emotions. She would face Becca and put on a good show for Michael. He had to know that she supported him, she was happy for him and she was there for him. Becca being his teacher made no difference. She had to be more involved.

Determined, Kimberly re-doubled her efforts to focus on her paperwork. She skimmed through the numbers, calculated their profit, decided raises were likely for most of her staff in the next few months with the trends she was seeing and put the plan into place. It wasn't much longer until her alarm went off, reminding her that she had to head home to shower and change before going to the school.

* * * *

Becca wrung her hands, her nerves once again taking over. Jessica had attempted to calm her down over dinner, but Becca had pushed her food around on her plate, not wanting to eat before she escaped back to the school and her work.

They had been spending most evenings together, and Jessica had been hinting about them moving into an apartment together. Becca was resistant to the idea. Although living with Drew was becoming more and more cramped as the weeks went on and Drew had been spending an inordinate amount of time away from the apartment. They claimed they were seeing someone over the last few months, but Becca had her doubts and fears.

She worried Drew was hiding and avoiding her, not only because she was in their space but because they really didn't like Jessica. Becca gave a heavy sigh as she pulled up at the school in her run-down Toyota. No matter how much she tried, Jessica and Drew did not get along and seemed to always butt heads when they were in the same room.

That had been partially why Becca had taken to going to Jessica's apartment across town and staying there more often than not. She didn't want to live through the tension between her best friend and her girlfriend. Shaking the feeling, Becca got to her classroom in time to help Miss Knorr with the final touches. They draped their students' latest craft project from the ceiling, Becca standing on a short stepstool while Miss Knorr handed her the photos to clip up with clothes pins.

They readied lemonade, water and coffee, along with cookies that Becca had spent the better part of three days making. They laid them out carefully and stood back to admire their work. It wasn't long before students and parents arrived. Becca interjected herself into different conversations here and there where appropriate, but most parents were interested in Miss Knorr, and rightfully so.

She kept looking toward the door, waiting for Kimberly to arrive. She wasn't disappointed when she did. She was dressed up, her dark hair curled into loose spirals and her eyes lined, the shadow bringing out the yellow hazel that was so rare. The red shirt she wore clung to her body and wrapped around her side slightly to accentuate her curves.

Once again Becca found herself unable to take her eyes off her former employer. Her heart was in her throat, her stomach spinning in circles. Michael grabbed his mom's hand and dragged her over to his desk to show her where he sat. Bradley trailed behind, his eyes set on Becca with determination. Becca had seen that look before, when she'd first met him. She swallowed hard and turned to distract herself and keep busy.

When she felt the hand at her elbow, she straightened. Bradley, in his gray power suit and purple-striped tie, towered over her with a glint in his eye. "We need to talk."

His low voice brooked no room for disagreement. Becca nodded, and they moved closer to the back of the room and away from the majority of the people inside. She clenched her jaw as she looked up at him. "What did you need to talk about, Mr. Thompson?"

He rolled his eyes. "Bradley, please. I may be a parent, but we know each other outside of here. I don't need you to put up walls where there are none."

She gave a curt nod and folded her hands in front of her. She hated how he affected her. His height made her small like a child, and his pristine outfits always made her feel a mess. He was so confident in how he moved and talked, so boisterous and bossy in his commands. She struggled not to follow them.

"I'm here to talk about Kimmie."

Becca opened her mouth, and she glanced over at Kimberly, who was staring at the two of them. Becca clenched her jaw as she looked at Bradley. "There's nothing to talk about."

"You know, you and she sound oddly familiar in that. However, I know her really well. I was married to her for ten years and knew her for years before that. You want to know what I learned about Kimmie Thompson in that time?"

Becca found herself nodding, even though she wasn't certain why. Even if she did want to know, it was beyond what she should be doing. She had curiosity, yes, but Kimberly wasn't a part of her life any longer.

Bradley leaned close to Becca's ear. "She's stubborn as a goat. She is blessed with this amazing ability to put different foods together and create the most delicious thing you have ever tasted. She's stubborn. She's an amazing mother and would do anything for our son. She's stubborn, did I mention that? Right. I did. Well, she's stubborn."

"Where are you going with this?" Becca interjected, once again risking a glance toward Kimberly and seeing her suspicion amp up with each second Bradley spoke to her. "Someone is watching us."

"Let her." He laughed slightly. "Maybe it'll prompt her."

"Prompt her?" Becca turned to him in surprise, their mouths nearly touching with how close he was to her. "What do you mean?"

"She's in love with you."

Becca's heart clenched hard. The wind was knocked out of her lungs, and she struggled to catch her breath again. She was sure Bradley could see the shock written all over her body, but she didn't care. They had never talked about how they felt. They had never once uttered a word of like, dislike or even dared to think about love...either of them.

With her heart thumping, Becca shook her head. "I think you're mistaken."

Bradley snorted. "I've known the woman for fourteen years, Becca. She has never looked at anyone like she looks at you, me included, and she has never wallowed so much in her own pain and stupidity and stubbornness before. She is hurting. And she's stubborn—pretty sure I mentioned that one before."

"I don't know what you want me to do about it."

That's when he smiled and leaned in again, whispering, "I dare you to love her back."

Becca shivered as his breath floated over her neck and down her shirt. Once again, she locked gazes with

Kimberly, who had both hands on her hips and was about to come over and break up their little chat, but Bradley stepped away just in time. Becca let out a shaky breath and leaned against the counter to steady herself.

With Bradley entertaining Kimberly once again and Miss Knorr distracted with other parents, Becca slipped out of the back door for some fresh air. She leaned against the hard stone wall of the classroom, facing the retaining wall, and pressed a hand to her chest.

Love.

Bradley had to be wrong. Kimberly couldn't love her. There was no way possible that could be the case. She'd been Becca's boss, she'd pushed boundaries to get what she wanted and Becca hadn't wanted to give in anymore, no matter how good it had felt. Closing her eyes and pressing her head back into the wall, she let the cool evening breeze wash over her and calm her racing heart.

"Are you okay, Becca?"

When Becca opened her eyes, she was faced with none other than Kimberly. Groaning, she stood, but Kimberly waved her hand.

"I'm sorry. I shouldn't have come out here, but I saw you slip out and you didn't exactly look well. I just wanted to check."

Becca's heart caught in her throat. Kimberly's neatly painted lips were only a few short feet away, and when she stared at them, Kimberly slipped her tongue out and licked. Becca closed her eyes again, not sure how to answer Kimberly's question but certainly not wanting her to go inside again so soon. Inside was stifling — the heat from everyone in there, the energy. If she listened to something other than her own breath, the joyous noise of kids and parents and teachers filtered in and out of classrooms. They were utterly alone, though.

Opening her eyes again, she was surprised to find Kimberly still standing in front of her, her head cocked to the side with curiosity and concern written all over her face. Without warning, Becca straightened, took one step forward, slid her hand behind Kimberly's head and brought their mouths together. Kimberly's surprise was echoed in her voice as she let out a small yelp before moaning.

It was furious and wild. Becca didn't want to stop, to even slow down. She wanted this moment to last forever, for the little bubble they'd created to never burst. She stepped backward until she was against the wall, dragging Kimberly with her as she went. Kimberly's teeth grazed over her lip, and she whimpered at the shots of pleasure coursing through her body.

Kimberly grinned, her lips curling against Becca's mouth, and she did it again. Becca shuddered, not sure what fresh hell she had just invited into her personal space but loving every moment of it. Kimberly's hands were against her hips, then on her belly, then on her breasts. Becca arched her back, trying to have more contact with Kimberly to increase their touch.

Once more, Kimberly smiled against her, and Becca's heart gave one deep thud, forcing the air from her lungs. She was drowning in a sea of Kimberly, and she didn't even have the wherewithal or the desire to try to swim back up. No, she was exactly where she wanted to be.

She dug her fingers into Kimberly's hair, making sure she had a tight hold and pulling Kimberly into her even more. She didn't want this moment to end. She slid her tongue around Kimberly's, drawing circles and teasing each time Kimberly squeezed her breast. Becca pushed away from the wall and flipped them so Kimberly's back was against the stone, and she pressed delicately into her.

Fear coursed through her at the thought of their kiss breaking, and she tripled her efforts to keep Kimberly exactly where she wanted her—with their lips locked. Becca reached under Kimberly's shirt, sighing when her fingertips touched warm, smooth skin. She heard Kimberly's sharp intake of breath and dug her nails in slightly in response—their old dance coming alive again no matter how much time had passed.

"Mama?"

Becca jerked away sharply and wiped her fingers over her lips as she stared wide-eyed at Kimberly, who was still heaving against the wall.

"Kim, are you out here?" Bradley's voice covered Michael's soft one.

"Yeah, I'm right here." Kimberly shoved her shirt into place and sent a longing look to Becca.

Becca couldn't discern what Kimberly was trying to tell her, but her heart was back in her throat and words had escaped her. Kimberly put herself together and looked up as Bradley rounded the corner beside the back door and stopped short. His gaze made quick work of the both of them before he grinned and turned around, stopping Michael in his tracks with a hand.

"Mama will be right in, bud. I think she just needed some fresh air."

He started toward the door, and Kimberly shot Becca another sharp look, her lips parting as if to say something. Becca shook her head and closed her eyes as she held up a hand to stop Kimberly. In a rush of air, Becca confessed, "I'm seeing someone."

"Oh," Kimberly answered, her gaze not wavering from Becca's face. Disappointment filtered through her eyes, and Becca's heart broke a little more. "Guess she can't be too great then."

With that comment, anger flared in Becca's chest. She focused on it, rode it out and used it to escape. She rolled her eyes, crossed her hands over her chest and glared. "Like you would even know how to be a girlfriend."

Kimberly put her hands out in surrender, but Becca brushed by them as she took a step onto the sidewalk, her shoulders stiff and jaw tight. She straightened her shirt again before she headed to the front door of the classroom. She left the wake of emotions behind her and ignored everything she could, focusing only on her anger for Kimberly and her joy for her students.

Bradley and Michael were back in the classroom, playing with one of the sensory tables Becca had set up after school and before she had met with Jessica for a meal. Her stomach twisted hard. *Jessica.* What on earth was she going to do about Jessica?

They had ridden out a relationship neither seemed to have too much interest in. The sex was okay, and the company was passable. *Why are we even together in the first place?* Sighing, Becca rubbed her temples and focused on work.

It wasn't too much longer until the students and parents were gone, and she and Miss Knorr were cleaning up the classroom in preparation for Monday. They could have come in early, but both of them were night owls and decided they'd rather be done Friday and sleep in on Monday. They worked mostly in silence, exhaustion seeping into the room.

Unfortunately, it gave Becca time to think. Jessica wasn't her soulmate, that much she knew, but their relationship was going well enough and served its purpose for both of them. Jessica had a date to tote around to different functions, and Becca had the distraction she was looking for. Whether or not she and Jessica would break up was not the question. It was just a matter of when.

Becca gathered the rest of the cookies and divided them into two containers. She didn't want to break up with Jessica. That was the point. That was the deciding factor, so she wouldn't. She would wait and ride it out as long as she could and as long as Jessica would let her.

But Kimberly... She sighed as she snapped the lids on the containers. Kimberly was going to be the death of her. She confused her. One minute they were yelling at each other, the next they were practically screwing against the wall behind her classroom in the middle of the school's open house. One minute Kim was her boss, and the next, Becca was Michael's teacher.

Everything about Kimberly confused her, but there was no way Becca could deny the attraction the two of them felt for one another, the tenuous pull of one of them to the other—and the inappropriateness of it all that felt so exactly right. Setting the cookies down, Becca turned to look around the room and see what else needed to be done. Miss Knorr seemed to also be making that assessment, and when their gazes locked, Miss Knorr nodded.

"I think we're all done for the night."

"Thank God. I'm beat," Becca answered. "I bet you are, too."

"Yeah. Open houses, while fun, also take their toll." Miss Knorr smiled and started for her jacket and keys.

Following suit, Becca grabbed her things. She handed Miss Knorr one of the containers of cookies and headed out of the door. She waited for the door to be locked, and together they walked to the small faculty parking lot at the side of the school's campus. They got into their vehicles, and Miss Knorr drove off.

Becca stayed put. She closed her eyes and put her head on her steering wheel. The scent of Kimberly's perfume lingered on her clothes, and even the smells of the clear evening or the cookies in her lap couldn't make it go away. Her lips tingled from the memory of Kimberly's mouth against hers, and her body ached, truly ached, for the woman she didn't think she could have.

Brushing away a single tear, Becca put her car in reverse and headed for Jessica's house with one thing on her mind. Forgetting.

Chapter Nineteen

Each time at drop-off, Kimberly would walk Michael to his classroom, even though she didn't have to. She wanted to see Becca. Each day that she saw Becca, Becca would immediately look somewhere else or walk to the far end of the classroom. Kimberly's hope faded.

She finally decided they had to talk. It was her day off, and she was supposed to pick Michael up from school, so she parked her car and headed toward his classroom. He was already outside playing and ran over when he saw her. Kimberly gave him a hug and a kiss.

"Kiddo, I've got to talk to Miss Kline for a minute, so you just keep playing here, and I'll be back to get you. Okay?"

"Miss Kline wasn't here today."

"What do you mean?" Kimberly's eyebrows drew together as she bent down to be eye level with Michael.

He shrugged. "She wasn't at school today. Miss Knorr said she was busy or something."

"Was she sick?"

"I don't know."

Kimberly clucked her tongue and stood up, rolling her shoulders. She looked around the playground and toward his classroom, hoping her son was wrong and Becca was somewhere inside the school's campus. After staring and looking for a few minutes, she didn't see her. Sighing, she glanced down at Michael and ran a hand through his hair.

"Come on, then. Let's go."

He grabbed his backpack and slung it over his shoulders. Kimberly walked with him right by her side until they reached the car. After he got into his seat and buckled in, Kimberly pulled out her phone and bit her lip as her thumb hovered over Becca's name in her text messages.

She hadn't deleted any of the texts Becca had sent her, the personal ones or the professional ones, the photos and videos of Michael. Nothing. She clicked the message thread open then closed it again.

"Let's go, Mom!"

Rolling her eyes, Kimberly started the ignition and threw the car into drive. She pulled out onto the road and headed toward their house. After they'd arrived and gone inside, Michael sat down at the table and worked on his homework, asking her for help on math when he was trying to learn how to add. She gladly sat down and ran through each problem with him until he understood what he was doing and sent her on her way.

Kimberly headed for the kitchen to start dinner and pulled out her phone again. She'd sent Becca a few texts here and there since she'd quit, but she'd never gotten a response. This time, she hit the call button and listened as the phone rang. And rang. And rang.

Suddenly Becca's sweet voice filtered over the speaker. "Hi, you've reached Becca Kline. Leave a message, and I'll get back to you as soon as I can."

With her stomach flipping flops she didn't even know were possible, Kimberly waited until the beep echoed. Her throat was dry and her voice failed her, so she hung up. If Becca were to question it, she could play it off as a pocket dial, but she didn't want to. One glance at Michael gave her the courage to call again, this time preparing herself for what to say.

When the final ring ended and Becca's voice came over the line again, requesting her to leave a message, Kimberly swallowed and wet her lips. "Hey, I know you probably don't want to talk to me, but I really do think we need to. Please, call me back."

Hanging up, Kimberly set the phone on the counter, glancing at it every two seconds to see if Becca was calling or texting back. She was so distracted by the phone that the steak burning in the cast iron didn't register until the smoke alarm went off and Michael screamed at the top of his lungs with his hands over his ears.

Cursing, Kimberly pulled the pan off the stove then ran to grab a chair from the table, standing precariously on it to reach up and hit the button on the alarm, effectively silencing it. As soon as the blaring was done, Michael stopped screaming and uncovered his ears.

"That was loud, Mama. Don't do that again."

She gave him a wan smile, pulling her lips tightly together. After opening as many windows as possible and the front and side doors, Kimberly went back to the kitchen to survey the damage. There was no salvaging the steak. It was completely black on one side and mostly raw on the other. She picked it up carefully between her thumb and forefinger, flipping it back and forth.

"Damn it," she muttered and flopped it heavily onto the pan. "Some chef I am."

"You're a great chef," Michael interjected.

"Thanks, kiddo, but I'm not tonight. I burned dinner."

"Oh no!" Michael skittered around the island and toward the stove. "Lemme see."

She lifted him up so he could have a good view of the burned meat and her failed attempted at dinner. Her buzzing phone shook her out of her reverie. She sent Michael to go wash his hands with an intention of ordering out for dinner. She grabbed her phone, and her heart skipped a beat when she saw the caller ID.

Becca.

She answered the call, pressing it nervously to her ear.

"Hey," she said, her voice wavering with a mix of nerves, joy, excitement and fear. There was no response. Confused, Kimberly asked, "Becca?"

She could hear breathing on the other end of the line. It was light at first, but it got heavier after a few seconds. Kimberly stared down the hall to make sure Michael wasn't coming back yet. He yell-sang his favorite nursery rhyme like Becca had taught him to time how long it took him to wash his hands.

"Becca, can we talk?" Kimberly tried again.

This time, without warning, the call ended. Kimberly pulled the phone away from her ear and stared at it, not sure what to make of it. She was about to call Becca back when Michael came into the room.

She set her phone down, deciding it would be a better conversation to have in private when he wasn't around.

Instead, she got down on his level. "Kiddo, since I burned dinner, what do you say we order out?"

"Yes!" He pumped his fist up and then down, squinting his eyes with joy as he did so. "McDonald's?"

Wrinkling her nose, Kimberly shook her head. "Something a little better than that. I was thinking pasta."

"Mac 'n cheese?"

"Sure, if that's what you want."

He nodded his head. "Thanks, Mom! You're the best."

He gave her a hug and went on his way to the living room. Kimberly placed the order then waited impatiently for it to arrive and even more impatiently for Michael to go to bed. She really wanted to try to call Becca again, maybe she would answer this time.

Finally, Michael was asleep, and Kimberly retreated to her bedroom. Lying on her bed, she opened up her phone and dialed Becca's number. It rang twice before it went straight to voicemail. Determined, Kimberly dialed again. This time it only rang once before going to voicemail.

After sending a text message, Kimberly closed her eyes and rubbed her temples. Her hope of ever being able to talk to Becca again was rapidly fading. She was obviously avoiding any calls, and perhaps it was time for Kimberly to take the full hint that Becca didn't want to talk to her, didn't want to see her.

But the kiss...

Brushing her fingers over her lips, Kimberly could still taste Becca on her tongue. That kiss had been something else entirely, something she had never experienced with Becca before. Complete unrestrained, Becca had let herself go in a way she had never dared. She'd taken control, and even then, two weeks later, just the thought of the kiss and the power Becca had wielded over her made Kimberly shudder with licks of pleasure at the edges.

She was near asleep when her phone rang. Grabbing it, she saw Becca's name and pressed it to her ear after answering. On a breath, she said her name. "Becca."

"Stop calling this number."

Confused, Kimberly tensed and sat up, wide awake. The voice didn't belong to Becca, and the anger laced in the tone was beyond what she would ever imagine coming from a wrong number. "Who is this?"

"I am Becca's girlfriend. You are not. Stop calling this number."

Swallowing, Kimberly paled. Becca had told her she was with someone, and it had completely slipped her mind. Nodding to no one but herself, Kimberly finally answered. "I will. I'm sorry."

She hung up. Staring at her phone, she let out a breath before tossing it to the far corner of her bed. She rolled onto her belly, pulling the covers with her, and buried her face in the pillow. Calling Becca had been a mistake. Now not only had she risked their relationship, but she had potentially ruined a good relationship for Becca. It seemed that no matter where Becca was concerned, Kimberly couldn't stop putting her into positions that compromised Becca's integrity.

Vowing to never do it again, Kimberly lay awake in bed for the rest of the night, wishing for morning. She wanted a new start to a new day to a new life. She had to move on. Becca was obviously not interested, and even though her hope had been rekindled by the open house, she had to back off and back away.

* * * *

Something had shifted in their relationship, and Becca couldn't put her finger on it. Jessica was colder toward her. She wanted to be with her less often, and their date nights often turned into bickering before dissolving into unsatisfactory sex as a resolution.

Becca had picked up more hours at the grocery store in hopes of finally having enough to move out on her own and not have to share an apartment with Drew. That had put a severe limit on her already limited time with Jessica, and Jessica had seemed to recoil at the thought.

When Becca arrived at Jessica's house that evening, she could truly say she didn't want to be there. In any relationship, that did not bode well. Forcing herself from her car, she dragged her feet going up to Jessica's apartment, using her key to get in. Jessica sat on the couch with her laptop balanced on her knees as she read something. She barely even looked up when Becca entered.

Bending down, Becca pressed her lips to Jessica's for a greeting kiss, and it hit her. She didn't love Jessica. She'd known that for months. She'd known that pretty much since they had first started dating.

She plopped herself down onto the couch and mulled over exactly how she wanted to bring it up. Jessica had a temper, and Becca certainly didn't want to end up in an argument with her. She'd had a long couple of weeks preparing for parent-teacher conferences and working extra hours at the store. She was bone tired, not just physically but also mentally. She had hardly anything left to give.

Thinking she could perhaps push it off a few more weeks until she was in a better state of mind, one glance at Jessica told her it wouldn't be worth it. No matter how she brought it up, there would be a fight, and she would be the one who would have to hastily pack her things and leave the apartment she'd refused to move into. It had been for the best in the long run.

Deciding to head off the insanity before it began, Becca stood up and went to the bedroom. She grabbed a tote bag and put her things into it one at a time while Jessica was distracted with whatever it was she was doing out there. It took her nearly ten minutes to have everything packed.

When she went back to the living room, she set the bag down by the door and went to sit next to Jessica. "Can we talk a minute?"

"Sure, what's up?" Jessica barely took her eyes off the screen.

"No, really talk."

Jessica scrunched her nose in disgust, but she did put her computer down and turned to focus on Becca. "What?"

"This... I didn't really have this planned, but I think we both know it's time."

Confused, Jessica shook her head. "It's time?"

"For this to end. We're not... We just don't really like each other."

Sighing, Jessica crossed her arms and closed her eyes. "Yeah. We don't."

Letting out a nervous chuckle, Becca held out her palm with the apartment key in the center. "I guess you'll need this back."

"Your things," Jessica said as she took the key.

"I already packed."

"That quick?"

"You were distracted." Becca shrugged. "I thought you'd be mad."

"I'm not. I was going to wait until after your conferences to talk to you about breaking up."

"I was too, but, well, I just didn't think it'd be worth the energy to wait."

"I'm glad you didn't." Jessica gave a small smile. "Though I'm not very happy about this, I do think it's for the better."

"Agreed." Becca sat on the edge of the couch, not sure whether she should leave or stay and talk some more. She didn't really want to talk. She wanted to hide and start fresh one more time.

Jessica pressed a hand to Becca's cheek, drawing her attention back. Slowly, she leaned forward and planted a small and tender kiss on Becca's lips. "It was fun while it lasted."

"Yeah, for the most part."

Grinning, Jessica stood up and dragged Becca with her. "Do you need any help?"

"I think I've got it."

Becca grabbed her small tote of the items she had left at Jessica's over the past few months. She slung it over her shoulder and headed out of the door with an awkward goodbye on her lips. As soon as she got to her car, relief flooded her, easing a tension she'd held in her chest. That had been the right decision. No matter how much she'd wanted to avoid it, she had done well in that conversation.

The next day, she felt lighter. She felt like she was floating on air when she walked into the school, then realized suddenly that it was officially parent-teacher conferences and she wouldn't get to see her kids for four whole days. When she looked over the schedule for the day, her stomach clenched. Kimberly and Bradley had their appointment set for just before the lunch hour, no doubt so she could go to work after and he could take his lunch for it.

She was newly single, and she'd have to see Kimberly. Mentally preparing herself during the rest of the day, Becca got her papers in order and waited for the Thompson family to arrive. When they came into the room, the air whooshed out of Becca's chest. She had to pause a minute to catch her breath before they all sat down at the small tables and waded through Michael's progress for the semester.

It didn't take too long. He was doing well, though math was certainly his struggling point, along with some social issues he had with a couple of classmates. At the end of the meeting, Kimberly waited behind as Bradley scuttled off to work. Becca's heart was in her throat again as she paused to wait for what was going to happen.

"Miss Knorr, do you mind if I steal Miss Kline for a few minutes? Do you have the time?"

"We were just about to take a break for lunch, so she's all yours."

Becca's breathing became rapid. She knew this was going to be a personal conversation, so after Miss Knorr left for the lounge with her lunch, Becca locked the door behind her. She turned to Kimberly, arms across her chest, bracing herself.

"I wanted to apologize," Kimberly started.

"A-apologize for what?" Becca stammered. This was twice in as many days that Becca was left confused and lost with the conversation. First she'd expected anger and hurt from Jessica and now a full apology from Kimberly? She had no idea what axis the world had turned on to give her these unexpected outcomes.

"For calling and texting and not giving you space and not respecting your boundaries. I shouldn't have done that, and I'm truly sorry."

"Oh." Her stomach fluttered. "Well, thank you. I appreciate that."

Awkward tension filled the space between them, and Becca silently begged Kimberly to leave her alone. She wasn't sure what to do with this new side of her. Kimberly stepped forward, but Becca tensed, and she stopped. Becca decided to put one foot forward and let her know how she truly felt—well, mostly.

"Look... I know whatever between us isn't exactly gone. But I already lost one job because of you. I am not willing to lose a second. I need this position."

Putting up both hands, Kimberly stepped away. "And I respect that, truly I do. I want you to graduate. In fact, if you'll let me, I'd love to be at your graduation. I want you to succeed in this. You've dreamed about it for decades."

Becca's breathing hitched as her nerves took over. She worried that if Kimberly came any closer, they would end up in the same position they had the other week. As much as she wanted that, she didn't at the same time. She had to put up the shield she'd created, and she had to keep it in place.

"I have," Becca finally responded. "I don't want anything to jeopardize that."

"I will respect your decision."

Becca's chest heaved.

"I guess I'll see you around then, probably at drop-off and pick-up only." Without another word, Kimberly spun on her toes and headed for the door, unlocking it and escaping.

Becca let out a breath she hadn't known she was holding. She leaned against the counter and melted as all the tension raced from her body. After months of avoiding each other, it seemed as if they had finally made a truce. Perhaps this time it would last.

Organizing her paperwork to keep her hands busy, Becca scarfed down her home-made lunch then busied herself as she waited for Miss Knorr to come back. It didn't take long, as they'd scheduled the appointments close together to get them done faster.

The rest of the day she spent in conferences, talking about the students she had come to love so much over the course of a few very short months. As soon as she was released, exhaustion hit her like a frying pan. She drove back to Drew's apartment and collapsed on the couch. Two hours later, Drew came in and shook her foot to wake her. Becca groaned and turned on her side so Drew could sit down by her feet. When she pried an eye open to look at them, they stared straight at her.

"You gonna tell me whatever it is that happened that has you less stressed? I know it's not just conferences."

Nodding, Becca answered, "First, Jessica and I broke up."

"Yes!" Drew jumped up and did a happy dance. Becca rolled her eyes but stayed plastered to the couch. "I did not like that bitch one bit."

"I know," Becca said wryly. "It was for the better. It was pretty much mutual."

"Oh good." Drew sat down and rubbed her leg up and down. "If that was the first, what's the second? Is there a third?"

"Just a second."

"Well?" Drew prompted when Becca didn't continue.

"Well, what?"

"Spill it already."

Chuckling, Becca turned on her back. "I talked to Kimberly."

"You did?" Drew gave her a sly grin and wiggled their eyebrows up and down. "Talked like you did at open house?"

"No." She glared. "We actually talked. Kind of. Well, I talked. I told her I was not going to lose this job over her, so she had to back off."

"Damn! Proud of you, sugar."

Rolling her eyes, Becca snuggled into her blanket, exhaustion seeping through her. "I feel like I can finally catch my breath."

"I bet you do." Drew trailed fingers up and down Becca's back in a soothing motion.

It had been a good week, even though it had been busy, and she wasn't sure she'd ever catch up on her sleep again. She'd done what she wanted, accomplished what she'd needed, and life finally felt like it was clicking into place. With Drew sitting next to her, it wasn't long before Becca found herself back asleep in the comfort of her best friend's home.

Chapter Twenty

She'd signed up to teach in the classroom for one day and had been agonizing over it for the previous two weeks. It was stupid. Kimberly was not a teacher, and she certainly wasn't a parent who entirely enjoyed small children either. Michael was the exception to the rule. Other than that, she wanted nothing to do with small kids running amok.

In the midst of her crisis of working every waking hour to avoid thinking about Becca, she had agreed to teach the kids in Michael's class how to make Thanksgiving cookies. It'd been a month or so since the open house, and she and Becca had managed to keep everything very professional, but now they'd be stuck in a classroom in close quarters together for hours.

Her nerves had been on high alert since she'd agreed to the project. Apparently, it had been Becca's idea, since in class they had been talking all about different Thanksgiving traditions. Sighing, Kimberly loaded up the supplies she needed into the back of her SUV and headed for the school. She was supposed to arrive at lunch and set up while the kids were eating, then bake with them for most of the afternoon.

It would all happen in the span of two or three hours — ones when she'd be very close to Becca and she'd have to be on her best behavior. As she slid behind the driver's seat, panic set in. She started the ignition and focused on driving as carefully as possible, still avoiding what she'd agreed to as best as she could.

Once parked, Kimberly had no other option. She pulled the tote of supplies from the back of her car and hit the button under the bumper with her foot to have the rear door shut. She waddled, carrying the heavy tote with both hands, to Michael's classroom. Luckily, the door opened just as she was about to reach it, Becca holding it open for her as she entered.

"Is that everything, or do you have more in your car?"

"This is it," Kimberly answered. She set the tote down onto one of the tables and stretched out her back. "Remind me next time to make two trips. That was a bit much."

"Gladly." Becca flashed her a wide grin while she turned to pull out the items they needed. "I figure we'll have the kids mix and what-not at the tables. Then we can set up the cookie sheets back here where I can run them to and from the ovens."

"Sounds good." Kimberly thinned her lips, not quite wanting to tell Becca she'd already thought this through — well, more than three dozen times. They were going to have close to sixty dozen cookies to make, but they could do it. "I have two kinds of cookies for the kids. Pumpkin snickerdoodles and some sugar cookies with candy for decorations. We'll do the sugar cookies first, then the pumpkin ones, then we can decorate while the pumpkin ones cook then pack them up for the kids to take them home."

"That's a lot." Becca eyed the room like she was debating if it was achievable.

"I know, but I think it's doable. The decoration will keep them entertained while they wait for the pumpkin cookies to come out, and it only took Michael about thirty minutes to make them without assistance."

Becca shrugged. "I guess. They'll have fun either way."

"Yes, they will. Did you happen to clean the desks yet?" After Becca nodded, Kimberly grabbed the measuring cups she had brought and set them out at each pair of tables, where two students would be working together. She'd brought sixteen sets of everything. Becca picked up what she was doing and followed suit, setting everything at the tables so it was all ready to go.

Kimberly then evenly divided the flour and different sugars into smaller containers for each grouping of tables to use and set them next to the measuring cups. That way they could still measure to learn but it wouldn't be a fight over one giant bag, and they wouldn't have too much extra to make messes. She took out the first grouping of small containers she'd gotten from Gamma's and put them on each table as well. Each one held the small dry ingredients such as baking soda and salt.

She was pleased with how she'd managed to plan it all out and make it so that it would work easily for a bunch of five- and six-year-olds. The bell ringing surprised her, and she jumped. Becca grinned at her. "It took me months to get used to that, and it still surprises me sometimes. The kids should be coming back, so we only have a few more minutes of quiet."

"All right." Kimberly hurried her pace to finish setting out the items they would need. "Will you have all the kids wash their hands before they sit down?"

"Absolutely."

"Good." Kimberly put her hands on her hips and surveyed the classroom. "I think we're set then."

Becca nodded as Miss Knorr opened the door with a line of students behind her. Becca didn't hesitate and stepped right up to give directions to the kids. She moved over to the head of the line and clapped her hands once, then twice. The kids copied her, and once she had all their attention, she spoke.

"Now, remember when I told you we had a special guest coming to teach us something this afternoon? Well, she is here, but before you sit down, I need you to do two things for me. I need you to get in a line and each of you wash your hands very well, then when you sit down, do not touch anything at your desk."

"Yes, Miss Kline," Kimberly heard as the students eagerly tried to look around her into the room.

As soon as Becca let the kids inside, Kimberly could hear the *ooo's* and *ahhh's* as they saw what was about to happen. Michael waved at her as he entered but dutifully stayed in his line to wash his hands at the sink in the back of the room. Kimberly's stomach twisted again, but she knew when she focused on the cookies and not on Becca, she would be in better shape and not as nervous.

Once all the students were seated, Becca gave her a small introduction then let Kimberly take it from there. Miss Knorr sat in the back corner of the classroom at her desk, observing and taking notes. Kimberly knew that as soon as they got into the actual baking, she was likely to join in the fray.

"Hey, everyone. As Miss Kline said, I am a chef, and what that means is when you go out to eat at a restaurant, I'm the one in the back, cooking up your food. You don't see chefs a lot because we're always in the kitchen, but we're there working on whatever it is you ordered to eat. Miss Kline asked me here today to teach you all how to bake some cookies for Thanksgiving. I know in a lot of families we have big feasts with lots of family and friends who come over to share in one big meal, right?" The kids nodded their heads. "Well, this is one of the things we like to eat in our family. We like to eat cookies. How many of you like cookies?"

Hands shot into the air.

"Then let's get started, because I'm not sure I can wait any longer to make cookies. We're going to make two kinds today, one you can decorate and one is just really good and my favorite. Let's start with the first one."

They spent the next forty minutes making sugar cookies. There was flour and sugar almost everywhere, but Kimberly was smiling and so was Becca when she risked a glance in her direction. Once they had the sugar cookies in circles and on parchment paper, Kimberly dragged them off to the sheet pans to prepare for baking. She wrote each kid's name on the paper associated with the ones they'd made so she could bring them back later.

Becca took the cookies to the ovens while Kimberly helped the kids clean up then set up for the next round. She had them come up to her two at a time and grab the necessary items. Once everyone was in place, Kimberly explained the directions one at a time. As she explained, the kids followed her instructions and added the right items in the right order.

All in all, everything went as planned. Once the kids were down to rolling the dough in the sugar and pressing them down with their tiny fists, Kimberly was ready to be done. She was just setting up the next rolling cart for Becca to take when she came back with the first cookies still warm.

Kimberly helped the kids clean up, then set out the candy corn for the feathers, the edible eyes and some frosting to glue everything on. She unloaded the cookies on the correct tables and let the kids have at it in their own decorating style after showing them a few of her and Michael's examples. When Becca came back with the pumpkin snickerdoodles, the kids were done decorating and starting the process of packing up their cookies in the to-go containers Kimberly had brought.

With all the baking said and done, Kimberly glanced at the clock to realize that the school day was about finished. Becca stood in front of the class and clapped her hands to get their attention. Once they all repeated her claps — this time it took her up to five — Becca smiled.

"We've got to clean up, you guys, and our time is running short! You know what that means? It means we need to be efficient. Who can tell me what 'efficient' means?"

One small girl raised her hand.

"Victoria."

"It means we have to work really well and really good and fast."

"Yes, but not super-fast. We don't want to accidentally make an even bigger mess, do we?" She shook her head. "Right, so I want you to each grab a washcloth and clean up your tables and your chairs. Wash your hands too, if you need to. Don't worry about the floor."

The kids moved swiftly and in order. Kimberly was in awe of the command Becca had over them. They listened to her so easily. Becca cleaned up what she could with the utensils Kimberly had brought, but Kimberly stopped her. "I'll just take them home and do it there."

"Are you sure?"

"Yeah. Rather, I'll take it to Gamma's and have the dishwashers do it. I pay them enough as it is, and all this stuff is from there anyway."

Becca laughed. "I guess that makes sense."

Kimberly piled the dirty bowls, measuring cups, whisks, spatulas and leftover ingredients back into her tote. Before she was done, the bell rang and the students all looked at Becca.

"If your table is clean, you may grab your backpack and head out to your parents, the bus or the playground to wait."

It was as if she had said magic words. The energy in the room doubled, and the kids were everywhere. As soon as they were all gone except for Michael, Kimberly sighed. The room was eerily quiet. Miss Knorr stood up. "I have bus duty, so I'm going to have to leave you to clean up."

"I'll see you in a bit," Becca answered as she waved her off.

Michael tugged on Kimberly's shirt to get her attention. When she looked down at him, he smiled. "Can I go play until you're done?"

"Yes, you may. Thank you for asking so nicely."

He beelined it for the door and stopped short when he heard Becca correct him to walk. After that, he took long steps to get to the playground faster, but steps that would still be considered walking. When Kimberly turned back around, her stomach dropped. Becca was like a whole different person in this classroom. She was confident and strong in ways she hadn't seen before. It suited her.

Surprised, Kimberly grabbed a washcloth to help re-clean the tables the kids had finished, making sure all the sugar and flour were gone. With her hands wet on the table, she looked up to find Becca staring at her. As soon as their gazes met, Becca looked back at the floor and she blushed pink. Oddly enough, Kimberly found herself satisfied at the reaction.

It made her feel wanted. Pushing her feelings aside, Kimberly finished with the desks and moved on to the floor. Carpet and baking did not mix, and she spent the next thirty minutes just trying to get the sugar out of the short blue carpet that seemed standard in a lot of public spaces. Eventually, Becca came over and laughed lightly.

"You'll never get it all out, so you might as well give up."

"I'm determined."

"I know you are." Becca put a hand on Kimberly's, stilling her furious vacuuming. Then she reached down and turned the machine off. "I know you are, but you're still not going to get it all out of there."

"I can certainly try." Kimberly set her jaw and straightened her back, knowing she wasn't going to win this battle, but also not quite sure they were still talking about vacuuming.

Becca gave her a sweet smile, but there was a hint of sadness to it. Kimberly cocked her head, trying to read as deeply into the look as she could. She wanted to know what was going on inside that smart brain of hers. Becca stepped forward, their hands still connected, and pressed a very gentle and sweet kiss to Kimberly's lips, humming when she pulled back with her eyes closed.

"I can finish up here so you can take Michael home. I know he's bound to get bored as soon as all the other students are gone."

Kimberly wanted to reject the notion. She wanted to stay, to be in the same room as Becca even longer, but she got the feeling the request was not negotiable. She wanted to respect Becca's decisions about her own life and that this was her place of work. Nodding, Kimberly stepped away from the vacuum, leaving it in Becca's hands.

She gathered the rest of her supplies, holding the tote tightly with both her hands. With her back against the door to push it open, she stared directly at Becca who had watched her the entire time. "I'll see you around then."

"See you," Becca answered with that same sweet and confusing smile.

Backing out of the classroom, Kimberly left.

* * * *

Becca sat down on the couch in a haze. Drew was already home, surprisingly, and cooking up something in the kitchen that smelled delicious. She ignored it as she tried her best to wipe the smile off her face but couldn't. Drew eventually came to sit next to her, shooing her feet off the side so they could sit together comfortably.

"What's got you so happy?" Drew asked.

"Nothing," Becca replied, trying to keep her joy hidden—but it was futile. She was too happy to contain it. She flushed and half-laughed, unable to avoid what she felt.

"No, really, what's got you so up?"

Becca shrugged. "Just a really good day at school."

Drew narrowed their eyes at her, studying. "Was today cookie day?"

The smile wiped from Becca's face as she stared at Drew directly.

"I knew it! So it went that well?"

"It finally felt like we could be in the same room as each other without all the tension and heartache and pain, without all the weird boundary issues we've had."

"And?"

"And what?" Becca said, the grin returning to her face. She wanted to tell them, but at the same time, she didn't. They would take it the wrong way and tease her endlessly about how she had never given up hope on a relationship with Kimberly—which she hadn't. The timing had been wrong.

Drew turned to face her fully. "There's something else keeping that smile on your face. What happened, sugar?"

Taking a deep breath, Becca grinned again. "I'm sorry. It was just a really good day."

"You kissed her. Again!"

Becca's face fell. "How did you know?"

"Oh my God! You did kiss her? I should have known! I was just guessing to see if I could get it out of you. You kissed her? In the classroom? Like in front of the kids?"

"No! No one was there, not in front of the kids. We were cleaning up. It had been such a good day. She respected the boundaries I had put into place. I respected hers."

"Except you kissed her."

"Yeah, well, I don't think she minded much."

"Oooo..." Drew raised their eyebrows up and down. "Do tell."

Becca leaned back onto the couch even more, glancing down at her hands then out of the window. "It wasn't anything special, just a quick peck. But for the first time, it really felt right."

Drew grinned.

Becca narrowed her gaze at them, trying to figure out what had gotten them so smitten. "What?"

"You're in love."

She rolled her eyes. "Well, that's not new."

"I— What?"

Becca stood up to head to the kitchen, but Drew was hot on her heels.

"Wait. You can't just say that then run away. What do you mean that's not new?"

"I think I've loved her for a long time. I just— I wanted to make sure it was real love and not just infatuation or her trying to wrangle me into anything."

"You really think you're that malleable that someone can wrangle you into a relationship?"

"Yeah, you're right. That didn't make sense." Snorting, Becca lifted the lid on the pot to smell whatever it was Drew had going underneath it. "This smells amazing. What is it?"

"Squirrel stew. Stop. Tell me what you mean by *'this isn't new'*."

Sighing, Becca put the lid back down and crossed her arms over her chest. "I think you know as much as I do how long I have loved Kimberly."

"Yes, but you never said anything."

"Because I didn't want to admit it. She was my boss. I was so infatuated with her that I couldn't think straight enough to even recognize my own feelings. That's why I quit and pretty much ran here. It wasn't right to be in a relationship with her. It didn't feel right on so many levels, while on others it felt perfect."

"But you're her son's teacher right now."

"And we're not in a relationship right now." She cocked her head and grinned. "That boundary issue isn't an issue at the moment."

Drew raised one delicately plucked eyebrow. "No, you're just making out in dark corners every chance you get."

"We did not make out today." Pointing on finger at Drew and wagging it up and down, she narrowed her eyes and lifted her chin. "We had one simple very nice kiss. That was it—like you'd kiss your mom."

"Sugar"—Drew raised one dutiful eyebrow even higher—"you do not kiss someone you love like you would kiss your mom, no matter how platonic it is."

"You're right, bad example. We did not make out today."

"But you did kiss."

"Yes."

"So you are in a relationship."

"No."

"I'm confused." Drew put a hand to their head and plopped down at the kitchen table. They turned back to look at her, head still in their hand. "So you love her, but you are not in a relationship with her."

"Correct."

"And you want to be in a relationship with her?" Hope slipped into Drew's voice.

Becca shook her head. "No. Not at this time."

"What?" Drew's head smacked down onto the table once and then twice. "This is why I don't date women. You don't make any sense."

"Same could be said about men." Becca came around and sat across from them. "Or gender queer. People are just confusing. I am her son's teacher, and until that changes, I will not consider a relationship with her. However, we kind of already tried the relationship thing, and we all saw how that turned out. Not good. I'm not sure I want to put myself in that position again. I like where I'm at. I'm enjoying life. I love teaching, I love my kids and I want to stay here for as long as I can. I want to continue to be a teacher and make that a priority in my life."

"But you love her?" Drew asked, although it didn't completely sound like a question.

"Yes. Or at least, I did at some point fall in love with her. I don't know whether or not I am still in love with her, but I will always love and respect and admire her. She's an amazingly strong woman who has pulled her life out of the shitter and made it the best she can for her and Michael."

"Oh God."

"What?" Becca asked.

"Don't tell me you're going to get up on your high horse and not date her because you think she'll be better off without you."

Shaking her head, Becca laughed. "That's not what I'm saying. What I'm saying is not right now, and I don't know about when yet — or if ever. We'll have to wait and see what happens before that decision is made."

"You're just going to die lonely, sleeping on my couch."

Chuckling, Becca patted their arm and got up again. "Is this done yet?"

"Yeah."

"Good. I need something hearty after cookies all afternoon."

She served up two bowls of whatever it was Drew had made. Becca was sure it wasn't squirrel stew, as much as Drew insisted it was. Settling into their normal banter, she relaxed, ready for the weekend to give her a break from her crazy routine.

Chapter Twenty-One

Her last day teaching was just before Thanksgiving, and the students threw her a party to send her off. All she had left were her finals with her one other class and the evaluation Miss Knorr would give her and she'd be done. She'd be a teacher. She'd have her degree, and her life would be on track.

Becca picked up as many hours as she could at the grocery store over the holiday break, racking up as much overtime as she could. They were glad for the help during the busy season. December first came quickly enough, and she was in the process of applying for teaching positions at local schools. It wasn't the greatest time to apply for jobs, as the school year was already halfway through, but she hoped someone would be leaving unexpectedly and she'd have the opportunity to slip in and finish out the school year.

She'd spent hours and hours filling out applications, so much so that it made her head spin. When a very proud Drew showed up at home with a small

Thanksgiving feast under their arm in a take-out bag, Becca laughed. She dug into the food, sighing as it hit her hungry belly. Drew happily chattered about work that day while Becca listened, only half paying attention as her mind swirled through what other schools in the area she could apply for. Moving home was not an option. She loved her mother dearly, but they could not live under the same roof again.

Drew gave up trying to distract her and instead asked all sorts of questions about her day. Becca laughed and leaned back in her chair. "Well, I had the weirdest dream last night."

"Oh?"

"Yeah. One of the perks of working at a grocery store during the Thanksgiving holiday, I bet. I had a dream that I was standing at my register, and there was just turkey after turkey after turkey that I had to scan. One after the other. No end in sight. Nothing. There were no customers, just the damn turkeys going by on my scanner one after the next."

Drew snorted. "That's bad."

"Yeah. It was bad. Woke me up out of a dead sleep for sure."

"Sounds more like a nightmare."

Chuckling, Becca agreed. "Yeah, let's call it a nightmare." She took another forkful of turkey and gravy and shoved it into her mouth. "And I just owned the turkey after that nightmare."

Letting out a roar, Drew brushed fingers under their eyes and wiped away nonexistent tears. "That was too far, now."

"Too far, but so worth it."

Drew rolled their eyes and went back to focusing on the food on the table. It wasn't the greatest

Thanksgiving meal, but since both of them had needed to work that day, it was better than nothing. Becca knew meals like this would be in her life for a long time.

"Any job offers?" Drew asked.

"No. I don't expect any for a few more weeks, anyway. No one is really focused on hiring during the holidays. I'll substitute in the meantime, if I need to."

"True enough." Drew went back to eating.

They sat in silence for a few minutes before the knock at the door disrupted them. Frowning, Becca shrugged and got up to see who it was. When she opened the door to find Kimberly standing outside in the light rain, surprise ran through her.

"What are you doing here?" Becca asked, pretty sure Kimberly hadn't even known where Drew lived.

"I — I needed to talk."

Rain droplets clung to Kimberly's dark brown hair, and Becca grabbed her hand to drag her inside and out of the weather. She shut the door and locked it, spinning around on her toes. "It's Thanksgiving."

"I know. I'm sorry. Are you — Are you busy with dinner? I can leave. This was stupid. I'm sorry."

Kimberly made for the door, but Becca grabbed her hand to stop her. "No. We were eating, but it's just the two of us with take-out. Nothing fancy. Did something happen to Michael?"

"No." Kimberly let out a breath and shook her head. "No, nothing like that. Michael's fine. He's — He's at his dad's for the first time ever on Thanksgiving, and it made me think, and well, you know me, thinking isn't the greatest thing to happen in the twenty-first century."

"Who is it?" Drew called from the kitchen.

Becca glanced at Kimberly with a questioning gaze, wondering if she should share. When Kimberly nodded, Becca called back. "My old boss... Remember the one where you puked all night in her bathroom?"

"Oh, that one," Drew said saucily.

Becca knew with her not-so-gentle reminder about that night that Drew would stay far away in the kitchen, too embarrassed to peek their head around the corner and see either one of them. With that settled, Becca focused on Kimberly. She was still damp from the rain, but it was soaking into her clothes and hair now. She was dressed simply in tight black leggings with cats on the knees and a simple green shirt that brought out the color of her eyes even more.

If anything, the simplicity of how she typically dressed made her that much more accessible. It was never any wonder why she succeeded so well in her television career, excluding her amazing ability to cook and to do so under pressure. Becca brought her gaze back to Kimberly's face, noting the uncertainty still reaching Kimberly's eyes and wanting to put her at ease as much as possible.

"Right, so what brought you here? Well, first, how did you even know where 'here' was?"

Kimberly looked over Becca's shoulder into the kitchen before glancing back at Becca. "Had some help."

"Oh." Becca's lips formed a perfect circle. She turned to look in the direction Drew sat and shook her head. "I'll deal with them later. What are you doing here?"

"I— I wanted to talk to you. Is there somewhere we could go that's private?"

Thinking for a second, Becca tossed a look over her shoulder at Drew's bedroom. It was the only other

room in the apartment besides the kitchen where Drew
was currently stashed away. Shrugging, Becca nodded
in the direction.

"There's the bedroom or there's a car, your choice."

"Bedroom. The rain was picking up pretty good."

"Okay." Becca took two steps to the kitchen
doorway and put on her serious face. "We're going to
steal your room for a minute. Don't you dare come in
there, and don't you double dare listen in on our
conversation."

"Sure... All you'll be doing is conversing," Drew
muttered under their breath.

"Drew!" Becca responded as a warning, her voice
low.

"I won't. I swear. I'll sit here with my cold turkey
and gravy and eat it."

"Good." Becca turned back to Kimberly and looked
down at the ground. "Sorry about that.
They're...they're ornery today, to say the least."

"It's okay. We're kind of taking over their space.
That can't feel normal or good."

"Yeah. Anyway, it's right through here."

Becca led Kimberly into the room and flipped on the
lights. As soon as Kimberly stepped all the way in, she
shut the door. The loud click sent a stab of fear straight
to her heart. Normally, when the two of them were in a
closed room together, clothes came off rapidly.

Becca anchored her feet to the ground, put her arms
over her chest in a protective manner and stared
directly at the back of Kimberly's head. Breaking the
ice, she started, "What's going on, Kimberly?"

Kimberly spun around. Her face fell, probably at
Becca's stance, and Becca felt a moment of remorse but
decided her plan was better.

"I—I just… I don't know even know where to start," Kimberly confessed.

"Start at the beginning."

"The beginning? Okay. The beginning. I was drunk, so were you." Kimberly pointed a finger at herself then at Becca.

"Oh." Realization dawned on Becca. She sat heavily on Drew's bed, waiting for the onslaught of emotions to catch up with her, like it always did when she thought about her relationship with Kimberly and the rollercoaster that it was. Her defenses had been knocked down with one swift mention of the past, and she was left broken open for the woman who had taken her apart one brick at a time. "*That* beginning."

"Yes, *that* beginning." Kimberly hissed slightly but then sat down next to Becca. "I can't stop thinking about *that* beginning."

"Neither can I," Becca admitted. "But I don't really want to think about it either."

"Same here," Kimberly confessed. She wrung her hands together in her lap, and Becca reached over to place her hand gently on top to soothe the motions. "But I can't stop."

"I know."

"You're not teaching Michael anymore."

"I know."

Becca's heart rate picked up. It didn't take a genius to figure out where the conversation was going. Becca had hoped for more time before it came up. Between working overtime and applying for jobs like it was a full-time job in and of itself, she hadn't thought about what to do with Kimberly more than her daydreaming had let her. And there had been a lot of daydreaming.

"So…that means this can be on the table again, right?" Kimberly tentatively asked.

"I don't know." Becca gave her a longing and conflicted look. She wanted to be as honest as she could this time around. She wanted to talk rather than just walking out with everything unsaid. Turning slightly to face Kimberly even more, Becca pressed a hand to her cheek. Kimberly immediately turned her head in that direction. "I don't know, and that's the best answer I can give you right now."

"Okay." Nodding, Kimberly straightened her back. "Okay, but just…just one thing."

"What's that?"

Kimberly's mouth on hers was hot. Becca closed her eyes and slid into the sensations Kimberly caused, rippling through her body. Kimberly's fingernails scraped up her scalp, sending shivers along her spine. Becca whined as she listed closer. She pressed her hand into the mattress to hold herself up as Kimberly had her way with her.

Drawing in a deep breath, Becca leaned into Kimberly's body and braced herself for the onslaught of emotions to hit her. It did every time they were together like this. Becca closed her eyes and focused on the sensations Kimberly caused to ricochet up her spine. When their tongues touched, Becca moaned. She shifted slightly to have a better angle at holding herself as close to Kimberly as she could.

With an arm pressed around Kimberly's back, Becca melted into the kiss. She relaxed and let Kimberly take the control Becca knew she very well could. She enjoyed it, even, allowing Kimberly to take command, but there was something in the far reaches of her mind that kept her from letting go completely.

Kimberly leaned back, tugging Becca with her. Becca covered Kimberly's body. Pushing up, she cupped Kimberly's cheek and grinned. This felt right, so unlike her time with Jessica. But that niggling feeling lingered. Ignoring it, Becca dove into Kimberly, burying her fear in soft lips and gorgeous curves.

Kissing a line down Kimberly's neck, Becca stopped when she hit the soft cloth of her shirt. She moved back up, kissing around her jaw to her ear then to her mouth. As soon as their lips touched, Kimberly reached for Becca's shirt and tugged it up. She scraped her nails lightly down Becca's back, and Becca pressed her hips into Kimberly's.

When Kimberly reached up to Becca's bra, Becca's heart thudded hard. She pushed herself up and away to break their embrace. Heaving breaths left her lungs as she stared wildly down at the woman below her. After a few long seconds, Kimberly pushed herself to sit up and reached for Becca's cheek, but Becca turned her head away to avoid the touch.

"Wait...just wait." Becca let out a breath, tensing her shoulders.

Respectfully, Kimberly didn't reach for Becca again. Taking the time she was given, Becca drew in a deep breath and closed her eyes in an attempt to clear her thoughts and figure out exactly what she was thinking and feeling. Becca turned to Kimberly, staring at her with what she felt was as much emotion as she could muster.

"I need time," Becca confessed. "I just need some time."

"You've had a lot of time," Kimberly countered. "I've been waiting and waiting. If this isn't what you want, tell me now."

"I-I can't answer that." Becca put her hands together in her lap tightly.

Kimberly hit her hand down on the mattress and lifted her chin. "I'm not going to wait around forever."

"I know." Looking down at her entwined fingers, Becca was lost. She felt completely alone, as though she were the one ruining whatever semblance of a relationship they had left. "I just need a little more time."

"I don't know what to say." Kimberly stood up and straightened her clothes. "I'll give you the time, but you're going to have to come to me, and I won't wait around much longer. You've given me hope again in having a relationship, and I think... I think I would like that in my life, for me and for Michael. It's a much better balance for me."

Becca nodded. Kimberly left the room without another word. The front door shut, and Becca watched her from the window as she got into her dark SUV and pulled out of the small parking lot with quite a bit of force on the gas pedal. She let out a breath she hadn't known she was holding as soon as Kimberly's car disappeared from view.

Drew came into the room and sat next to her on the bed, their mood oddly somber compared to what it normally was. "And here I thought you two were getting hot and heavy in my bed."

Rolling her eyes and shaking her head, Becca refused to look at them. "Not in the slightest."

"You sure? I could hear some heavy panting from the door."

Narrowing her gaze, Becca pursed her lips. "That is gross. And I told you not to listen in."

"I didn't, but thanks for answering my unasked question."

"You told her where we live?"

Drew shrugged then nodded sheepishly.

"You're an ass."

"Yes, and a mighty fine one at that." They grinned and winked at Becca. "You want to talk about it?"

"I don't know. I just don't know anymore." When Becca turned to Drew, tears brimmed in her eyes and fear took over.

Drew held out an arm for her, and she snuggled into their side, sighing a breath of relief at their familiar scent of honeysuckle and aftershave. They stroked fingers through her hair and kissed the side of her head, allowing Becca time to breathe and center herself again.

After about an hour, Drew shifted and looked Becca straight in the face. "Why are you so afraid to love her?"

"I'm not."

"Okay, sugar. Better question. Why are you so afraid to let her love you?"

Becca whimpered as Drew hit the nail on the head. "I don't know."

"It's not like you've had bad experiences or something. So be honest, what's really holding you back?"

Shaking her head, Becca snuggled into Drew. She wanted to hide even more and avoid answering Drew's questions. They were the same questions that had been running through her mind for months. What was she so afraid of?

"What did you tell her?"

"That I needed time."

"That was stupid." Drew sat straight up and about knocked her off the bed. "So stupid. She is not going to wait around, Becca. If you want her, you have to jump now and not look back. Answer me this. Can you live without her?"

Becca's breath hitched. The word was on the tip of her tongue, but she couldn't bring herself to say it. She couldn't bear to hear the word. Fear ran rampant in her heart and she struggled to breathe. Drew wasn't letting her off the hook. They waited patiently for the answer.

Shaking her head, Becca whispered, "No. I don't want to."

"Then there is your answer. Stop being so stupid about it and go get her."

"I can't."

"Becca!" The frustration rang clear. "You have got to stop playing games with this poor woman's heart. If you want her, go get her. If you don't, then tell her. But stop being so mopey about it and *do* something."

Becca shot up out of the bed and cut her hand across the air to tell Drew to stop. She panted as she stared at them. "I don't want to talk about it."

"You never want to talk about it. You always avoid it, and it's time to stop. It has been nine months of this shit. Stop. Just stop. It didn't work out with Jessica, but Kimberly? There is something different about her. You know that and I know that. It's been this way from the beginning. Remember? Remember all those months ago when you came hiding out here over the weekend because you were scared to death because you had a crush on your boss? Since when has a crush ever been scary? Yeah. It started then. Kimberly was always different. I have never seen you act like this with anyone else. So get off the freakin' scared wagon and get back on her — literally. You need to get laid."

Letting out a wry laugh, Becca rubbed her temple. All the emotions swirled around her heart and belly. She plopped down on the bed, her energy leaving her. "You're right. Not about me getting laid — well, maybe about that — but you're right about the rest. I need to remember that, remember it before all the complications."

"You just scared yourself for no reason."

Smiling, Becca nodded. "Yeah. Again, you're right."

"So...? Does this mean I get to be the flower girl?"

Scoffing, Becca punched them lightly in the arm. "Don't go getting ahead of yourself now."

"Come on! I've always wanted to be the flower girl."

Becca chuckled and laid back in their bed, staring at the ceiling. "I'm really going to do this, aren't I?"

Drew lay down next to her, grasping her hand and squeezing tight. "You are, and you are going to love it. I promise you. It is about damn time. That whole thing with Jessica was just stupid, too. You've been doing a lot of stupid lately."

"Shut it. Like you're one to talk with taking E."

Drew paled. "Yeah, that was stupid."

Their voice wavered, and Becca caught it. She turned on her side, resting her head on her palm as she stared at her best friend. Secrets filtered over their face. She touched their chest briefly and gently.

"It was just the once, right?"

"Uh...yeah. Just the once."

"Drew!"

"What? I didn't bring it home like you asked."

She rolled her eyes and sat up. "Drew, how often?"

"Not often."

"Drew. Don't you dare lie to me."

"Not often."

"What is 'not often' to you?"

They balked. They rolled off the bed and stood straight. "This is my apartment, Becca. I'll do as I damn well please in it."

"Yes, you can. But this isn't about your apartment. This is about your wellbeing. How often, Drew?"

"I don't have to answer that."

"You don't. You're right. I'll just leave you to your own demise then."

Storming out of the bedroom, Becca slammed the door behind her. Suddenly the apartment felt small, too small. She grabbed her jacket and went for a walk outside in the soft rain. She had to get out. Drew was right about her and Kimberly, but now her fear shifted away from her relationship troubles to her best friend and the odd drug habit they were hiding.

By the time she got back to the apartment, the lights were off. She debated whether or not to sleep in her car for the night but decided against it. Their neighborhood was far from safe. While she couldn't solve Drew's problem for them, she could certainly solve her own love problem and perhaps finally get a place of her own to stay. Sighing, she headed inside and crawled under the covers on the couch, sure that she wouldn't be sleeping any time soon.

Chapter Twenty-Two

She and Drew had avoided each other for the rest of the week. Becca had finished out her finals, worked overtime and finished even more applications. Drew had barely come home. She knew she'd outstayed her welcome and looked at apartments for rent she could potentially afford, but she really needed a teaching job first. It was going to be tight on her grocery store budget, but she could make it if she cut a lot of other corners.

Receiving her final evaluation from Miss Knorr set her plan in motion. She skimmed it over, pleased to see it was a relatively positive evaluation and that it might even secure her a position in the future. Setting her computer aside, Becca glanced at her watch, noting Kimberly would most likely be getting ready for work in the next few hours, so she had the time to talk.

Getting in her car, Becca put it into gear and drove the familiar route to Kimberly's large house up on the hills just outside of LA. She parked in the driveway and let out a breath. She was perhaps more nervous than she had been when she'd shown up for her first day of work at Kimberly Thompson's house.

Bolstering herself, Becca got out of the car and went to the dark-wooded French doors. She took a deep breath and let it out before she reached out to ring the doorbell. The sound echoed through the house, and her heart caught in her throat. She heard Michael shout and smiled to herself. Seeing him again was an unexpected and happy benefit of coming to see Kimberly.

When Michael pulled open the door, he screamed and ran straight into her outstretched arms. He clung on tightly, and she rubbed his back and bent down to smell his hair, reminding herself of why she was there. Kimberly came around the corner, her bare feet on the tile floor and a dish rag in her hands as she dried them. She stopped short as she caught sight of Becca, a small smile tugging at the corner of her lips.

"Michael, stand back and let the woman in already."

He jumped away from Becca, keeping his hand firmly around hers as he dragged her into the house. "I miss you at school! You have to come see these new action figures Mom got me. Here."

Michael dragged her down the hallway as fast as he could. Becca sent a look over her shoulder at Kimberly, who shrugged and followed them. As soon as they got to his room, he dropped her hand and dug around in a toy box for whatever he was looking for.

He threw out a few items onto the floor, but when he found the toys, he tugged Becca's hand again until she was seated next to him, cross-legged. "Look. I got Iron Man and Spider-Man. They fight the bad guys who are coming to take over the world."

"Really? How bad are they?" Becca asked. When she glanced up at Kimberly, she was leaning against the doorframe, smiling at the two of them.

"Really bad," he answered, his eyes wide with the seriousness of the situation.

Becca chuckled and grabbed the Spider-Man figurine he offered her. She played with his arms and his legs, making them move in different directions. Michael then took it back out of her hands and set the two action figures next to each other so they could battle it out.

When Becca looked back at the door, Kimberly was gone. She spent the next hour focusing on Michael and rekindling their relationship in a way she hadn't been able to for months. She'd missed this — the simple time spent playing with him outside of teaching. While she loved teaching, there was something special about this one kid that made her wish for more opportunities for them to be together that weren't so structured.

They battled the big bad robot who was coming to take over the world, and they managed to save Earth just before the bombs exploded and tore down the city. She found herself laughing and relaxed in a way she hadn't been in the better part of ten years. She truly enjoyed the simplicity.

The knock on the door startled both of them out of their imaginations. Kimberly stood there, this time with the dish towel flung over her shoulder. "I made some brunch if you want to join us."

"Yes!" Michael jumped up and ran toward the kitchen.

Becca was much slower to stand, and as she went to leave the bedroom, Kimberly stopped her with a gentle hand on her wrist. "Am I to assume you being here is a good thing?"

"Depends on your definition of a good thing," Becca said back, a slight tease in her tone, and a twinkle in her eye.

"Becca..." Kimberly answered in a warning.

Grinning, Becca bent down and kissed Kimberly briefly. As she was about to deepen the kiss, Michael's voice filtered down to them. "You coming? I'm starving!"

Kimberly closed her eyes and tapped the side of her head against the doorframe. "I guess we can talk about this later."

"Hmm, yes, I suppose we can." Becca trailed her fingers over Kimberly's shoulder and back as she walked around her, squeezing through the suddenly small doorframe to reach the other side and head to the kitchen. When she looked over her shoulder at Kimberly and bit her lip, Kimberly stared at her with a longing look.

Becca loved that she could do that, that she could make Kimberly want her so much. She sauntered down the hallway with an extra sway in her hips to tease Kimberly even more. When she reached the kitchen and living area, she stopped so as not to alert Michael to what she was doing.

Kimberly followed behind a few seconds later and grabbed the platter of eggs, gravy, sausage and biscuits. She set it on the table in front of Michael, who had already grabbed plates and silverware for the three of them. They ate in good company, Michael keeping the conversation going as Kimberly and Becca shared heated looks.

As soon as the meal was done, Kimberly checked her watch and glanced at Michael. "Kiddo, go pack up your bag to head to Daddy's today, okay?"

After that, Kimberly's gaze locked on Becca as Michael took his plate to the sink then walked to his room without another word. As soon as he was out of earshot, Kimberly picked up her fork and shoved some of the food around her plate.

"I suppose I should start, since I'm the one who just showed up at your door," Becca jumped in. "I will only do this if you are honest with Michael. I will not hide from him anymore."

"Of course," Kimberly answered, shooting Becca another glance. "I realize I was wrong to put that on you before, along with everything else."

"*Everything* else?"

Kimberly sighed. "Look... Like you have had time to think, so have I. I was in the wrong, and it was my fault. I should not have put it on you to keep us a secret, and I should not have asked you to be in a relationship with me—any kind of relationship—while you were my employee, and for that, I am truly sorry. I hope you can forgive me."

"It's not like I said no," Becca countered. She reached forward, grabbed Kimberly's fidgety hands and held them in hers. "I wanted to."

"You did, and you didn't. You made that very clear."

"I was confused."

Kimberly nodded. "I think I was, too."

Silence took them over, but it was a comfortable silence. Becca enjoyed being in Kimberly's presence again. With her heart in her throat, she took a risk and leaned over, pressing their mouths together. Kimberly sighed, and Becca closed her eyes, leaning into the kiss and parting her lips. Everything about it felt completely right. It felt good and near perfect.

They took it slow, which was rare for them. Becca drew in a deep breath and slid her tongue along Kimberly's, bringing up a hand to cup her cheek and hold her in place. For the first time ever, Becca reveled in the moment without boundaries, without confines, without anxiety.

The squeal sent Becca trying to pull back, but Kimberly held on to her tightly, ending the kiss slowly and with a grin on her lips. She pecked Becca's lips once more before she turned to Michael, who had dropped his bag in the middle of the living area and had his hands together, clapping.

"Mama! Are you and Becca together now?"

Kimberly sent Becca a shy look. "We might be. How do you feel about that?"

"It's about damn time!"

"Michael!" Kimberly scolded. "Where did you learn to say that?"

"Umm...Daddy?" He grinned and ran around the table to give Becca another big hug before turning to his mom and giving her a hug. "I'm so happy!"

Kimberly laughed and patted his butt. "I'm glad you're happy about it. Your dad is about here, so you're all packed?"

"Yes," he answered.

Kimberly turned to Becca and shrugged. "Bradley has been wanting extra nights with him. It's sweet but also hard."

"I can imagine the house feels empty."

With a sidelong look, Kimberly nodded. "Perhaps not as lonely as before."

They chatted until Bradley came to pick up Michael. He sent them both curious glances, which Kimberly as well as Becca ignored. Kimberly shut the door and locked it behind them as they left and turned to Becca. "I suppose we should talk a bit more."

"Probably, maybe figure out some details," Becca responded as she trailed a finger over the back of one of the dining room chairs.

Kimberly let out a low chuckle as she leaned against the door. "Maybe a few details." She raked her gaze up and down Becca's body, her chest tightening with hope and desire. "But details can always wait, too."

"They can."

Their gazes locked. Kimberly's chest heaved as she stayed rooted to the spot. She wanted Becca to come to her. She wanted this to be the one last test of what their relationship could be. "I called in to work this morning."

"Did you now?" Becca took a step toward her, and Kimberly's heart raced.

"I did. I figure I can afford a day at home."

"So we're not going anywhere?" Another step.

"I don't really want to go anywhere. Do you?"

Another step. Becca was almost within reach.

"Not really," Becca almost whispered, her long legs carrying her one more step. "What should we do then?"

Kimberly growled low in the back of her throat. "I'm pretty sure we can come up with a few things."

"You sure?" Becca asked.

One more step. If Kimberly wanted, she could reach out and touch Becca's soft red hair, run her fingers along her arms to her hands. How she wanted to.

"I mean, I'm not that creative a person," Becca whispered.

Kimberly swallowed hard. "Somehow, I don't believe that."

With one last step, Becca was only millimeters away from her. Kimberly gripped the door handle to try to keep from reaching out. She dragged her gaze up Becca's body, stopping briefly at her breasts, her lips and finally resting on her eyes.

"I don't believe that at all," Kimberly said on a breath.

Becca planted a hand above Kimberly's head on the door and leaned in even more, so their lips were only a hairsbreadth apart. "Maybe we'll have to put that to the test. Is that something you would like to do?"

Her breath shuddered when she let it out. "I would. I would very much like that. Would you?"

Becca hummed as if she were contemplating. Kimberly's heart thudded loudly, and she was sure it was all Becca could hear, but she didn't care. If it meant Becca knew how much she wanted her, then she'd grovel as much as she could.

"I think I would." Becca bowed her lips into a devious smile, and finally she bent her head and captured Kimberly's in a kiss.

Drawing in a deep breath, Kimberly gasped at the fire of pleasure coursing through her. This was a different side of Becca than she had ever seen, one she had only glimpsed on occasion, but it was one she was completely in love with—the confidence, the control, the strength. Becca pressed Kimberly hard against the door and cupped her breast firmly.

"Do you want this?" Becca whispered in Kimberly's ear.

Kimberly whimpered.

"That's not an answer, Chef."

"Yes." Kimberly's chest fell as she breathed. Her words came out on a whisper. "Yes, I want this."

"What do you want?" Becca's lips brushed against Kimberly's neck. "You have to tell me what you want."

Kimberly closed her eyes, listening to the confidence in Becca's voice and the command she held in her tone. She made sure she had complete eye contact with Becca when she spoke next. "I want you...all of you."

"You have me."

Drawing Becca's mouth back to hers, Kimberly locked their lips together in a heated kiss. She pulled at the buttons on Becca's shirt until she could tug it off then skimmed her nails across her chest and breasts. Becca pulled off Kimberly's shirt and threw it on the ground, immediately pressing their skin together. Becca broke their kiss and pressed her lips to Kimberly's ear.

"Tell me what you want."

"I want fast. Make me come fast...then we'll go slow."

"Yes," Becca answered.

She didn't hesitate as she shoved her hand down the front of Kimberly's pants, not waiting as she slid two fingers inside her. Kimberly's lips parted as she arched against the door in pleasure. This was exactly what she wanted — Becca in full force, all her attention focused.

"Keep going," Kimberly whispered. "Don't stop."

Becca complied and moved her fingers and thumb in tandem. Kimberly's mouth opened as a small noise escaped. Pleasure hit her, bringing her higher and higher as Becca kept her hand moving.

"Like that?" Becca asked.

"God, yes." Kimberly opened her eyes and stared straight into Becca's blue eyes. "I want you to look at me when I come."

"Always," Becca answered and jerked her wrist harder.

Kimberly bit her lip, trying to stave off her orgasm so she could stare into those beautiful eyes one minute longer. When Kimberly came, she scrunched her eyes tight and gripped Becca's hand to slow her motions. Once her breathing calmed, Becca's lips were on hers again in a long, sweet kiss.

Coming around, Kimberly smiled. "While I would love to continue this here, you are twenty-eight and I am absolutely not."

"Bed?"

"Yes."

Becca removed her hands and licked her fingers carefully as Kimberly grabbed her free hand and led her to her bedroom. The last time they had been in there didn't hold sweet or good memories, but Kimberly knew this time would be different. Instead of shutting the bedroom door, she left it open. She went to her bed, turned around and beckoned Becca forward with a curl of her finger.

Becca grinned and pulled her bra off as she walked. When she reached Kimberly, she toyed with the ends of her hair, curling them around her fingers. Kimberly smiled sweetly, the light of the sun floating on Becca's skin and making it glow, something Kimberly had never seen, since all their trysts had happened at night.

When Becca bent down to kiss Kimberly again, she kept it brief. Kimberly reached up but hesitated before she touched Becca's breast. "May I?"

"Yes, please do. And you know what else you can do?"

"What's that?" Kimberly asked, her palm running along Becca's hardened nipple, mesmerized by the way it moved into a peak.

Becca licked her lips and whispered in Kimberly's ear. "Remember that night...in here?"

"Fondly."

"I want to do that again."

Chuckling, Kimberly moved back slightly. "Liked it, did you?"

Becca moaned. "More than you can imagine."

"Well, I think that can be arranged." Kimberly pinched Becca's nipple. "Strip."

Letting out a chuckle, Becca undid the belt on her jeans and slid them off her hips and down to the floor. She toed out of her shoes and flicked the pants behind her with her foot. "Everything?"

"Well, yes, if you want your wish to be my command. That's a bit necessary, don't you think?"

Grinning, Becca shucked her panties and crawled onto the bed. She sat on her knees, her back to Kimberly. Her curves set Kimberly's desire into overdrive. She grinned and slipped a hand down Becca's side from her breast to her hip to the curve of her butt, pinching gently before giving a light smack. After tugging off her own bra and pants, Kimberly crawled onto the bed behind Becca.

She pressed her front to Becca's back and rolled her hips into her. "First, I want to take you like this if you'll have me."

"Yes." Becca leaned backward into Kimberly's chest, jutting her breasts out and spreading her knees.

Kimberly kissed gently down her neck and slid her hand to Becca's belly. She moved her hands, teasing, heating up then soothing. "I have waited months for this."

"Me too," Becca confessed.

"I can't deny how much I love it."

Becca didn't answer. When Kimberly turned Becca's chin to face her, her eyes were closed. Kimberly kissed her gently and waited patiently until she finally looked at her. Kimberly smiled.

"How much I love you."

The smile that bloomed on Becca's face was all the answer she needed. Slipping her fingers between Becca's legs, she started a gentle rhythm. Becca moved against Kimberly, and Kimberly held on to her tightly. When Becca came, she brought her to a second orgasm, loving the flush in Becca's cheeks, the slight part to her dry lips, her fluttering eyelids, her heavy breaths.

"Once more, Becca. You can do it."

The order was all she needed, and Kimberly felt the sweet tug of Becca's muscles on her fingers. Kimberly kissed her neck again.

"There you go. Easy now."

When Kimberly moved her fingers from Becca's body and Becca let out a whimper, Kimberly eased her down onto the bed on her hands and her knees. She covered her with gentle touches and kisses.

"Are you ready?"

"Yes. Do it."

Kimberly licked down Becca's spine. She moved Becca's hips so her ass was higher in the air. Brushing her hair from her face, she bent to slip her tongue between Becca's legs, tasting her as gently as she could. Becca let out a yelp of surprise then eased backward into Kimberly even more. Kimberly spread Becca's cheeks and spun her tongue in circles around her anus.

Kimberly moved slowly, wanting to draw this out for Becca as long as possible. As soon as Kimberly felt Becca was calmed enough, she moved her forearm under her hips to keep her upright. Using her other hand, she slipped her thumb and fingers between Becca's legs and once again built a slow pattern.

Becca rocked back and forth, and Kimberly followed her cues. When Becca's pace picked up, Kimberly moved faster. Becca arched her back and pushed in closer. Kimberly gave two more swipes and Becca came for a third time.

This time, she let Becca fall heavily to the mattress, completely spent. Kimberly covered her, using her elbows to prop herself above Becca as she smiled down at her. "I meant what I said."

"I know," Becca breathed out. "I love you, too."

Kimberly's breath rushed from her lungs, relief washing over her. Kimberly closed her eyes as tears threatened to spill, tears of joy. When she opened her eyes again and looked down at Becca, she grinned as widely as she had in years. "You have no idea how long I have waited to hear you say that."

"Probably about as long as I've waited."

"Probably." Kimberly laughed and kissed Becca again. She rolled to her side then curled into Becca's spent body. "It's about time."

"It is." Becca kissed Kimberly, twining her fingers through Kimberly's hair. "Does this mean we're a thing now?"

"Is that what kids are calling it these days?" Kimberly chuckled. "I guess it does."

"Good, because I think it's your turn again."

Kimberly's laugh turned to a squeak of pleasure as Becca climbed on top of her. "I guess it is."

"Shall we?"

Nodding, Kimberly put her hands on Becca's hips. "Let's do this."

Want to see more like this?
Here's a taster for you to enjoy!

More Than This
Alexa Milne

Excerpt

It had been two years since I'd seen her. Cassandra Forster, there in the flesh, as perfectly turned out as always. Every so often during the meeting, she glanced at me, but gave no indication we'd known each other in the past. Today, she wore a deep purple fitted dress with buttons up the front, a dress that hugged every curve. Shit, those curves. I couldn't see a line of any sort impacting the smoothness of the fit. The highest of black stiletto heels graced her feet. Her legs were encased, as always, in black. She hated tights, so they were probably hold-ups with those lace panels at the top stretched around her thighs. Wet welled between my legs at the thought of her pale flesh. Her long dark hair, lying straight and loose down her back, shone.

I shut my notebook. "And that's everything, I think, unless anyone has anything else to add?" I glanced at everyone, hoping no one would say anything. No one did.

"Thank you all for coming. I'm sure the merger will be a success. We'll set up teams for each section within the next week." People stood, scraping their chairs back to leave the room, chatting as they exited.

This was my first time in charge of a merger meeting since my promotion to partner in the company. I needed this to go well. The last person I'd expected to appear was Cass, especially in the role of personal assistant to the CEO of one of the companies we represented in the negotiations. Melanie Kneale was renowned for her impatience with subordinates, and I couldn't see Cass putting up with her style of management for long...unless...

I pushed the thought away and shuffled my papers, waiting for the room to clear, even though I was desperate to get back to my office, away from her, away from our past. Or at least, I told myself I was. Before I'd had to leave abruptly, I'd begun to think that maybe we could have more than what we'd had, satisfying though it had been, but I had no idea whether she'd felt the same.

And now, it would be so easy to get lost in her again. I breathed a heavy sigh of relief, watching her leave. I grabbed a mug of black coffee and, once back in my office, closed the door then sat in my chair staring out of the window. After a few minutes, I heard a noise behind me. I swiveled. Somehow, I knew it would be her. She closed the door behind her and stood waiting.

I'm the boss. I'm in charge here. I needed to believe those words. "Hello, Cassandra. Has Ms. Kneale let you off her leash?" *Do I sound confident? I need to sound confident.* I clutched at the arms of my chair and gazed at her, hoping maintaining eye contact showed strength, but I was drawn to her as always.

Cass shook out her hair. "I told her I'd be back after lunch, so I have an hour. A whole sixty minutes. It's good to see you, Ronnie."

No one else called me Ronnie. To everyone else, I was Veronica. I sat up in my executive chair, chin held high and back straight. "I'm surprised to see you here *and* working for Melanie. She has a reputation for chewing up assistants and spitting them out."

"She'd certainly never swallow. I'm not sure I've ever seen her eat anything but those godawful protein shakes full of kale. I've never understood a woman who doesn't like her food. Not like you. Food is too sensual not to experience it all."

Automatically, I pulled in my stomach.

Cassandra crossed the room. Her heels sent her hips swinging. Without any hesitation, she came around to my side of the desk, pushed back my chair and stood in front of me. Inches separated us.

Say something. Tell her this isn't appropriate. Tell her to go. The voice screamed in my head. I, of course, ignored it. *But I want you to stay. I've missed you. I'm sorry I left without saying goodbye. I had reasons.*

She picked up my phone. "Hello, Matthew. Could you hold all Ms. Smith's calls for the next hour? Thank you." She replaced the receiver. "So, we have sixty minutes. What do you think we should we do with them?"

"This isn't appropriate, Cass." My voice barely managed a whisper. I swallowed, trying to wet my arid mouth then, without thinking, licked my lips. "I have work to do." *Please don't go.*

"Since when has appropriate mattered to me?" She ran a perfectly manicured nail down my cheek, and I had to fight the urge to lean into her touch. "You're looking well, Ronnie, but you've changed your hair. And you're doing well, judging by this office."

I nodded.

"Power is such an aphrodisiac, don't you think?" She took hold of a strand of my hair and twirled it around her finger. *So close.*

"Is that why you're working for Melanie Kneale?" I asked, my voice shaking.

She stroked my cheek. "Do I detect a smidgeon of jealousy?"

I waited for her to ask me where I'd been for the last two years, and why I'd left New York so suddenly, but instead she sat on my desk and crossed her long legs.

"The position suits me for the moment. And as for Melanie, I wouldn't say no to giving her a little discipline, but she's far too fond of pegging her secretary over her desk for my taste."

Her hands went to the top of her dress. She undid each button slowly, revealing a stunning black lace bra which pushed her ample breasts together to make a wonderful cleavage I longed to get lost in. Goosepimples popped up on my arms. *I should tell her to stop. I should tell her to leave.* I didn't. *Who am I trying to fool?* She stopped at the waist and, without warning, uncrossed her legs and pulled the arms of my chair forward until my face was level with the small pink bow in the center of the lace. My pulse quickened. She knew me too well. Her fingers, with their immaculately painted nails, undid a hidden hook, letting her breasts spring free.

She licked her finger and used it to lazily circle one nipple. *Oh God.* "You always had a thing about my boobs, didn't you, and I had a thing about you liking them." She lifted one breast until the dark pink nipple rubbed my lips.

"Lick it," she said.

I shook my head. The rest of me shook with desire. We'd played this game so many times before and both knew how it always ended.

"Lick it. You know you want to. I can see it in your eyes. You want to lick and suck like you always did."

It was true. Losing myself in her made the world go away better than any drug. I let my tongue slip between my lips and touched, ever so slightly. The nub and areole hardened, and I was back on the hook, being pulled in.

"Go on, you know that's not enough. Lose yourself. Do what you're told."

I did. I couldn't help myself. Leaving her had killed me. What must she have thought? How mad she must be. How would she punish me? It had been two years, and there had been no one since. *When you've tasted perfection...* I wrapped my lips around the glorious nub. She curved her hand around the back of my head and held me there. It was like coming home. I wouldn't have cared about anyone else entering the room. The sky could have fallen, or the world ended. My mouth was made for this.

"Enough." Her usual command. She placed her hands either side of my head, tilting it upward. "Now the other one." I moved sideways.

"Oh yes. You haven't lost any of your skill, have you, Ronnie? Such a gorgeous mouth and talented tongue." She kept me there for minutes, alternating between each nipple while I licked and whimpered into the wetness I'd created so greedily. It had been too long.

"Enough." Immediately, I stopped. The dance moved on, as carefully choreographed as ever.

"Undo the rest of the buttons."

I did as I was told, one by one, until I reached the last. She wore matching black lace panties and, as I'd suspected, hold-ups, the kind with the lacy tops rather than the purely functional. I desperately wanted to kiss the pale flesh above the elastic lace. She stood and shimmied out of her briefs. She never fully shaved like many others, but chose to trim. She loathed wax. I wanted nothing more than to sink my face between those white thighs and she knew it. I could practically taste her on my tongue. My pussy ached and I was so wet my knickers would be damp all day.

She reached between her legs with one finger, rubbed herself then held her hand up to my mouth. I could smell her. I needed to taste her so badly. She slipped the finger into my mouth and I devoured the salty flavor with its subtle hint of mango from the shower gel she always used.

"You want more, don't you?" she said. I couldn't speak. I nodded. "Then you shall have more."

She edged back farther on the desk and opened her legs. Her body glistened. "Move closer," she said. She pulled open her lips to reveal her clit.

"Oh God," I whispered, staring up into those dark eyes. "Can I?" Would she refuse? Would that be my punishment for leaving her? I couldn't bear the thought of not seeing her again. *Please don't say no.*

She stroked my hair. "Oh yes, my pet. Make me come like only you can."

Tension leached out of me. I wheeled closer. Sitting like this, I could concentrate. I glided my tongue over her clit.

"That's it, my pet. Take it. Take me."

I buried my face in wetness. I loved the feel of it on my skin, the taste and smell. I took her clit between my lips and sucked hard. Now, the tables were turned a little. I had the power. This was how it worked between us. I did what she told me. Anything she told me. She liked the power and I liked the danger. Did we have a chance for more?

The door wasn't locked. Anyone could come in, but I didn't care. Every memory of every time came flooding back along with the need—the need to lose myself. I slipped one finger inside her. I loved to feel her contractions as she came.

"Oh yes. No one has ever done this as well as you." She wrapped her legs around me. I could hardly breathe. I pushed harder, licked harder, moaned into her flesh, waiting for the moment when she pulled away before she came. I knew how she moved. When she did, I followed her, not letting up my attention to her body through the convulsions as she came with more wetness covering my face. I loved the feeling of being surrounded by her. I kept going until she put a hand on my hair then raised my head to meet her gaze. She lifted my chin and leaned down to kiss me, tasting herself on my lips.

"Thank you." Those simple words made all the difference. She always thanked me. Those words gave me hope. Had she forgiven me?

I said nothing, letting my breathing return to normal while I licked my lips.

She stood, fastened her bra, put on her briefs, then buttoned her dress and brushed herself down. She checked and reapplied her lipstick and ran her fingers through her hair. I sat in silence, knowing there wouldn't be anything for me to relieve the ache between my legs. At least not from her, not now, not here. Not in this dance.

"It's been good to meet again," she said as if we'd merely had a coffee together. "I missed you, my pet." She dug into her bag and pulled out a card. "Call me." It wasn't a suggestion. Could we be more than this?

"I don't know," I whispered. But I did. I'd call. Probably.

PUBLISHING

Sign up for our newsletter and find out about all our
romance book releases, eBook sales and promotions,
sneak peeks and FREE romance books!

About the Author

Adrian J. Smith has been publishing since 2013 but has been writing nearly her entire life. With a focus on women loving women fiction, AJ jumps genres from action-packed police procedurals to the seedier life of vampires and witches to sweet romances with a May-December twist. She loves writing and reading about women in the midst of the ordinariness of life. Two of her novels received honorable mentions with the Rainbow Awards.

AJ currently lives in Cheyenne, WY, although she moves often and has lived all over the United States. She loves to travel to different countries and places. She currently plays the roles of author, wife, mother to two rambunctious toddlers, and occasional handy-woman.

AJ loves to hear from readers. You can find her contact information, website details and author profile page at https://www.pride-publishing.com